D0427893

Welcome to a
World of Darkness. . . .

Where strange creatures live among humans. Creatures of lightning speed, inhuman strength, and undeniable power. Immortal creatures—with a thirst for blood.

This is the world of the vampire. A world where nothing and no one is what they seem.

And a world from which there is no escape.

BOOKS BY R.L. STINE

Fear Street Super Chillers
PARTY SUMMER
SILENT NIGHT
GOODNIGHT KISS
BROKEN HEARTS
SILENT NIGHT 2
THE DEAD LIFEGUARD
CHEERLEADERS: THE NEW EVIL
BAD MOONLIGHT
THE NEW YEAR'S PARTY
GOODNIGHT KISS 2
SILENT NIGHT 3
HIGH TIDE
GOODNIGHT KISS COLLECTOR'S EDITION

Fear Street Sagas
A NEW FEAR
HOUSE OF WHISPERS
FORBIDDEN SECRETS
THE SIGN OF FEAR
THE HIDDEN EVIL
DAUGHTERS OF SILENCE
CHILDREN OF FEAR

The Fear Street Saga
THE BETRAYAL
THE SECRET
THE BURNING
COLLECTOR'S EDITION

Fear Park
THE FIRST SCREAM
THE LOUDEST SCREAM
THE LAST SCREAM

99 Fear Street: The House of Evil
THE FIRST HORROR
THE SECOND HORROR
THE THIRD HORROR

Fear Street Cheerleaders
THE FIRST EVIL
THE SECOND EVIL
THE THIRD EVIL

Available from ARCHWAY Paperbacks

For orders other than by individual consumers, Pocket Books grants a discount on the purchase of 10 or more copies of single titles for special markets or premium use. For further details, please write to the Vice-President of Special Markets, Pocket Books, 1633 Broadway, New York, NY 10019-6785, 8th Floor.

For information on how individual consumers can place orders, please write to Mail Order Department, Simon & Schuster Inc., 200 Old Tappan Road, Old Tappan, NJ 07675.

FEAR STREET®
R.L. STINE

GOODNIGHT KISS

COLLECTOR'S EDITION

A Parachute Press Book

AN ARCHWAY PAPERBACK
Published by POCKET BOOKS
New York London Toronto Sydney Tokyo Singapore

The sale of this book without its cover is unauthorized. If you purchased this book without a cover, you should be aware that it was reported to the publisher as "unsold and destroyed." Neither the author nor the publisher has received payment for the sale of this "stripped book."

This book is a work of fiction. Names, characters, places and incidents are products of the author's imagination or are used fictitiously. Any resemblance to actual events or locales or persons, living or dead, is entirely coincidental.

AN ARCHWAY PAPERBACK *Original*

An Archway Paperback published by
POCKET BOOKS, a division of Simon & Schuster Inc.
1230 Avenue of the Americas, New York, NY 10020

Goodnight Kiss copyright © 1992 by Parachute Press, Inc.
Goodnight Kiss 2 copyright © 1996 by Parachute Press, Inc.
"The Vampire Club" copyright © 1997 by Parachute Press, Inc.

All rights reserved, including the right to reproduce this book or portions thereof in any form whatsoever. For information address Pocket Books, 1230 Avenue of the Americas, New York, NY 10020

ISBN: 0-671-01377-7

First Archway Paperback printing July 1997

10 9 8 7 6 5 4 3 2 1

FEAR STREET is a registered trademark of Parachute Press, Inc.

AN ARCHWAY PAPERBACK and colophon are registered trademarks of Simon & Schuster Inc.

Cover design by Jim Lebbad, tip-in art by Bill Schmidt

Printed in the U.S.A.

IL 7+

GOODNIGHT KISS

COLLECTOR'S EDITION

FEAR STREET®
SUPER CHILLER

Goodnight Kiss

PART ONE

FIRST KISS

Chapter 1

FIRST KISS

Jessica's sandals clonked over the wood planks of the walk as she made her way quickly past the small shops and restaurants. She stopped in front of the Beach Emporium, the largest clothing store in Sandy Hollow, and peered into the window.

A hand-painted sign read: BIKINIS HALF OFF.

Jessica chuckled to herself. Was that meant to be a joke?

No. Mrs. Hopping, the quiet old woman whose family had owned the Beach Emporium for a hundred years, had no sense of humor. She was a stern, unfriendly woman who smiled only when punching down the buttons on her old-fashioned cash register to ring up a big sale.

Mrs. Hopping will soon be smiling a lot, Jessica thought. Just beyond town, Beach Haven Drive was already clogged with cars as the summer people were arriving to open up their beach houses. In a few days the white-skinned tourists would be lying on the sand all day, soaking up the rays, then jamming the tiny town at night, all pink and sweaty, eager to party and shop, shop, shop.

Jessica let her eyes roam over the bathing suits in the window. A very bright orange bikini caught the light. It probably glows in the dark, Jessica realized, rolling her eyes. How tacky.

The sun had disappeared behind the low, shingle and clapboard buildings along Main Street. The evening air carried a chill from the ocean to the east. Loud voices and laughter rang out from the Pizza Cove restaurant across the street.

It's exciting, Jessica thought. A new summer. A new season. New people.

Sweeping her thick mane of copper-colored hair back behind the shoulders of her black cotton sweater, she pushed open the door to the shop. The bell on the door jangled as Jessica stepped inside. She was surprised that Mrs. Hopping was not at her usual perch behind the jewelry counter.

The shop smelled of sweet spices, clove and cinnamon, the fragrance wafting from a display of potpourri. I'll bet that's a big seller, Jessica thought, picking up a sachet and holding it close to her face to smell it. The summer people would do *anything* to get the musty, mildewy smells from their houses.

She headed past the bathing suits and beach cover-ups to the racks of colorful summer skirts, tops, and sundresses against the wall. I need something sexy but not obvious, she thought, pulling out and immediately rejecting a red and yellow flower-print skirt with matching midriff top.

Before she could look any further, she heard footsteps on the wood floor, and a voice from behind her called out a cheery hello. Jessica turned, surprised to see Lucy Franks, a girl she'd known for years, another townie.

They exchanged greetings. "Are you working here?" Jessica asked, her eyes returning to the dress rack.

"Yeah. Just evenings," Lucy replied brightly. "Town is filling up. I'm glad."

"Me too," Jessica said, holding up a maroon top.

"Not your color," Lucy said helpfully. Then she added, "Your hair's so great. Mine's always a mess. It curls up because it's so damp here."

"The damp air is good for your skin," Jessica said, pushing the maroon top back into place, then moving her hand down the rack. Jessica's skin was pale and flawlessly smooth and creamy white, her best feature.

The almost-translucent skin contrasted with her dark brown eyes and her full red lips. The long cascades of red hair framed her high cheekbones and made Jessica appear very dramatic, very sophisticated.

"It's so nice to see people in town," Lucy said, straightening a stack of oversize T-shirts. "Sandy Hollow is so *boring* in the winter."

5

"Yeah. It's like living in the Antarctic or somewhere," Jessica agreed.

"What are you doing this summer?" Lucy asked.

"Just hanging out, I guess," Jessica told her. "What do you think of this?" She held up a short, navy blue sundress with a halter top.

"Well, what are you looking for?" Lucy asked, giving the T-shirts one last pat and walking up to Jessica. "Something a little dressy?"

"Not too dressy," Jessica said thoughtfully, holding the sundress up. "I have a blind date tomorrow night."

Lucy giggled. "A blind date? Wow. Do people still do that?"

Jessica's dark eyes lit up. "I sort of got talked into it—you know. A friend of a friend said there's this really nice guy, and—"

"What's his name?" Lucy asked. "Do I know him?"

"Gabriel Martins," Jessica replied. "Everyone calls him Gabri."

Lucy shook her head. "Don't know him." She took the navy blue sundress from Jessica and studied it. "Try it on. It'll probably look fabulous on you. You're so tall and have such great long legs. You really look like a model."

Jessica laughed. "Lucy, you really know how to make a sale!"

Lucy blushed. "No. I mean it, Jessica. Really." She handed it back, and Jessica hurried to the dressing room to try it on. She scrambled out of her jeans and sweater and pulled the sundress on. It fit perfectly.

"There's a mirror out here if you need it," Lucy called.

"That's okay. It fits great," Jessica called out.

A few minutes later, having bought the dress, she waved good-bye to Lucy and headed out onto Main Street. Across the street some teenagers were piling into the Pizza Cove. Next door, the Mini Market was crowded with shoppers choosing food to stock their houses. Cars honked as drivers looked for parking places on the narrow street.

Summer, here I come! Jessica thought happily, gripping her plastic shopping bag tightly as she crossed Main Street, mission accomplished, and headed for home.

Gabri Martins was tall and very thin, with a pale, narrow face, straight black hair swept back from his forehead, intense, black eyes, and a broad, friendly smile that didn't seem to belong on such a serious face.

He's really good-looking, Jessica thought as he approached in his black denim jeans and pale blue T-shirt, stepping under the flickering lights of the marquee of the Harbor Palace, the town's only movie theater. The smile on his face seemed to indicate that he liked Jessica's looks as well.

She had arrived at the theater first, feeling nervous and uncertain. How will I even know which one he is? she had wondered. As the line of laughing, chattering summer people filed into the theater, Jessica waited under the marquee, nervously straightening her new sundress, asking herself why she had let herself be talked into a blind date.

After a while she realized she was the only one still waiting. The movie must have started, she told herself, glancing at the big clock outside the Mini Market. Gabri isn't even going to show up.

But then he stepped under the marquee lights and flashed her his open, friendly smile, and her nervousness melted away. "Sorry, I'm late," he said, taking her arm and guiding her inside.

It was dark and warm inside the theater and smelled of cats and mildew. Jessica stumbled in the aisle, her eyes adjusting slowly to the darkness. Gabri caught her before she fell.

Good move, Jessica, she scolded herself. Way to make a good impression. Now he knows you're a clumsy ox!

They sat in the back row. Jessica found herself glancing at Gabri every few seconds, too distracted to concentrate on the movie. His dark eyes glowed in the flickering light of the movie screen. His expression remained serious even though the movie was a comedy.

About halfway through the film, he leaned close to her and whispered, "Do you like this movie?"

"Not really," she answered honestly.

"Let's go," he said, standing up immediately, smiling reassuringly at her.

A few seconds later they were back outside. The air smelled fresh and salty. Narrow wisps of dark clouds snaked across a full moon hung low in the sky, so low it seemed to hover over the shingled roof of the darkened barbershop across the street.

Swanny's, the ice-cream parlor and video-game arcade next to the movie theater, was packed with young people. A line had formed at the outdoor take-out window, people standing in clusters of two and four, talking and laughing as they waited for cones and milk shakes.

"Want to get something?" Gabri asked, pointing to the line.

Jessica shook her head. "Not unless you want to."

"Why don't we check out the beach?" he said. "It'll be quieter. We can talk." His dark eyes seemed to capture hers. As she stared back at him, she felt hypnotized by him.

"Uh . . . okay," she finally replied, forcing herself to snap out of it.

He must think I'm a real jerk, she thought glumly. I'm usually so self-assured, so confident. Why do I feel so awkward, so unsure of myself with him?

They walked along Dune Lane, which meandered from town across the tall, grassy dunes down to the beach. It was a short walk, about ten minutes. The low, bright moon with its shadowy wisps of cloud seemed to move with them, leading the way.

After sliding down the dune, they took their shoes off and stacked them beside a clump of grass. The sand felt cold and soft and wet under Jessica's feet. She slid her toes in, enjoying the sensation, enjoying the fresh, salty air, enjoying the white moon that sent a trembling path of light across the billowing ocean waves, enjoying sharing it all with someone new.

She took a deep breath, closing her eyes. "It smells so clean," she said happily, wrapping her bare arms around her chest as if hugging herself.

"Are you cold?" Gabri asked, his voice suddenly concerned.

She opened her eyes to see him staring at her. "I like your dress," he said. "I just thought you might be cold. I mean . . ."

She shook her head. "Know what I feel like doing? I feel like running."

Before he could reply, she took off, running along the shore, her bare feet kicking up clumps of wet sand, the rush of the waves in her ears, the ocean wind lifting her coppery hair.

It took her a while to realize that Gabri was right beside her, matching her stride for stride, moving over the sand as effortlessly as she. His dark eyes searched out hers, his arms outstretched as if he were about to take flight.

She turned and headed away from the water, her feet pounding the sand. He soared with her, grinning, staying at her side, now a step behind, now a step ahead.

Without a signal, they both plunged headfirst into the soft, grassy dune, tumbling together happily, both laughing as if they were little children, rolling in the sand, the high grass soft against their skin.

When they finally stood up, still laughing, not the slightest bit out of breath, brushing sand from their clothes, he took her hands.

And pulled her close.

He looked so handsome under the low, low moon.

She knew he was going to kiss her.

She wanted him to.

He didn't say a word. He didn't have to. Those dark, intense eyes, so serious, so hypnotic. Those eyes said it all.

And before she realized it, his arms were around her.

His face drew close. Closer.

She stared into his eyes and once again came under their spell.

And then she saw his mouth open.

And the pointed fangs emerged.

So bright and sharp, sparkling in the moonlight.

Gently, so gently, Gabri tilted her chin up.

And dug his fangs deeply into her pale, tender throat.

Chapter 2

THIRSTY

Jessica groaned. She raised her hands to Gabri's shoulders and shoved him away.

"Hey—" he cried out, startled by her strength. His fangs still gleamed in the shadowy moonlight.

"You idiot!" Jessica snarled, pushing him again. "I'm an Eternal One too!"

"Huh?" Gabri took a step back, bewildered.

Jessica's eyes widened, glowing red embers against the darkness. Her fangs lowered, curling down toward her chin. She laughed scornfully. "Idiot," she repeated, shaking her head, her long, thick hair swinging behind her.

"Well, how was I to know?" Gabri asked angrily, his features tightening in a dark scowl.

The light faded from Jessica's eyes. "I bought a new dress and everything," she muttered.

"Well, why didn't you say something?" Gabri asked, crossing his slender arms in front of himself.

"What was I supposed to say?" she cried heatedly. "Hello. Nice to meet you. I'm an Eternal One. How about you?"

He groaned and kicked at the sand, avoiding her stare.

"A blind date," Jessica muttered. "I should've known better than to go on a blind date with a townie."

"You wasted my whole night," he said peevishly, his arms still crossed.

"Boo-hoo," she replied nastily. "Break my heart, why don't you? You really are pitiful, you know? Is that how you do it all the time? Have someone arrange blind dates with poor, unsuspecting girls? You're too pitiful to get a date on your own?"

"Why don't you shut your fangs?" Gabri snapped, staring out over the water. "I'm not the pitiful one. *You're* the one who agreed to go on the blind date. I can't believe you. Acting so sweet and innocent."

Jessica laughed. "I *am* sweet," she insisted. And then she added coyly, "But it's too late for *you* to find that out."

Gabri uttered a cry of disgust. "But I *need* the nectar!" he cried, turning to her. "Without the nectar, I'll perish."

"Where'd you get that line? Out of an old horror movie?" Jessica joked, shaking her head. She repeated it in a high-pitched, desperate voice, imitating him meanly. "Without the nectar, I'll perish."

"You're not funny. You're pitiful," he said softly. "Really."

The wispy cloud trailed away from the moon, and the beach brightened as if someone had turned on a light. In the white light, Gabri aged a hundred years. He has a teenager's face, like mine, Jessica thought, studying him. But his skin is so pale and brittle, stretched so tightly over his bones. And in the light his eyes are old—ancient and evil.

"Listen, Gabri," Jessica said, softening her tone a bit, "I need the nectar too, you know. It's been a long, cold winter here."

She pushed her hair back over her shoulders as a group of teenagers, carrying drink coolers and Boogie boards, walked past. One of the boys, a straggler, stopped to stare long and hard at her before hurrying to catch up to the group.

"Guess this dress *isn't* bad," Jessica said, smoothing the front of it with both hands. Her eyes followed the boy who had stared at her. "Fresh blood," she said hungrily.

"Fresh blood," Gabri repeated in a low voice that barely carried over the wind. "Fresh blood all up and down the beach—and I end up with you."

"Sucker," Jessica said.

He scowled again.

"Idiot—that was a *joke!*" she cried, shoving him playfully into the dune. "Don't you even have a sense of humor?"

"Don't shove me again," he warned, his tone turning menacing. He seemed to float up from the sand, weightless like a kite, and hovered over her. "I don't have a sense of humor, not where the nectar is concerned."

"Back off, will you?" she yelled. "I don't care if you're an Eternal One or not. You're the biggest jerk I've ever met."

He stared at her coldly as if trying to decide how to react to her, as if trying to decide what to do to her.

He's trying to frighten me, Jessica thought.

Well, he's got a surprise coming. He can stare at me all he wants. I don't scare easy. And if he tries anything, I'll slash him to pieces.

She and Gabri slid into the shadows as two boys walked by their dune. The boys were hurrying to join a group of kids who had started a small bonfire down the beach.

"Fresh blood," Gabri said, his voice a whisper. "Maybe it isn't too late. Maybe I haven't wasted the whole night with you."

"What are you going to do?" she asked, not even trying to keep the mockery from her voice. "Try to get another blind date?"

He ignored her. "I need the nectar," he whispered, not bothering to hide his desperation. "I *need* it." Then, raising his arms above his head, he began to spin.

Clouds drifted over the moon, casting the dunes in total darkness. The ocean roar picked up. The wind swirled in wide circles.

Invisible in the dark swaying dune grass, Gabri spun. When the clouds drifted away and the pale light filtered down again, and the ocean hushed, and the wind calmed, he emerged as a bat, purple and black. The dark animal eyes stared down at Jessica with the same intensity, the animal mouth open, revealing pointed fangs covered in white drool.

He hissed at her, swooped at her face, forcing her to stumble backward and shield herself with her arms. Then, still hissing, up he fluttered until he disappeared against the black sky.

Seconds later Jessica was spinning in the tall grass. Moments after that she fluttered up to join her winged companion in the sky.

I'm so thirsty. So thirsty.

I need the nectar too, she thought.

I need the nectar. I need it so badly.

Monica Davis carried her sandals as she walked, her feet sinking into the wet sand, studying the rippling light on the ocean as the clouds moved across the moon. Her friend, Elly Porter, bent to pick up a smooth, white stone, then skipped it across the water.

"I'm cold," Elly complained, jogging rapidly to catch up, her knees high, as if that would keep her warm.

"Feels good," Monica said, closing her eyes, ocean spray clinging to her curly blond hair. "I'm just glad to get away from the cottage," she added, picking up her pace, enjoying the sound her feet made squishing over the sand.

"When did you get here?" Elly asked, turning to face her friend, walking backward, the wind fluttering her oversize T-shirt.

"Late last night," Monica replied. "And, of course, Dad threw a fit. He always does."

"What was it this time?"

"Two of the screens were torn. And there was some kind of bug nest in the house. Wasps, I think. So he started ranting and raving about how we're paying all this money for a summer house, the least the owner can do is make sure the screens aren't torn. Poor Dad," Monica said, shaking her head. "He's just so stressed out. It always takes him a month to unwind. And by that time—"

She stopped suddenly.

Elly stopped too, and followed her friend's gaze up to the blue black sky. "Oh!" Elly cried out, grabbing Monica's arm. "Are those—bats?"

Monica let out a silent gasp as the two dark forms hovered above. Their wings flapped like bedsheets on a clothesline.

"Run!" Elly screamed, pulling Monica's arm.

Monica held back. "The beach is full of bats at night," she told her friend, keeping her eyes on the two hovering forms. "They live on that island over there. See?" She pointed to a dark, wooded island out in the ocean beyond a small dock, its outlines visible against the purple horizon.

"Do people live on the island?" Elly asked. "It's completely dark."

"I think there used to be some beach houses there," Monica replied. "But you can only get to the island by boat. I don't think there are any people left. Only bats."

"They're so creepy," Elly said, close to Monica, her eyes trained on the two bats that seemed to be flying together.

"They flutter around," Monica said softly, "but they're harmless."

As she said that, one of the bats plunged toward Elly.

Elly didn't have time to move or cry out.

She saw gleaming red eyes.

Heard the hiss of wind, a shrill whistle, a screech of attack.

She felt it grab her hair. She felt it brush her face. Hot and wet. Hairy. Sticky.

It scratched her.

It beat its wings against her cheek.

"Help me!" she shrieked. "Oh, Monica—please help!"

Chapter 3

CHOOSING VICTIMS

"Help! Monica!"

Frantically waving her arms, Elly tried to beat away the attacker.

Monica hesitated for a second, horrified by the struggle, then lunged forward to help her friend.

As she moved toward Elly, the second bat swooped down. Monica cried out and raised her hands to shield herself.

She could feel a cold rush of air as the creature darted past her.

Then, to Monica's surprise, the second bat appeared to attack the first, flying at it, pushing it with its wings, hissing at it, bumping it away from Elly.

Screeching its anger, the first bat resisted the attack. But the second bat, its red eyes aflame, snapped and swooped until it pushed the first one away.

And then, as both girls stared openmouthed, their hands still held up protectively in front of their faces, the two bats lifted up into the darkness and disappeared over the dunes.

"Are you okay?" Monica cried, rushing to hug her friend. Elly was trembling all over. Her skin was cold and hard with goose bumps.

"I think so," she whispered uncertainly.

"Let's go," Monica said.

They began to run back toward the cluster of beach houses at the north end of the beach.

The whole struggle had taken less than ten seconds, Monica realized.

But it was ten seconds she would like to forget.

What's *with* these bats, anyway? she wondered, studying the inky black sky as she ran.

On the south end of the beach, beyond the clusters of beach houses, beyond the grassy dunes, a tall rock cliff jutted out over the ocean, leaning into the water as if trying to reach the dark, wooded island across from it.

In the shadow of this granite cliff, deserted and silent except for the relentless wash of waves against the shore, two bats descended to where sand met rock. Whirling furiously in the sand, they transformed themselves and stepped out to confront each other as humans, a boy and a girl.

"What is your *problem?*" Gabri demanded, glaring at Jessica and thrusting his hands angrily on his hips.

"I had no choice," she replied heatedly, standing her ground.

"But I'm so *thirsty!*" he declared. "One sip—"

"No," she said firmly.

"It's none of your business—" he started.

She tossed her long hair behind her with a sharp snap of her head. "Did you see how crowded the beach was?" she asked. "Did you see how many people were watching?"

She didn't give him a chance to reply. "Do you want to have everyone terrified before summer even begins? Use your brain, Gabri. Or has that dried up too?" Then she smiled as she made a joke: "You could give vampires a bad name!"

He snarled furiously at her, a frightening animal sound. His fangs curled down on his chin.

Jessica didn't back away. "One stupid attack like that, and all the fresh blood could be scared away. The town could close the beach until the bat problem was solved."

He turned away angrily, unwilling to admit that she was right, that he had acted foolishly. "She was so soft and ripe," he muttered.

"You're a jerk," Jessica said. "Have I mentioned that before?"

He kept his back to her and stared at the rocks sloping up to the cliff. "I'm sick of your insults," he hissed bitterly.

"That wasn't an insult. It was a compliment," she joked.

Angry, he spun around to face her, his features tight with fury. "How old are you?" he demanded.

"Huh?" Her full lips formed an O of surprise. "Old enough to know more than you," she replied, laughing, pleased at her own smugness.

His eyes continued to burn into hers. She tried to look away, but he held her with his stare. "You really think you're hot stuff, don't you?"

She nodded.

"You really think you're better than me."

She nodded again.

Again she tried to turn away from him. But the powerful hold of his stare was too overwhelming.

They stared at each other in silence for what seemed a long time, locked together by ancient, invisible forces.

"How would you feel about a little challenge?" he asked finally.

"A challenge?" She felt herself pulled toward him, pulled against her will.

"A bet," he said, a smile slowly forming on his handsome face.

"I'll win," she said flatly, her face expressionless, only her eyes alive.

The smile faded quickly from his face. "No, you won't. You will lose."

"What's the bet?" she asked softly, drawn toward him, caught in his grip, a prisoner of his eyes. "Do you want to bet on the Red Sox?"

He didn't laugh. "I hate your sense of humor," he said heatedly.

22

"Jealous," she accused. And then screamed, "Stop staring at me, Gabri!"

To her relief, he obediently averted his eyes. But the curve of a smile on his face revealed that he enjoyed having power over her. "Do you want to hear the bet or not?" he asked sharply.

"Sure." She moved beside him and leaned back against a sloping rock. It felt cool against her back. Soothing.

"We both need the nectar," he said, reaching up and sliding his fingers through her long hair. "We need it so badly."

"Cut to the chase," Jessica said sharply.

Ignoring her impatience, he continued to comb her hair with his long, slender fingers. "Why not see which of us is better at getting the nectar?" His fingers moved slowly, rhythmically through her hair, giving her chills. "Why not see which of us is more successful with the young humans, which of us is more attractive, more appealing?"

She shuddered, then grabbed his arm, gently pulling his hand from her hair. "What are you suggesting, Gabri?" she asked, not releasing his arm.

"I will get a girl within my power before you can get a boy to succumb to you," Gabri said, his entire face lighting up with the challenge.

Jessica's face expressed disgust. "You mean you will fly onto the beach and attack a girl before I can attack a boy—like that disgusting, babyish display you put on tonight?"

23

He squeezed her hand. "No, no," he said softly. "Not like that. Three sips, Jessica. Three small, measured sips on three different nights. That's what it takes to turn a human into an Eternal One. Take too big a drink, and the human dies. Three small, measured sips—and the human lives *forever,* as we do."

"So what are you suggesting?" Jessica asked, becoming more interested. "Are you saying that you will choose a girl, a living girl, and take three sips on three different nights, and change her into an Eternal One?"

"Yes!" he agreed excitedly. "I will do that before you can do the same to a boy. What do you say, Jessica? Do you accept the challenge?"

She closed her eyes and shook her head. "No."

"No? Why not?"

"It's too easy," she replied, a mischievous smile forming on her full lips. "I'd win too quickly. You're no competition. By the time you arranged a blind date, I'd have my victim in my power." She tossed her head back and laughed.

Gabri stuck his tongue out at her. "That's what I think of you. You're all talk, Jessica. You're afraid to compete with me. You know that girls can't resist me."

"I can resist you," she replied, crossing her arms over her chest.

"Then why won't you accept my challenge?"

She reached out and playfully squeezed his chin. "Don't get all pushed out of shape, Gabri honey," she teased. "I just want to make the bet a little more even. You know, give you a tiny chance to win."

He jerked his chin from her grasp and uttered an exasperated groan.

Jessica snapped her fingers. "I've got it! This'll make our little bet more interesting."

He turned his eyes to hers. "Well?"

"You select the boy I'm to work on, okay?" she said, pleased with her inspiration. "You select my victim, Gabri—and I will select yours."

"Yes!" he cried. "Excellent!"

Before they realized it, they were spinning together, whirling with the wind beneath the smooth, steep rock cliff, whirling together—and then rising apart, rising into the dark sky, soaring high, then diving low over the beach, still dotted with groups of young people.

Tender young people, Jessica thought hungrily, swooping low and hovering.

Tender young people.

Fluttering just high enough not to frighten them, she studied their full, happy faces.

And tingled with excitement.

Chapter 4

JUMPED FROM BEHIND

*A*pril Blair knew she was trapped.

She backed helplessly into the corner and awaited her fate.

"Oh, no! Stop!" she cried, raising her hands to protect herself.

But her two sisters, Courtney and Whitney, the Terror Twins, as April called them, closed in on her. Giggling madly, Courtney held April's hands, while Whitney dived and began a ferocious tickling attack.

"Stop! Stop!" April cried through tears of laughter.

The two blond-haired, round-cheeked, six-year-old monsters knew that April was extremely ticklish, and they made the most of their knowledge.

"I can't breathe!" April gasped, sinking to the floor. "Really! I can't breathe!"

That only encouraged them.

April tried to roll away from them, but Whitney quickly jumped on her, pinning her against the straw mat that partially covered the living-room floor. Courtney continued her attack, concentrating on the most sensitive spot—the back of April's neck.

April was squealing with helpless fury when Mrs. Blair burst into the room, loaded down with shopping bags. "April—what are you doing?" she asked, sighing as she set the heavy bags down.

Mom certainly has a flair for asking the obvious, April thought. "I'm being tickled," she answered.

"We're monsters," Whitney explained, still straddling April's back, her yellow sneakers digging into April's sides.

"I *know* that," Mrs. Blair said sarcastically. "But, April, why aren't you helping? There's still plenty to unload from the car."

"Sorry," April said quickly, trying unsuccessfully to unload her little sister. "They won't let me help."

"April, you're ten years older than they are," Mrs. Blair said impatiently. "Why do you let them push you around the way you do?"

"Mom—" April cried, turning it into a three-syllable word. "They've got me outnumbered, you know?"

"Yeah!" Courtney agreed and resumed tickling April's neck.

"You haven't even opened any windows," her

mother wailed. "It's so stuffy in here, April. The house has been closed up all winter. At least you could open the windows and let some fresh air in."

"She can't get up," Whitney said, pushing April's head against the straw mat.

"You girls are old enough to help too," Mrs. Blair said, hoisting the shopping bags.

"No, we're not. We're only six," Courtney insisted.

"You have a smart mouth, young lady," their mother said, exasperated.

"So do I!" insisted Whitney. "I'm smart too."

Mrs. Blair laughed. "Get up and help your father unload the car. You know, we didn't come all the way from Shadyside to roll around on a dusty floor. The sooner we get unpacked, the sooner we can get to the beach."

Whitney gave April a final push and jumped to her feet. "Let's go to the beach now," she demanded.

"Yeah!" echoed her twin, tugging April's hand, trying to pull her to her feet.

April groaned and stood up. "I'm going to need a vacation after a summer with these two!" she declared, dusting off her tennis shorts and sleeveless top, which had started out white but were now gray and streaked with dirt.

"Oh, I imagine you'll be spending all of your time with Matt," her mother called from the back bedroom. "We won't see you all summer—as usual."

"Let's go to the beach," Courtney demanded, tugging on April's hand.

"Ow!" April broke away from her little sister and hurried to the back bedroom to confront her mother. "Don't start in about Matt," she said heatedly. She blew a strand of straight honey blond hair off her forehead.

"I didn't say a word about Matt," Mrs. Blair said defensively. "It's just that—"

"Just that *what?*" April demanded. "Go ahead. Say it."

"It's just that I thought we'd have a nice family vacation," her mother said, avoiding April's stare as she made the bed. "And that maybe you'd meet a bunch of nice new kids here at Sandy Hollow. Instead of hanging around with the same kids you hang around with back in Shadyside."

"You mean Matt and Todd," April said angrily.

"Calm down. Sshh," Mrs. Blair said, raising a finger to her lips. "I guess I *was* disappointed that Matt and his family decided to summer here again."

"What's wrong with Matt?" April demanded, unable to calm down. "We've been going together more than a year, and—"

"April—we've had this discussion before," her mother said with a hint of weariness in her voice. "Matt is perfectly okay. He's very nice, actually. Especially compared to a lot of the boys you've brought home."

"Gee, thanks," April said sarcastically.

29

"It's just that he's—well, you know, a little immature for you, don't you think? I mean, he's only interested in sports, video games, and horror movies. Don't you think you should look around? Find someone with more intelligent interests? I mean—"

"You're right, Mom," April said curtly. "We've had this discussion before." She turned and strode quickly from the room.

"April—where are you going?" Mrs. Blair called after her, realizing she had gone too far, said too much.

"To help Dad," April called back from the hallway. And then peevishly added: "That's what you *wanted*—isn't it?"

April spent the rest of the afternoon helping her parents. There was so much to do at the summer house—unloading the car, unpacking all the bags, airing out the stuffy rooms, cleaning the house, buying food and supplies—and fighting with Courtney and Whitney.

As the sun lowered behind the dunes, Mr. Blair made the first barbecue of the season. Hot dogs and hamburgers sizzled on the grill, the smoke trailing over the tall reeds bending in the breeze.

Mr. Blair lived to barbecue. It was about the only thing at the beach he did like. He had delicate, fair skin, so he avoided the beach for the most part. He was happy to lie in a hammock and read, waiting for evening so he could barbecue.

30

After dinner April excused herself and hurried upstairs to change. Glancing at the clock on her small antique dressing table, she saw that she was already late. She had arranged to meet Matt in town at seven-thirty.

He'd better wait for me, she told herself, pulling off her shorts and tossing them on the floor. Then she searched the closet for a pair of denim cutoffs.

"Why do you let your sisters push you around?"

Suddenly her mother's words from that afternoon came back to April.

"Because it's easier than fighting with them," April answered the question.

"Because it's always easier to give in, not to fight with people.

"Because I'm a pushover."

All of these answers seemed right to April. And wrong.

She brushed her straight blond hair, her emerald green eyes staring back at her from the scratched dressing-table mirror.

Am I really such a pushover? she asked herself, examining her face in the spotted mirror. She liked what she saw—for the most part. If only her nose were a little longer. She wasn't as pretty as her sisters, but she was okay.

I'm *not* going to be a pushover about Matt, she decided, pulling her brush through her hair one last time before standing up.

I'm not going to let Mom put him down anymore.

Matt is a great guy. I'm glad he's going to be at Sandy Hollow too. We're going to have a really awesome summer together.

She waved good-bye to her parents, who were still on the deck in back, playing some kind of leapfrog game with the Twin Terrors. Then she headed around to the front of the house and, half walking, half jogging, headed along Beach Haven Drive toward town.

Beach Haven Drive.

She had to laugh. It was such a fancy name for what was nothing more than a narrow, unpaved path.

It was about a ten-minute walk from the cluster of summer cottages, past a sandy patch lined with tall reeds, then flat, grassy fields dotted with an occasional oak or willow tree, to the small town.

Following the path, April was only about five minutes from her house when someone leapt out of the shadows of the tall reeds and grabbed her roughly from behind.

Chapter 5

COLD FOREVER

"Gotcha!" Matt cried.

He let go of April and stepped onto the road, a taunting grin on his face, his dark eyes challenging her to retaliate. "April Fools'!"

"Matt—you jerk!" April cried, swinging a fist and missing him as he dodged to one side, laughing. He was always scaring her and crying "April Fools'!" and she really hated it.

She turned to Todd, who had followed his friend out from the tall reeds, his hands shoved into the pockets of his faded jeans. "Tell him he's a jerk," she said, her heart still thudding hard in her chest.

"You're a jerk," Todd obediently repeated to Matt.

Matt's grin didn't fade. Despite the cool of the evening, he was wearing red and blue baggy shorts and a sleeveless blue T-shirt. Matt stood over April, tall and broad-chested, a little pudgy. With his short brown hair, black eyes, and round cheeks, he reminded April of a big teddy bear.

Todd formed a complete contrast to his friend. He was short and lean with curly, carrot-colored hair and a serious expression punctuated by piercing blue eyes. He seldom smiled. He was quiet and shy, especially compared to Matt. Even though the three of them hung out together constantly, Todd often seemed uncomfortable, reluctant to tag along with the other two.

In the past few months April had tried arranging dates for Todd with some of her friends. He was painfully shy around them and never mustered up the courage to ask any of them out a second time. April gave up trying, and Todd just hung out with Matt and her.

"When did you get here?" Matt asked, putting an arm possessively around April's shoulder.

"This afternoon," she replied. "The house is in pretty good shape, but my parents will be cleaning it for a week!"

"My mom had a fit when we arrived yesterday," Matt said, "because one of the windows was broken and some kind of animal had gotten in and left a few surprises on the carpet."

"Yuck," April said. "Your mother is such a neat-freak, she must have dropped her teeth."

"Oh, no. She took it very calmly. She just said she wanted to turn around and drive back to

Shadyside and never come back," Matt said, chuckling.

"Hey, this sure beats Fear Street," Todd said, a few paces behind them. Todd lived in a ramshackle, old house across the street from the Fear Street cemetery. *Any* place would be better than that, April thought.

"You won't *believe* what a great place this is," Matt said to Todd. "It's awesome. Bodysurfing all afternoon, soaking up the rays. Then party on the beach all night. Then throw up all morning and start all over again!"

Matt laughed. April playfully shoved him away. "You're really gross."

"What else is new?" Todd asked quietly.

"Hey—whose side are you on?" Matt asked, pretending to be offended. He slung his arm back over April's shoulder and they continued to follow the curving dirt road past flat, grassy fields, a cluster of small, white clapboard houses, and finally into the town.

The air grew warmer as they stepped onto the wood-plank walk that lined Main Street and stopped to look around. April reached up and unloaded Matt's arm from her shoulder. His arm seemed to weigh a ton.

"Hey, look—" Matt said, pointing. "They added a video-game arcade next to Swanny's." He turned back to Todd. "You bring any money?"

Todd searched his jeans pockets but pulled out

only the blue plastic butane lighter he always carried. He shook his head.

Matt turned back to April. "No way," she told him, her green eyes flaring. "We're not hanging out in a stuffy arcade tonight. I thought we were going to walk around town, check out who's here, then go to the beach."

"Oh, yeah. Right," Matt said, giving the arcade one last, longing look.

They made their way slowly up one side of Main Street, stopping to check out the shop windows before heading down the other side of the street. Even though the season had just begun, the town was crowded. Main Street was clogged with slow-moving cars, the walks filled with new arrivals chatting, greeting one another, aimlessly moving in pairs and small groups.

"Hey, check out the movie theater," Matt cried enthusiastically, staring up at the old-fashioned marquee across the street. "A Living Dead festival!" He slapped Todd a high-five. "All *right!*"

He pulled the two of them across the street to study the movie posters displaying the coming attractions. "Looks like it's all horror, all the time!" he declared, slapping Todd another enthusiastic high-five.

April groaned. She hated horror movies. She couldn't understand why Matt thought they were so terrific.

"Come on, Matt." She pulled him away. "What's going on over there?"

The old movie theater was the last building on the street. The little town just came to an end there, giving way to a small, asphalt rectangle used as a parking lot, and then a wide, grassy field that was used for town picnics and all kinds of sporting events. That night the field was brightly lit with several spotlights, and the dark outlines of several trucks and vans could be seen on the grass.

Hurrying across the parking lot, April and her companions saw what was going on. A carnival was being set up. As they approached, they could hear the shouts of the workers, the whine of saws, and the steady thud of hammers.

It didn't seem real. The spotlights, aimed at the sky, created more shadow than light. Workers busily moved in and out of the shadows. Like a dark, silent giant, a Ferris wheel loomed over the field. Colored lights were being strung from poles. Food and game booths were being hammered into place. Men struggled to bolt a small roller-coaster track together.

April, Matt, and Todd huddled together at the edge of the field, watching the dreamlike spectacle. "Wonder if they'll have a Gravitron," Todd said quietly, breaking their silence.

"What's that?" April asked.

"You know. It's the thing that spins around and then the floor drops out and leaves you pressed against the wall."

"Sounds great," April said sarcastically.

Matt stared at Todd in surprise. "You like that ride?"

"No way," Todd said quickly. "I wouldn't go on it. I just wondered if they have it."

"I love Ferris wheels," April said, turning her eyes to the dark structure that towered over the field.

"They're for wimps," Matt said scornfully. "I mean, what's scary about a Ferris wheel?"

"Why does everything have to be scary?" April demanded.

He took her hand. "Come on. Let's check out the beach. This is boring."

The night sky was clear, bright, and cloudless, and the sandy beach shimmered like a broad, silver ribbon under the light of a full moon.

Couples walked barefoot along the shore, gentle waves lapping over their ankles. Groups of kids, blankets spread over the powdery sand, sat and talked and laughed. Music boomed from portable radios and tape players, a jangle of sound, rising and falling over the rush of water as it lapped at the shore.

At the base of a low dune, some kids had built a small bonfire. Making their way toward it, their bare feet moving silently over the soft sand, April and Matt recognized some of the kids, townies they had met the summer before.

"Hey—Ben!" Matt called out to a boy with shadows playing over his face from the fire as it darted and flickered.

"Whoa!" Ben Ashen, tall and gangly with short, spiked black hair, wheeled around at the sound of his name and peered at Matt. "Hey—the Mattster! How you doin'? You still so ugly?"

"You still so stupid?" Matt gave Ben a hard slap on the back.

Ben groaned. "Do that again and I'll hurl on you."

"What a class guy!" Matt exclaimed, and raised his hand to give Ben another hard backslap, but Ben edged away.

Several other kids greeted April and Matt. They lowered themselves onto a communal blanket, feeling the warmth of the crackling fire. Huddled in the red glow, everyone began talking at once.

"Hey, Todd, there's room for you," Matt called, suddenly remembering his friend. Todd, who had been left standing awkwardly in the shadows, hands in his pockets, hesitantly lowered himself to the blanket on the other side of April. "Hey, everyone, this is Todd," Matt announced.

"You see the new arcade?" Ben asked Matt. "It's excellent."

"I saw it, but I didn't bring any money," Matt said.

"I've got some," Ben told him, rising to his knees. "Come on. Let's go."

Matt started to get up, then remembered April. "Uh, not tonight, man." He put an arm possessively around April's shoulders and turned to smile at her. Her emerald eyes glowed, reflecting the firelight. She smiled back at him and lowered her forehead affectionately against his chest.

"Well, I'm outta here," Ben announced, climbing to his feet.

"Later," Matt said, without looking up.

Ben started jogging over the dune. "Bring some money tomorrow night," he called back to Matt. "Steal it if you have to."

"He's a class guy, isn't he?" Matt said quietly, holding April close.

She made a face, then glanced over at Todd, who was by himself at the edge of the blanket, staring at the fire, not talking to anyone. She saw that he was twirling the blue plastic lighter between his fingers, moving it back and forth in his hand, the way he always did when he felt nervous or uncomfortable.

April started to say something to him, but before she could, Matt put his hand on her chin, tilted her head up to his, and began to kiss her.

"That one," Jessica said, red eyes aflame, peering at Gabri in the darkness.

"Which one?" Gabri asked, floating beside her, the wind filling his outspread wings.

"The blond girl," Jessica said impatiently.

The two bats lowered themselves toward the ring of teenagers around the campfire, but stayed high enough to remain in the dark and out of sight.

"She's perfect for you, Gabri," Jessica said, her voice a wet whisper through her slender, pointed fangs. "Look at that blond hair, those rosy, milk-fed cheeks, that wholesome good health. She's just your type!" A hiss of laughter escaped her small opening of a mouth.

"No!" Gabri whispered, fluttering his black wings in agitation. "That big lunk of a boy has his arm around her. He's kissing her. She has a boyfriend, Jessica. I really must protest."

"I really must protest." Jessica imitated his voice, mocking him. "You really sound like a bad movie, Gabri."

"I don't care. I protest. The girl you've chosen for me has a boyfriend. How am I to win her affections if—"

"You didn't think I'd make it easy for you!" Jessica declared, another hiss of laughter spraying the night sky.

She soared high as he attempted to bump her, then allowed herself to float back beside him. "Of course, if you'd like to give up now . . ." she teased.

"No!" Gabri cried, tilting toward the leaping flames below, then swooping easily away. His tiny red eyes peered through the darkness, attaching to April like evil radar, studying her carefully.

"Well?" Jessica asked impatiently.

"I accept the challenge," Gabri replied, a gob of white spittle sliding down the fur of his chin. "The girl is so luscious—so *ready*—so ripe."

"Save the poetry for when you're alone with her," Jessica snapped. "You really are the biggest jerk. Were you this bad when you were alive?"

Gabri's bat eyes narrowed as he stared hard into

hers. Even in bat form, the eyes revealed deep sorrow. "I don't remember," he whispered. "I don't think I ever *was* alive."

Jessica refused to allow herself to be touched by his words. She filled the air with dry, scornful laughter.

"Never mind!" he cried hoarsely, ruby eyes lighting with fury. He tilted away from her, swooping just above the yellow light of the fire.

Suspended in the night air, wings outstretched, allowing the wind and currents to carry him this way, then that, Gabri stared down at the shifting figures around the fire.

"Have you found a victim for me?" Jessica asked, her voice drifting down from somewhere above.

"Yes," Gabri hissed, encircling his rodentlike body with his wings, then shooting them out and soaring back up to meet her.

"Which one?" Jessica asked eagerly, her lips wet with anticipation, the thought of fresh nectar making her heart flutter faster than her wings.

"That one," Gabri declared. "The little skinny one with the red hair."

Jessica peered down into the firelight, training her eyes on Todd. "The one sitting by himself, not talking to anyone?"

"Yes," Gabri replied, obviously pleased with his selection. "That guy won't warm up to anyone— not even you, Jessica."

"I'm afraid you've lost our bet," Jessica taunted,

deliberately brushing Gabri out of her way. "I'll warm that boy up easily—and then he'll be *cold* forever!"

Her dry, hoarse laughter ruffled against the wind.

Having selected their victims, the two bats slid low in the sky, then floated high, soaring into the dark emptiness high above the dunes.

Tucked next to Matt, April raised her eyes just as the bats swooped near and uttered a loud gasp. "Matt—did you see them? Two of them," she cried.

"Don't pay any attention to them," Matt told her, pulling her close. "They're perfectly harmless."

Chapter 6

TODD AND JESSICA

It took Todd a while to realize that the small dots hopping along in the puddled shadows were birds. He stood on the low, smooth rock watching them, trying to focus on them. They're terns, he decided, his eyes following them as they made their way along the shoreline, zigzagging around one another until the darkness swallowed them up.

His hands shoved into the pockets of his cutoffs, Todd turned and allowed his eyes to follow the sloping line of rocks up to where they flattened out, forming a shelf on top of a steep cliff. Then turning back to the water, he could just barely make out the low, black outline of the small island, like the top of a submarine coming up for air, the island where all the bats supposedly came from.

Why *are* there so many bats on this beach? he

wondered, searching the hazy purple sky for the fluttering creatures. He saw none.

He couldn't see very far. Low clouds pushed over the shore, filtering the moonlight, making the beach shadows long and strange. Wisps of fog trailed along the shoreline. The air was cool, heavy, and damp.

This end of the beach, south of the rowboat dock, across from the mysterious, wooded island, was usually deserted, he had discovered. That's why he liked it so much. He could lean peacefully against the smooth, cool rocks and stare out at the water for as long as he wanted.

How long had he been standing there watching the clouds lower and the fog drift in? Todd wasn't sure. He knew he was supposed to meet April and Matt down the beach. He was probably late.

Hope you're not turning into some kind of weird loner, he warned himself, stepping away from the rocks and starting to trudge up the beach.

This could be a great summer, he thought. If only I could shape up and stop being such a drag. If only I could stop feeling so awkward, so out of place all the time, and—

His thoughts were interrupted by a fluttering sound overhead. Turning his eyes to the low, hazy sky, he saw several bats swooping and soaring, disappearing into the thick cloud cover, then suddenly scooting low enough to be seen again.

Bats are good, he told himself. They eat insects.

But their fluttering sound so near, echoing off the steep rock cliffs, and the shrill chatter they made gave Todd a chill.

He took a few long steps, wet sand invading his rubber thongs—and then stopped.

He was no longer alone. Someone was there.

Behind him. Back by the rocks.

He hadn't seen anyone. He just had that feeling. He knew.

The fluttering sound overhead grew louder, closer, then quickly faded. The wind off the ocean whipped at his sweatshirt.

Todd turned around.

And saw the girl staring at him.

She stood a few feet from the rocks, barefoot. As she approached, the beach seemed to light up, and Todd could see her as clearly as if it were daytime.

She was beautiful.

"Hi," she said softly, staring at him shyly with big, dark eyes. She was wearing a flowered sarong skirt and a matching bikini top. With a toss of her head, she waved her long red hair behind her bare shoulders. She smiled at him with full, dark lips.

"I—I didn't see you," Todd stammered.

What a dumb thing to say, he told himself, immediately wishing he could sink into the sand and never be seen again.

"I mean I—"

"I think I'm lost," the girl said, coming closer, close enough that he could see how pale her skin

46

was, close enough that he could smell her perfume, the scent of lilacs.

"Huh? Lost?"

She nodded, her full lips forming a pout.

She's the most beautiful girl I've ever seen, Todd thought. He realized he was gaping at her. Embarrassed, he cast his eyes down to the sand.

"My family is renting a cottage," she told him, gliding even closer. "Right near the ocean. We just arrived this afternoon, and I think I'm all turned around." She shrugged, a helpless gesture, her shoulders as smooth and pale as ivory under the hazy night sky.

"Yeah. Well—" Todd cleared his throat.

Why does my voice sound so tight and choked?

"Most of the summer houses are on that end," he managed to get out, and pointed to the north end of the beach.

"Up that way?" she asked hesitantly.

"Yeah. I'll show you," Todd said. "I mean, I'm going that way. I'm—uh—meeting some friends."

"Thanks," she said and, to Todd's surprise, reached out and took his arm. Her flowery scent invaded his nostrils, seemed to encircle him. He suddenly felt dizzy, but forced himself to walk, his thongs sinking into the wet sand.

"I've never been here before," she said softly. "It's so beautiful. I know it's going to be fun."

"Yeah. It's very—pretty," Todd said.

I'm walking on a dark beach with the most beautiful girl I've ever seen, he thought.

And all I can think of to say is that the beach is *pretty*. Yuck.

"It's very foggy," he said. "That's why the beach is so empty and dark tonight."

Oh, great. Now I'm giving her weather reports! he thought.

"You're lucky to have friends here," she said, turning to smile at him, still clinging to his arm. "I don't know anybody."

"That's too bad," Todd replied awkwardly.

"Maybe *you* can be my friend," she said and giggled self-consciously.

Wow, Todd thought.

"Where are you from?" she asked.

Todd told her.

He continued to lead the way, walking slowly, breathing in her perfume, stealing glances at her, wishing the beach were longer so they wouldn't reach their destination so quickly.

He tried to think of things to say to her, but she was so close, and so beautiful that he was even more tongue-tied than usual.

Luckily, she kept up the conversation, asking him questions about school and his family, telling him about her family and her life in Maine.

I wonder if she likes me, Todd thought.

I wonder if she'll go out with me if I ask her.

If I ask her. The big if.

Could he summon the nerve to ask?

They both heard it at the same time. The fluttering of wings so low, so close overhead.

"Oh!" she cried out and squeezed his arm.

"It's okay," he said, trying to sound assured. "The bats don't bother anyone."

She laughed. A surprising laugh.

Why did it strike her as funny?

"By the way, my name is Jessica," she said. He realized she was still squeezing his arm.

He told her his name. Her perfume was so sweet.

The white beach seemed to tilt beneath him.

"Oh. My house is right up there," she said, pointing. "You were right!"

He followed the direction of her finger. It was suddenly so foggy, so gray and foggy, he could barely make out any houses beyond the dunes.

There was no one on the beach. The water seemed far away. Beyond the fog. Beyond the clouds that seemed to lower around him.

"Thanks for helping me, Todd," she whispered.

He loved the way she said his name.

"That's okay," he said.

Should I ask her out?

Should I ask her to meet me on the beach tomorrow?

Will she say yes?

Will she laugh at me?

Before he could decide, she was kissing him.

He nearly toppled backward in surprise.

Before he could decide. Before he could say anything. Before he realized what was happening, her arms, so pale, so light, were around him.

She pulled on him ever so gently, pulled his face to hers, lowered her face to his.

Those lips. Those dark, dark lips. Pressing so tenderly against his.

Tenderly at first. And then harder.

Oh, wow, he thought. Oh, wow.

She likes me.

Then she was kissing him as no girl had ever kissed him before.

Kissing his mouth. His cheek.

His neck.

Kissing his neck as the clouds lowered and the fog circled in. Kissing his neck as the sand tilted beneath him.

She was holding his head and kissing his neck hard, harder.

The smell of the perfume, the roar of the ocean, the soft wetness of her lips, the fog, the thick fog—it all swept over Todd, swept over him, over him, over him.

Until he sank into a cool, waiting darkness.

Chapter 7

APRIL AND GABRI

Where *is* he?

April made her way through the crowded aisle of the arcade, explosions, automatic gunfire, space battles, and car races roaring in the narrow, dimly lit room.

Where *is* he?

Near the back of the arcade past a row of flashing pinball machines, she thought she saw him, trying to push a dollar bill into the change machine. The dollar went halfway into the slot, then came sliding out. He tried again.

"Matt!" she called.

When he finally succeeded in getting his game tokens and turned around, she saw it was some other big-shouldered, round-faced brown-haired boy.

Matt isn't here.

Back on the street, she pulled down the sleeves of her olive sweater and pushed back her blond hair, which felt damp and heavy from the humid air.

Fog was drifting in from the ocean, creating strange, shifting shadows beneath the streetlights. Searching for Matt, April turned her gaze down Main Street, jammed with summer people floating in and out of the restaurants and shops. They emerged from the fog, brightened quickly into focus, then faded just as quickly back into the mist, as if stepping through a heavy curtain.

Where are you, Matt? April wondered, glancing at her watch for the thousandth time. Lost in a fog?

She poked her head into Swanny's, her eyes quickly surveying the brightly lit ice-cream parlor, then stepped aside to let a middle-aged couple enter.

He wasn't in there, either.

He was supposed to have met her nearly twenty minutes earlier. The plan was to meet in front of Swanny's, then head to the beach and hook up with Todd.

"Hey—April!"

April spun around hopefully. "Matt?"

No. It was a couple of guys she had met at the bonfire on the beach the night before. She waved. "Lookin' good!" one of them called. Then they disappeared into the lowering fog.

I *am* lookin' good, April thought. She and the twins had spent the afternoon at the beach, and now she could feel the warm glow of her sunburn. She always got so pale during the winter. Now she was getting some color, feeling warm despite the cool, foggy night, feeling alive.

So where was Matt?

He really takes me for granted, she decided.

He keeps me waiting all the time. And then he shows up without an excuse or anything. He usually just says, "Sorry I'm late. I got hung up." And that's supposed to be okay.

The flash of warmth she felt now wasn't from her sunburn—it was from anger. Matt is a great guy, she thought. But maybe her mother was a little bit right about him. Maybe he *is* a little immature.

April stepped to the corner and peered up and down Dune Lane, one of only two cross streets in town.

I'm not going to wait for Matt all summer, she thought.

Gazing at the shadows on the street created by swirls of fog under the corner streetlight, April suddenly sensed that she was being watched.

She turned to see a tall, thin boy in a black sweatshirt and dark, straight-legged denims. He was standing on the opposite corner in front of the camera store. The curtain of fog seemed to part in front of him, and as he stepped under the white light of the street lamp, April could see him with almost exaggerated clarity.

He was very handsome, she saw, with straight black hair, very pale, almost white skin, a slender, serious face, and dark eyes, which he turned away when he realized she was staring back at him.

He looks like an actor or a model, April thought. He's almost *too* good-looking.

She wondered if he was waiting for someone. Then the fog seemed to close in around him, and he became a solitary, still shadow among many moving shadows.

I'm giving Matt five more minutes, April decided, pacing angrily back and forth between the corner and the front of the arcade. Then I'm going home.

This is a bad start to the summer, she thought. She decided she'd just have to be straight with Matt. There were two kinds of people in the world—those who always showed up on time and those who never showed up on time. April was always punctual. And if they were going to have a good time this summer, she decided as she paced, Matt would have to be punctual too.

Glancing at her watch, she was about to give up on him when a hand touched the shoulder of her sweater.

Startled, she spun around, expecting to see Matt.

Instead she stared into the penetrating, dark eyes of the handsome boy she had seen across the street.

"Hi," he said shyly. "Sorry. Did I scare you?"

"No," April lied. "I mean—no."

"Are you lost or something?" he asked. "I saw you here and I thought . . ." His voice trailed off. He stared into her eyes.

"No. I'm not lost," April said with a sigh. "I'm waiting for someone."

"Oh. Sorry." The boy took a step back.

He couldn't be a townie, April thought. He's so pale.

But so good-looking.

He flashed her an embarrassed smile. "I didn't mean to bother you."

"That's okay," April said. She realized she didn't want him to leave. "Is this your first summer here?" she asked.

He shook his head. "No. I've been here before. It doesn't usually get this foggy in town."

"I know," April said. "By the way," she added, feeling a bit awkward, "I'm April Blair."

"Gabri Martins," he said and reached out and briefly shook her hand.

"Gabri? That's an odd name," April blurted out.

He nodded. "Yeah. I know. It's short for Gabriel."

"Well, it's nice to meet you, Gabri," April said.

He was so thin, half the size of Matt.

He stared into her eyes and seemed to be reluctant to leave. He was wearing a lemony aftershave or cologne, April realized, sweet and tart at the same time. She felt drawn to him, more than just attracted because of his good looks.

She had to concentrate hard to hear what he was saying.

"Maybe your friend got mixed up or something. Did he know to meet you here?"

April nodded. "We were supposed to meet here, then go to the beach." Why did she suddenly feel uncertain?

"Maybe he got mixed up and went straight to the beach," Gabri suggested, taking a step closer to her as a group of teenagers squeezed past on the walk.

"Maybe," April replied thoughtfully.

Matt usually got things right. But maybe he *did* get mixed up.

"The beach isn't very crowded tonight with this heavy fog," Gabri said. "It shouldn't take long to find him if he's there."

"Yeah. I guess," April said reluctantly. "But it's so dark tonight. . . ."

"Tell you what. I'll go with you," Gabri offered. He smelled so lemony, so good. He leaned toward her, his handsome face brightening out of the shadows, his eyes locked on hers.

"That's really nice of you," April said. "But—"

"I'm a nice guy," Gabri said, smiling to let her know he was joking, not seriously boasting. And then he quietly added, "You'll see."

"But you don't have to take me—" April started.

"No problem," he assured her. "Come on."

She felt his hand on her back as they turned the corner and began to follow Dune Lane to the ocean. To April's surprise, the curtain of fog grew lighter as they neared the beach.

"The town of Sandy Hollow is low," Gabri explained. "Sort of in a gully. When a fog floats off the ocean, it hovers over the town and stays there."

"Are you a science expert?" April asked, teasing.

"Ask me anything," he said, his hand still lightly on her back.

A heavy layer of low, gray clouds hovered over the shore, but the beach was clear. No fog at all.

The waves were high and rough. April could see the white froth on the towering wave tops, even in the darkness.

A few couples walked near the water. A group of teenagers huddled around a small bonfire, sounds from their tape player competing with the rhythmic thunder of crashing waves.

No sign of Matt. Or Todd.

April and Gabri, walking close together, occasionally bumping shoulders, made their way south toward the rock cliff. As they walked, he told her about a whale that had somehow lost its direction and washed ashore in the early spring. He made her laugh by imitating the frightened look on the whale's face. And then he described the heroic actions of the townies who managed to pull the whale back out to the water and send it on its way.

He's really smart. And funny, April thought.

And interesting.

I'll bet he doesn't waste his time at stupid horror movies.

She stopped and peered down the empty beach.

Was she really attracted to Gabri? Or was she just angry at Matt?

A little of both, probably.

"He's not here," she said softly, staring at the

steep rock cliff beyond the rowboat dock, feeling Gabri standing close behind her. "But the beach is really awesome tonight. The waves are so rough."

Gabri checked in all directions, making sure they were completely alone. The ocean waves thundered, black against an even blacker sky.

They were surrounded by the blackness. And alone.

And Gabri could resist her no longer.

She was so beautiful. So perfect. So sweet.

Yes, the nectar would taste so sweet.

He needed it now. He needed the nectar.

Not just because of his silly bet with Jessica. But because he needed the nectar to survive. It was the nectar that kept him going so many long years after he had died. It was the nectar that made him an Eternal One.

And now he was about to drink.

She stood in front of him, her back to him, arms crossed, staring at the dark, tumbling waves.

He leaned forward as his fangs slid wetly down his chin.

Gently, gently he raised his hand and pushed the hair away to reveal the back of her neck.

So pale. Such tender skin.

Breathing heavily, Gabri opened his mouth wide and lowered his head to bite.

Chapter 8

"TWO CAN PLAY DIRTY"

Watching the waves, nearly hypnotized by their dark, rolling splendor, by the soft explosion of sound as they hit the shore, April felt Gabri somewhere close behind her.

Matt isn't here, she thought. No one else is here. The beach is so empty.

I've got to get home.

It seemed as if a soft rush of wind was moving her hair to one side.

She started to turn toward Gabri, preparing to thank him for accompanying her through the darkness. But before she could move, she felt warmth on the back of her neck. Gentler than the wind. Soft, like breath.

And then she heard the fluttering sound, followed by a hideous metallic screech.

And then a dark shadow dropped from the sky.

A shadow at first, then a living, screeching, clawing creature.

April saw the red, glowing eyes and knew instantly that it was a bat.

She cried out and raised her hands.

Too late.

Screeching shrilly like a car alarm gone out of control, the bat dug its talons into April's hair.

"Oh! Help!"

She could feel its wings flapping against her head, feel its warm body bumping against her, feel it tangling itself in her hair, struggling, tearing, clawing.

"Help—*please!*"

She closed her eyes, dropped to her knees in the sand, helplessly flailing her arms above her head.

The creature hissed and clawed, struggling to free itself from the long tangles of her hair.

Then Gabri was there, swatting at it with his hand.

The shrill screech echoed throughout her head. The wings beat furiously.

Then with a final, sickening *yelp,* the bat broke free—and was gone, soaring silently up into the blackness.

April leapt to her feet. Even though she knew it was gone, she could still feel the creature bumping against her head, could still feel the beating of its wings.

The ocean roared louder. The roar circled her, came at her from all sides. She pressed her hands against her ears, but the roar continued, as if it were *inside* her head!

She suddenly realized that the sound *was* coming from her. She was screaming. Screaming out her terror.

And suddenly the whole beach started to roll. The sand was moving beneath her feet.

No.

The beach isn't moving.

I am.

She was running hard, running over the sand, running away from the shore, away from the rock cliff, gasping for breath, her chest aching, running too hard to scream now.

Running, running—into Matt's arms.

"Whoa!" he cried. "April—what's wrong?"

She held on to him tightly, waiting for her heart to stop racing, waiting for her chest to stop heaving, waiting for the feeling of the clawing bat in her hair to fade.

"What happened? *Tell* me!" Matt demanded, still holding her tight, wrapping her safely in his arms.

"I—was looking for you," April finally managed to get out, pressing her forehead against the warmth of his sweatshirt. "Here. On the beach."

"And?" he demanded impatiently.

"And a bat flew into my hair. It got tangled somehow. It was screeching at me. So loud. I panicked. It was trapped. I couldn't get it out. But then Gabri—"

61

"Who?" Matt asked. "Who's Gabri?"

"That boy over there," April said, pointing behind her without turning around. "He was so nice. He pulled the bat out. He—"

"Who?" Matt demanded.

April pulled away from Matt and turned to call to Gabri.

"Hey—"

There was no one there.

Far down the beach, on the high shelf of the dark rock cliff, slippery from the mists and heavy dew, two bats landed silently. As dark as the night, they began to whirl, folding and unfolding their wings as they spun in an eerie, tuneless dance.

They emerged from the dance in human form.

Gabri, his red eyes flaring, raged at Jessica, backing her to the sharp cliff edge. "You jealous fool!" he shrieked. "You saw that I was about to drink the nectar. Why did you interrupt?"

She responded with scornful laughter. "Are you going to push me off the cliff?" she asked casually, ignoring his rage. "You can't kill me, Gabri. I've been an Eternal for years."

"Answer my question," he insisted, not backing away, not giving her room to move. "Why were you spying on me? Why did you *do* that?"

"Calm down and we can talk," Jessica said, holding her ground. She straightened the hem of her dark sundress, then started to button the cardigan sweater she wore on top of it.

62

"I'm not going to calm down," Gabri said heatedly. "Answer me!"

"All right, all right," she replied, rolling her eyes. "You weren't playing by the rules."

"Huh?" Some of the fury drained from his eyes, replaced by bewilderment.

"You can't just attack that girl," Jessica said, shaking her head, her mane of red hair bobbing behind her. "You have to make her desire you first."

"Are you crazy?" Gabri cried, his dark features distorted by his anger. "She *liked* me."

"I saw what you were doing," Jessica insisted. "She wasn't even looking at you. You can't do that, Gabri. That's not our bet."

Gabri raised his face to the sky and let loose an animal cry of rage. When he stopped, he seemed a little calmer. "I should've let you strangle in her hair," he muttered.

She laughed, a dry, humorless laugh.

"Stop laughing at me," he snapped. "You think you're so funny."

"Yes," she agreed smugly. "I do."

He pointed at her, his eyes narrowing. "I'm warning you, Jessica. Two can play dirty at this game. Laugh all you want, I can play just as dirty as you. You'd better watch out."

Jessica yawned loudly. "You don't scare me, Gabri."

"You'd better watch out," he repeated, starting to spin himself back to bat form.

It's those two teenagers who had better watch out, Jessica thought, smiling as she thought about Todd, about the nectar, about how easily she was going to win this bet, and how much she was going to enjoy winning it.

A few seconds later two bats floated up from the rock cliff, circled the dark sky briefly, dipping low over the wildly leaping waves. Then hissing angrily at each other, their glowing red eyes met, locked in challenge. Then they soared off, swallowed up by the heavy clouds, retreating to their lairs to wait, to plan, to dream of how they would soon quench their relentless thirst.

Chapter 9

A QUICK BITE
IN TOWN

"How's the ocean?" Mr. Daniels asked, padding to the kitchen counter in the baggy bathing suit he always wore around the house. Sleepily he poured himself another cup of coffee.

Matt had gotten up early, before eight o'clock, and feeling energetic, he had slipped out of the house without waking his parents and taken a long walk along the beach. "It's wild," he told his father, pulling open the refrigerator door and removing a carton of orange juice.

"Very descriptive," Mr. Daniels said sarcastically, standing at the counter, sipping coffee, staring out the kitchen window at the orange sun in the clear sky.

"No. I mean, the waves are wild. Very high. Coming in at different angles," Matt said.

"Don't drink from the carton," his father scolded. "Get yourself a glass."

"I only wanted a sip," Matt told him, returning the carton to the fridge, wiping his mouth with the back of his hand. "Did Todd call?"

Mr. Daniels glanced up at the kitchen clock before replying. Nine-thirty. "No."

"I was supposed to meet him last night, but we never hooked up."

"He didn't call," Mr. Daniels said, yawning. "You want to play some tennis today?"

"Maybe later," Matt replied. "I want to go bodysurfing this morning. It should be awesome with the waves so wild." He walked over to the wall phone and picked up the receiver.

"Who are you calling?" his father asked, scratching his bare chest.

"Todd. He'll probably want to go to the beach with me."

"Hey, look—a hummingbird!" Mr. Daniels exclaimed, pointing out the window.

Matt replaced the receiver and started to the window. "Where, Dad?"

"In that flower. Oh. Too late. You missed it."

"Are you sure it wasn't just a big fly?" Matt joked. "I had flies in my room last night as big as bluejays!"

"I've got to get those screens fixed," Mr. Daniels muttered, shaking his head. Carrying his coffee cup, he slid open the glass door and slipped out on the deck. "Isn't it a little early to call people?" he called in from outside.

"No. Todd always gets up early," Matt said, picking up the receiver again. He found the number of Todd's beach house on the pad on the counter and quickly dialed it.

The phone rang five times before Todd's mother picked it up.

"Hi, this is Matt. Can I speak to Todd?"

"Hi, Matt," she said breathlessly. "Sorry. I was out back in the garden." She took a few seconds to catch her breath. "I don't think Todd is awake yet. He came in very late. I'll go check."

"What a lazy bum," Matt said, glancing at the wall clock. Todd was always a morning person. Since when did he sleep till quarter till ten?

He heard a clunk as Todd's mother put down the phone. Then he heard her footsteps receding as she left the room to get Todd. After a long wait, Matt heard footsteps approaching, then Todd's voice, hoarse and sleep filled. "Hello?"

"Todd? Were you still asleep?"

A pause. "Yeah. I guess." A yawn.

"Sorry, man. Where were you last night? April got attacked by a bat."

"Huh?"

"It flew right in her hair. But she's okay. Where were *you*?"

Todd cleared his throat. "I met a girl."

"Yeah?" Matt couldn't hide his surprise. Todd

was always so shy and awkward with girls. "That's why you're so wrecked this morning?"

Todd yawned. "She is awesome, Matt. I mean, she's *hot.*"

"Yeah? You met her on the beach?"

"Uh-huh. She was lost. So we started walking on the beach. You know. I was helping her find her house. And we were talking and everything. She's beautiful, Matt. I mean, like a TV star or something."

"Hey, not bad," Matt said. "Go on, man. Details. Details."

Todd groaned sleepily. "I can't wake up this morning," he said, his voice still hoarse. "I don't know what my problem is."

"Who cares?" Matt interrupted. "What's this girl's name?"

"Jessica. It got really hot and heavy, Matt. I mean, there we were on the beach. You know. In the fog. And she started really coming on to me. I mean, really." He coughed. "You should see the hickey on my neck."

Matt whistled in reply. "Wow."

"Yeah," Todd agreed. "She's incredible."

"Well, let's get to the beach," Matt said. "We can do some bodysurfing, and you can tell me more."

"No, I don't think so," Todd said sleepily. "I mean, not this morning, okay? I really don't feel too well. I'm so sleepy. I don't know. I feel kind of weak or something."

Matt laughed. "Maybe you and Jessica overdid it, man."

Todd didn't laugh. "I think I just need some more sleep," he replied seriously. "Tell you what. I'm supposed to meet Jessica in town tonight. Why don't you and April come too."

"For sure," Matt agreed enthusiastically. "But come on, Todd. The waves are excellent this morning. The water'll wake you up."

"No, I don't think so," Todd said, sighing wearily. "I'm just going back to sleep, okay?"

He had hung up before Matt could reply.

Matt replaced the receiver, trying to imagine Todd making out on the beach with a beautiful girl. Todd rarely had the nerve to ask any girl out. It had taken him months before he was comfortable enough to have a long conversation with April, Matt remembered, even though the three of them went everywhere together.

Well, way to go, Todd! he thought. He wondered if this Jessica was as fabulous as Todd described. She must be *awesome,* he thought. Todd sounded like a total vegetable!

Leaning against the counter, his hand still on the receiver, Matt wondered who he could call to go bodysurfing with him. April had already told him that she had to spend the day taking care of her sisters.

Maybe Ben is around, he thought. He *can't* be at the arcade this early in the morning.

He looked up Ben's number in the slim local phone directory and dialed. He let it ring eight times, then hung up, disappointed.

"Hey, Dad—" he called out to the deck. "Want to play some tennis?"

Todd and Jessica were already side by side in a booth at the Pizza Cove when Matt and April arrived a little after eight o'clock.

"They sure look cozy," April whispered, waving to Todd across the crowded little restaurant as she squeezed past the line of kids waiting for tables. Jessica, she saw, had her arm around Todd's neck in an affectionate hug.

Todd blushed as April and Matt slid into the seat across from them. "Hey, guys."

"Hi, I'm Jessica," Jessica said, brushing her coppery mane of hair behind her slender, pale shoulders. She was wearing a green midriff top that revealed ivory skin above and below.

April spotted a dark lipstick stain just beneath Todd's ear. Jessica certainly seems to *like* Todd, she thought. She seems sort of sophisticated for him.

She scolded herself for thinking that. I'm just jealous because she's so great looking, she thought.

"I already ordered a pizza," Todd said, grinning across the table at Matt.

"Are you from Shadyside too?" Jessica asked.

April and Matt answered yes at the same time.

April found herself staring at Jessica's fingernails, long and perfect and painted a dramatic dark purple to match her lipstick. Leaning close to Todd, Jessica absently ran her hand up and down his arm.

Wow—is Todd enjoying this! April thought.

They chatted about the beach, about the town, about their parents. April told about how Courtney buried Whitney up to her chin in the sand that afternoon, and then poured water on her head before April could stop her, and how both little girls became hysterical because April had so much trouble pulling Whitney out.

As April talked, Jessica rubbed Todd's arm and playfully sifted her fingers through his curly hair, smiling at him and leaning close.

Matt and I were a little like that when we first started going together, April thought. And then she found herself thinking that it wasn't like that between them anymore.

The pizza arrived, steamy hot on a round metal platter. April, Matt, and Todd hungrily pulled off slices and deposited them on their plates. "I had a big dinner," Jessica explained, unable to hide her disdain as the platter was slid across the table to her. "I couldn't eat a bite."

"Just one slice?" Todd urged.

"No. Really," Jessica replied, looking a little ill. Just then her brown eyes opened wide. April realized she was staring at the front of the restaurant. She turned and followed Jessica's gaze.

Gabri, trying to maneuver his way through the

crowd in the doorway, waved to April from the street entrance. "Hey—there's Gabri!" she cried, motioning for him to join them. She turned to Matt. "He's the boy I told you about last night."

Matt had a mouthful of pizza and a gob of cheese running down his chin. He nodded but didn't raise his head.

Gabri made his way to the table and stood in the aisle, his dark eyes trained on April. "Are you okay? You ran away last night and—"

"I'm so sorry," April said. "I'm really embarrassed. I acted so babyish, I know. But I'm just terrified of bats." She pushed Matt to get him to move closer to the wall and scooted over, gesturing for Gabri to squeeze in.

Gabri was dressed in baggy gray shorts and a white polo shirt. His dark eyes lit with pleasure at April's invitation, and he flashed her a warm smile as he slid in beside her.

"This is Matt, and Todd, and Jessica," she said, nodding in the direction of each. "Do you know Gabri?" she asked Jessica.

Jessica shook her head. "No," she said, her hand resting possessively on Todd's shoulder. "Are you a townie?"

"Yes," Gabri told her. "I've lived here all my life."

"Have some pizza," Matt said, pushing the tray toward Gabri.

"No. Thanks," Gabri said, smiling warmly at Matt. "I just ate."

"Gabri saved my life last night," April gushed. "He was so brave."

Gabri raised his hands modestly, as if fending off her compliments. "No. Really. Come on."

"Tell us what happened," Jessica urged, glancing at Gabri.

"Well, if Matt hadn't been half an hour late, it wouldn't have happened," April said, giving Matt a sharp poke with her elbow. He made a disgusted face.

"Please—don't keep us in suspense," Jessica said, holding Todd's hand, squeezing it.

April told them what had happened on the beach the night before. She could tell that Matt wasn't enjoying the story at all. He's jealous, she decided. Jealous of how Gabri rescued me. Maybe he's even jealous that I was walking with Gabri on the beach at night.

"That's so scary!" Jessica declared when April had finished. "I'm terrified of bats too!"

"Nothing to be afraid of, really," Gabri said, leaning across the table toward Jessica. "Bats don't really bite. That's just myth."

"They're just so creepy," Jessica exclaimed, holding on to Todd, making it hard for him to finish his pizza slice.

Gabri told them that in a way, he was envious of bats. He talked about how he'd always wanted to be able to fly. "It must be neat to have that freedom, to be able to spread your wings and soar," he said.

He's really good-looking, April thought. He has

the greatest smile. She pulled another slice of pizza onto her plate. "Matt, could you pass the garlic powder, please?" she asked.

"Sure," he said somewhat grumpily, obviously annoyed that April found Gabri so interesting.

She took the glass shaker from Matt and was about to sprinkle some garlic powder on her pizza —when to her surprise, Gabri grabbed her wrist.

"Please," he said, immediately loosening his grip. "I'm sorry, April, but I just hate the smell of garlic. I think I'm allergic to it or something." He let go of her, his expression embarrassed.

"No problem," April said, reaching across Matt to set the garlic powder down at his end of the table. She turned to Gabri with a puzzled pout. "I've never heard of anyone being allergic to garlic."

He shrugged. "It's no big deal."

"I'm allergic to garlic too," Matt interrupted, tapping April's shoulder to get her attention. "Especially when it's on your breath."

Everyone laughed except Jessica.

"It's so hot in here," she said, fanning herself with her hand. She lowered her face to Todd's. "Are you finished? I'd love to take a walk on the beach to cool off."

Todd nodded and hurriedly swallowed his last bite of pizza. "Yeah. Okay. Let's go. Anyone else want to come?"

Annoyance briefly crossed Jessica's face. She

stood up, tossing back her long hair, pulling down the hems of her magenta short shorts.

April saw Matt's eyes bulge.

Okay, okay, she thought. So Jessica is gorgeous.

She gave him a sharp jab in the ribs. "Don't drool on your pizza."

"Huh?" He pretended he didn't know what she was talking about.

"Catch you later," Todd said happily, allowing Jessica to pull him to the door.

"Yeah. Later," Matt repeated, still staring at Jessica's long, slender legs.

"Nice to meet you," Gabri called after them.

But Todd and Jessica were already out the door.

"I like your friends," Jessica said, holding on to Todd's arm as they made their way along the shore.

It was a warm, clear night. The low moon surrounded by twinkling stars made the sand glimmer. The beach surface was cream-colored, furrowed by shifting blue shadows.

"It's so crowded tonight. Not like last night," Todd said.

Enjoying the warm night, people swarmed over the beach—couples, groups, strollers, joggers, little kids out past their bedtime, collecting shells in the bright moonlight.

Jessica kicked off her sandals and pulled Todd toward the water.

Green-purple waves leapt to the shore, then

flattened out with a gentle *whoosh,* rolling up the sand, puddling at their feet.

"Where are you going?" he asked, pulling back.

"How about a swim?" She gazed at him enticingly, her bare shoulders gleaming like ivory. She tugged him gently back toward the water.

"No way," he said, shaking his head.

She pressed her lips into a dark pout. "Don't you want to swim with me?" Her expression turned mischievous. "You don't need a swimsuit."

He laughed. "It's not that. It's the undertow."

"Oh," she said, her eyes narrowing, her expression still playful, still tugging him by the hand. "You mean you're chicken?"

"Yeah. That's it," he confessed. "I'm chicken. I mean, I'm not really that good a swimmer."

"Sure you are," she whispered, the wind catching her hair, sending it soaring behind her.

"No. Really. I'm not," he insisted. "And I hear the undertow on the beach at night is unbelievable." Watching her face fill with disappointment, he quickly added, "Besides, I just like walking with you."

He's getting over his shyness, Jessica thought, pleased with herself, with the way things were going.

He hasn't much personality, but he's kind of sweet.

The nectar is sweet, that is. Very sweet.

Her thirst suddenly became overwhelming.

"Let's walk on the dunes," she said breathlessly,

squeezing his hand. "It's too crowded down by the shore."

He agreed without hesitating and, putting an arm around her bare waist, led her up the sand, the rhythmic, regular wash of the waves following behind them as they half walked, half skipped.

Soon they were alone in the soft valley between two mounds of sand, walking barefoot in the tall grass. Breathless and eager for each other.

Jessica kissed his lips first, her eyes burning into his. Then, her lips quivering in anticipation, she felt her fangs descend as she lowered her mouth to his neck.

She closed her eyes dreamily and was about to bite when the scream rang out.

"Help me! Somebody—please *help!*"

A girl's scream. So shrill. So terrified.

So near.

Chapter 10

GABRI DID IT

Jessica groaned, disappointed.

So close, so close.

And I'm *so* thirsty.

She opened her eyes to see Todd turn toward the screams and begin to run over the dune, his sandals kicking up sand, sliding as he made his way over the soft, grassy hill.

By the time Jessica descended the dune, a crowd had gathered around the distressed girl. The hushed voices of the concerned and curious onlookers were drowned out by the girl's hysterical sobs.

Jessica made her way to the front of the circle. A man and a woman had their arms around a teenage girl's shoulders, trying to calm her. When the girl removed her hands from in front of her face, Jessica saw that she was plump and round faced, with crimped black hair down to her shoulders. She was dressed in black spandex bike pants and an oversize pink T-shirt.

She stopped sobbing, but her shoulders continued to heave.

"Try to tell us what happened," the woman holding her urged. "Try to tell us."

The girl opened her mouth to speak, but burst into another round of sobs. She held her hands up to her face, then lowered one hand gingerly to her neck.

"What's going on?"

"What happened?"

"Is she hurt?"

The voices of the crowd grew louder as more onlookers joined the circle. Jessica searched for Todd, finally spotting him on the far side of the crowd.

"It bit me," the girl finally managed to get out through clenched teeth. "It bit me."

The voices quieted, the questions stopped as people pushed forward, straining to listen.

"A mosquito bit her," a teenage boy behind Jessica joked in a loud whisper, and his lanky companion snickered.

"A bat!" the girl cried, pointing to the sky with one hand as she continued to hold her throat with the other. "It swooped down. It grabbed on to my shoulder. It bit me!"

Jessica heard hushed cries of surprise, of horror. A little girl at the back of the crowd burst into tears.

Her father quickly picked her up and started to walk away from the circle.

"Get her to a doctor," someone called out.

"I vant to bite your neck!" the teenager behind Jessica said softly to his giggling companion, doing an exaggerated Bela Lugosi—vampire imitation as he grabbed his friend by the throat with both hands.

"That's not funny," a tall, dark-haired girl said sharply. "That bat might have rabies."

"You might have rabies!" the boy snapped back. His friend thought it was a hilarious comeback.

The man and woman were leading the girl off the beach in the direction of town. She had stopped sobbing but was still holding her throat.

"Where are your parents?" the woman was asking the girl.

"I don't know," Jessica heard the girl reply, her voice high and frightened. "I don't know."

"We'll get our car. We'll drive you to the hospital," the man said.

The girl said something, but they were too far away for Jessica to hear. As they made their way off the beach, the crowd of bystanders came to life. Everyone started talking at once. Some people, Jessica saw, were frightened. Some were horrified. Some were shaking their heads in disbelief.

"What happened?"

"Did the girl fall or something?"

"What's going on?"

"Did someone drown?"

Hushed voices, confused voices, rising over the steady rush of the ocean waves, mingled with nervous laughter.

Fixing her face in an expression of fear, Jessica started to tremble as Todd made his way to her. "Jessica—are you okay?" he asked, concerned.

She hugged herself and shook her head. "Oh, I just hate bats!" she exclaimed. "They're so creepy."

Todd took her hand. "You're ice-cold!" he said, squeezing it.

"That poor girl," Jessica cried with a convincing shudder. She raised her hand to her throat, as if imagining what it would feel like.

"It's like a vampire or something," Todd said.

"*Please*—stop," she said, holding on to his arm. "I'm really scared." Warily, she turned her eyes up to the dark sky, as if searching for bats. She smiled as Todd put his arm around her trembling shoulders.

Gabri did this, Jessica thought bitterly as she pretended to be frightened.

Gabri was the bat. Gabri bit the girl.

I know it was Gabri.

He saw that I was having success with Todd. He saw that I was about to taste the nectar for the second time. And so he created a diversion. He knew I couldn't succeed with a girl screaming her head off a few yards down the beach.

What a dirty trick.

It's obvious that Gabri will do anything to stop me.

Well, you *can't* stop me, Jessica thought angrily, her anger serving to renew her determination.

You can't stop me, Gabri. You're too late.

Two more sips of the nectar and poor unsuspecting Todd is mine.

She gazed timidly at Todd. Look at him, she thought, forcing herself not to laugh out loud. Poor baby. He's madly in love with me. He thinks this is the luckiest summer of his life.

I wonder if he'll still feel so lucky when he finds out what he's become. I wonder if he'll still feel lucky when he knows he's an Eternal One, unable to die, unable to live.

So thirsty. Always so thirsty.

She sighed and pressed her face against his arm. Her mouth suddenly felt so dry. She could taste the nectar, ruby dark, thick and warm.

"Come on, Todd," she whispered. "Take me away from here. I'm just so . . . scared."

He nodded, holding her close, and she led him away into the darkness.

Chapter 11

FIRST DATE

A couple of nights later April made her way through the crowds on Main Street to meet Matt. The shops and restaurants she passed were brightly lit and jammed with people. She stepped onto the street to get around a large group of window-shoppers. She moved through the sea of glowing, sunburned faces, smiling people in colorful shirts and white shorts or skirts.

From halfway down the block, April could see that Matt wasn't on the corner in front of Swanny's where they had arranged to meet. I hope he isn't late again, she thought, glancing at her watch as she crossed the street.

A motorcycle roared past right behind her, and she jumped to the curb. "Hey—" She turned in time to see the backs of two boys with long blond hair, speeding in the direction of the carnival grounds.

I wonder if the carnival has opened, April thought, searching the crowded walk for Matt. April loved carnivals. She loved the rides and the dumb games, and the smell of popcorn and cotton candy. Maybe Matt would like to check it out, she thought.

She had promised her sisters she'd take them as soon as it opened. That meant an entire night of arguing over which ride to go on next and who got to sit in front and who had to sit in the back.

"Matt—where *are* you?" she said aloud.

She poked her head into the arcade—and saw him near the back. He and Ben were leaning over a game, staring intently at the screen as another boy frantically spun a steering wheel.

"Hey, Matt! Matt!" She couldn't make herself heard over the explosions, gunfire, loud whistles, sirens, and crashes that echoed through the long, narrow room.

When he finally turned toward the doorway, he seemed surprised to see her.

Didn't he even remember that we were supposed to meet? April wondered.

He pushed himself away from the game and hurried toward her, a guilty expression on his face. "Oh. Hi." He followed her out onto the walk. "You just get here?"

"Yeah." She nodded.

"You look great. Is that a new T-shirt?"

April was wearing a pale blue T-shirt with a V neck that she had worn about ten thousand times. "No, Matt. What's going on?"

"Uh . . . I ran into Ben. We've been playing some games with a few other guys. You know. Just goofing."

"So what do you want to do tonight?" April asked, her eyes following a cream-colored Jaguar convertible as it turned the corner onto Dune Lane.

"Nice car," Matt said.

"I think Jaguars are cute," April said, smiling at him.

"The prices are real cute too," he said, grinning back at her.

"You didn't answer my question, Matt. Did the carnival open?"

He shrugged.

"Want to go check it out?" she asked, turning in the direction of the carnival grounds. Yellow beams of light streaked the sky in that direction, spotlights announcing that the carnival was open.

"Well . . ." he hesitated. "There's this *Friday the 13th* triple feature tonight." He motioned across the street to the movie theater, where a line had already formed, mostly teenagers, waiting for the box office to open. "Ben and I really want to see it. How about you?"

April groaned angrily. "You *know* I hate those films! Why do I want to see a bunch of pretty girls get sliced and diced? It's such sexist garbage, Matt!"

"Yeah, I know," he replied, his eyes on the growing line at the movie theater.

I can't believe this! April thought, feeling her anger grow. He's spending all his time with Ben and the guys. He was so excited about this stupid triple feature, he didn't even remember he was supposed to meet me!

"You sure you don't want to come?" he asked, avoiding her eyes. He brushed his hair back nervously with one hand and glanced into the arcade, checking on his friends.

"Yes, I'm sure," April said, not bothering to conceal her anger. "Don't you ever get tired of that horror stuff?"

"No," he replied quickly, grinning.

April made a disgusted face. "Guess I'll go then," she said quietly.

She expected him to protest, to ask her not to leave. She expected him to change his plans, to tell Ben and the other guys that he was going to skip the movie.

"Well, we'll do something together tomorrow night," he said instead. "You know. Go to the carnival or something."

She turned away from him. "Yeah. Okay," she muttered and started to walk up the street.

"Call you tomorrow!" he shouted after her.

Why didn't I tell him how angry I am? April

asked herself, shoving her hands into the pockets of her shorts and taking long strides away from the arcade. Why didn't I let him know that I'm upset with him? Why did I just say, "Yeah, okay," and walk away?

She realized that she was as angry at herself as she was at Matt.

Maybe I should have just gone along to the movie with him, she thought.

No. No way.

She quickly erased that thought.

I'm always the one who gives in, always the one who compromises. He thinks he can do whatever he wants.

This vacation is turning out to be the pits, April thought, her anger soaring. All day long I take care of my bratty sisters at the beach. Then at night Matt would rather hang out with the guys than spend time with me.

April began to cross Seabreeze Road by the Mini Market, walking rapidly. She was so distracted by her angry thoughts that she crashed right into someone crossing from the other direction.

"Oh!"

Startled, she stumbled back, struggling to keep her balance.

First, she saw a maroon pullover, then black denims.

Then she saw a narrow, pale face, its expression as startled as hers.

Then she recognized the face. "Gabri!"

"Oh, hi!" he cried, still somewhat shaken. "I didn't see you."

"I didn't see you, either," she replied, embarrassed. "Are you okay?"

"Yes, I think so." He smoothed back his black hair and flashed her a reassuring smile. "You're in a hurry. Where are you going?"

"Nowhere," she admitted. "I'm going nowhere fast."

She thought she was making a joke, but he didn't seem to get it.

A horn honked. They both jumped and realized they were standing in the middle of the road. "Come on," he said. She followed him to the walk as the car rolled by, honking again as it passed.

"Are you with Matt?" Gabri asked, stopping in front of the Mini Market.

"Bad subject," April muttered.

Gabri's eyes seemed to light up. "Huh?"

"No, I'm not with Matt," April said, realizing her anger hadn't subsided.

Gabri stepped under the streetlight, making way for a woman who had just come out of the grocery store, struggling with three full bags of food.

"You have to be the *palest* townie in the world!" April blurted out, laughing.

Again, Gabri didn't smile. In fact, for a brief moment, he appeared alarmed by her comment. But he quickly recovered and his warm smile returned. "It's my job," he explained, moving from under the light, back into the shadows near the wall of the building. "I work all day. I never get to the beach till night. It's kind of hard to get a tan by moonlight."

"Where do you work?" April asked.

"In the next town," he said after a short pause.

"What do you do?"

"Whatever they tell me to," he replied. "It's not a very exciting job."

April realized that he was gazing into her eyes as they talked. Doesn't he ever blink? she wondered. And then she thought: His eyes seem so . . . deep. Like tunnels. Like tunnels that draw you in, deeper, deeper.

Feeling dizzy, she raised a hand to the building wall to steady herself.

"The carnival opened tonight," Gabri said. "Want to check it out?"

"Yes," April replied, without even thinking.

And then she pictured Matt. And thought, Matt won't like this.

I'm going to the carnival with another boy.

And then she thought: I don't care. He'd rather spend his time with Ben and the guys at that stupid horror movie.

He doesn't care *what* I do.

I have a right to have some fun too.

Her anger flared, then slipped away as she gazed into Gabri's eyes.

He smiled warmly at her. "Well, let's go."

This is so easy, Gabri thought, slipping an arm around April's shoulder as they made their way to the carnival grounds.

This is almost *too* easy.

April's going to be no trouble at all.

Chapter 12

NO TIME TO
REFLECT

"**H**ow about the Twister?" April urged, staring at the lurching and spinning metal cars. The squeals of the riders punctured the soft night air.

Gabri shielded his eyes from the glare of the flashing colored lights that ran all along the top frame of the ride. "No thanks," Gabri said, shaking his head and holding on to April. "I like *some* rides, but not the kind that make you dizzy."

"Me too," April agreed, gazing around the carnival grounds at the blaze of colored lights and the long row of game booths with their back walls covered with enormous stuffed animal prizes.

"Have you ever been on the Gravitron?" she asked.

"What's that?" he asked warily, still shielding his eyes.

"I guess you haven't," she said, teasing him.

They walked for a bit, surveying the rides. Many of them were still and empty, awaiting riders. The carnival had opened only an hour earlier, and not many people had arrived.

The breeze off the ocean was warm and gentle. April was glad she had decided to come with Gabri. He was fun and charming in a sort of old-fashioned way. The complete opposite of Matt, she thought spitefully.

Her anger had passed, but she wondered if Matt would even care that she had gone out with another boy.

"Do you like the carousel?" Gabri asked as they came to it. "This one is kind of drab, isn't it? Look—part of that horse's head has come off."

"It's gross," April agreed. "Carousels are too slow and babyish." I'll take the twins on it tomorrow night, she thought.

"You're in a reckless mood tonight, aren't you!" he asked, his eyes locked on hers.

"Maybe," she replied coyly, feeling the pull of those dark, dark eyes.

They walked along the row of game booths. A little kid was standing up on the counter of one booth, about to throw darts at a wall of balloons. The girl working behind the counter was ducking out of the way, about ten feet away.

Suddenly April grabbed Gabri's hand and tugged. "Come on. I know what'll be cool."

He pulled back, hesitating. "What is it?"

"I'll show you," she said. "Stop being such a chicken." She tugged his arm hard, and he reluctantly allowed himself to be dragged across the grass, past the game booths to a tall structure at the back of the field.

"Come on—" April urged impatiently. "The House of Mirrors!"

"No!" Gabri protested.

But April had already bought two tickets from the old, bored attendant and was pulling her reluctant companion up the ramp to the entrance.

"Really! I *hate* these things!" Gabri cried, holding back.

April wouldn't let go. "You really *are* a chicken," she chided him. "Come on, Gabri. This isn't even scary! You'll see!"

She dragged him inside, a bit surprised by his fear.

Inside, a narrow maze of glass and mirrors twisted endlessly. Staring at six reflections of herself, April laughed. Where was the opening? "Hey, Gabri—"

But he was far behind her.

"Gabri—you okay?" she called.

"I think so!" she heard his voice somewhere behind a mirrored wall.

Are we all alone in here? she wondered. She didn't hear any other voices or any feet clomping along the metal floor.

She leaned down as she made her way through a doorway, blinking at her several reflections, then turned a corner into an identical corridor of mirrors.

"Hey, Gabri!"

Was that him or just a reflection?

"Hey, Gabri— *Ouch!*"

Pain throbbed across her forehead as she walked into a mirrored pane she had mistaken for an opening. She closed her eyes and rubbed the ache away, laughing at herself for being fooled.

When she opened her eyes, there were at least eight reflections staring back at her. In one mirror, her images seemed to repeat forever, growing smaller and smaller and less distinct as they receded to infinity.

"Hey, I think I'm lost!" she called. "Where are you?"

"Over here," came a muffled reply. April spun around, thinking he was behind her, but saw only several surprised reflections of herself.

Feeling along the glass, she found the doorway, stepped into a darker chamber. The fluorescent light in there flickered, casting her reflections in eerie green shadows, as they stared back at her. Her expression grew troubled, exasperated.

This isn't as much fun as I thought, she realized, mistaking a pane of clear glass for a doorway and bumping her knee. "Ow."

Am I going in circles? she wondered.

Am I ever going to get out of here?

"Hey, Gabri?"

No reply.

"Gabri?"

She decided to wait right there, not to move until he caught up.

Why hadn't he answered her? Maybe he wasn't heading in her direction.

She decided to make her way back, to retrace her steps. But that wasn't as easy as it sounded.

Walking carefully, trailing her hands along the glass, she followed her reflections to the chamber with the flickering fluorescent bulb.

"Gabri? Where are you?"

And then she glimpsed him, crouched low, staring straight ahead.

Was that his reflection? Or was it him?

She moved closer, could see only one image.

"Gabri?"

That must be him. Where were his reflections?

It's so hot in here, she thought, suddenly flushed and prickly all over.

So hot. So uncomfortable.

Her knee and forehead still throbbed, reminders of her collisions with the glass.

"Gabri—over here!"

Gabri closed his eyes for a minute, then opened them to stare at the reflectionless mirrors, so blank, so empty, so . . . accusing.

It's so hot in here, he thought. The ceilings are so low. It's like—a coffin.

A glass coffin.

I'm so thirsty now. So hot and thirsty.

I need the nectar so badly now.

"Gabri!" He could hear her calling him, as if she knew that he needed her. "Gabri—over here! Can you see me?"

April and I are all alone in here, he realized.

All alone. And I'm so thirsty.

I can't wait any longer.

I must have the nectar.

The empty mirrors glared back blank at him as he eased his way silently toward her.

There she is, he thought, gliding around a glass-walled corner, searching for me. Searching the mirrors for me.

Well, you won't see me in the mirrors, April.

I'm alone tonight.

I come for you.

He reached for her—and hit glass.

Startled, he recoiled, momentarily dazed by the reflected light.

He spun around and saw reflected movement.

"Gabri!" she called to him.

He pounced, his arms outstretched, coming at her from behind. Once again, his hands hit glass.

These reflections are protecting her, he thought. They're mocking me. Mocking me!

His anger grew to meet his thirst.

I must drink now! I *must!*

April saw him approach, his hands stretched in front of him, moving uncertainly, as if blinded by the lights. I shouldn't have dragged him in here, she thought guiltily. He doesn't look as if he's having a very good time.

96

Surrounded by her reflections, she called to him. "Gabri—over here!"

He lowered his hands and turned to her, a strange smile on his face, a relieved smile, yet somehow . . . unpleasant. "There you are." His voice seemed to float from far away.

As he moved toward her, sliding along the glass walls, his eyes burning into hers, the narrow chamber seemed to close in on her, and the mirrors all fogged up.

"Gabri—" she started, but the fog descended.

The only light now came from his eyes.

He moved closer still, until he appeared to hover over her.

"Gabri—where are your reflections?" April asked dreamily.

"It's too dark for reflections," he replied, sounding so far away, miles away, far across the fog.

"But I can't see your reflections."

"I'm right here," he said, the cold gray light from his eyes penetrating hers.

April backed into her reflections. As Gabri moved nearer, she could feel herself slipping into the infinity of images, growing smaller and less distinct as she blurred into the mirror world, a world growing darker.

As she slipped back, Gabri leaned forward.

Then, uttering a moan of triumph from deep within his throat, he hungrily lowered his head for the kiss.

Transform his reflections, slithering to turn...

Below in their path.

He lowered his hands and turned to her, a master-
mind of pure evil, a relentless snake, yet a man, human once ... Have you ever saw was scared to
their ruin for ever.

Chapter 13

WHEEL OF FORTUNE

"**W**hat's happening?" April wondered, floating in the darkness of the mirror world. "Is someone kissing me?"

Then she heard the thunder of sneakers on the metal floor.

Laughter. Shouting kids' voices.

The fog began to lift. The mirror images grew clearer, brighter.

A loud *crack*.

A little girl began crying, loud sobs of pain.

"What's that?" April cried, the mirrored chamber suddenly blindingly bright, all of her reflections opening their eyes and asking the question at once.

Six Aprils stepping away from the glass, six mouths asking, "What's that?"

Gabri turned his head, willing the fangs back into

his mouth, trying to stop his breathless panting, to stifle his groans, to hide his disappointment.

When he turned back, April was running to the little girl who had smacked her head on the glass. She picked her up and tried to comfort her as several other kids gathered around.

Feeling vulnerable without any reflections in this mirrored chamber, Gabri darted around a corner. "Meet you outside," he called to April, shouting over the crying little girl, the squealing kids, the echoes of other footsteps approaching in the maze.

He burst out of the exit into the warm night, moving into the shadows, his features still tight with disappointment.

So close. So close.

He thought of Jessica and that eager boy Todd. Was Jessica having success tonight? Was Jessica tasting the nectar, satisfying her thirst, winning their bet?

He snickered, remembering how he had ruined Jessica's chances a few nights before, how he had interrupted her just at her moment of triumph, how he had attacked the girl, how the girl's terrified screams had denied Jessica her nectar.

Keeping to the shadows, his eyes on the exit from which he had just emerged, Gabri sighed. He enjoyed thwarting Jessica, but he knew that Jessica was ahead. Jessica had already tasted the nectar. The unsuspecting boy was nearly in her power, nearly an Eternal.

He couldn't let Jessica win. He couldn't.

Perhaps I'll have to do something drastic to stop her, something a little more exciting than creating a diversion on the beach, he thought, watching as April stepped out of the House of Mirrors.

Fixing his mouth into a pleased smile, Gabri stepped out of the shadows and approached her. "There you are. Is the little girl okay?"

"Yeah. Fine," April said, hurrying to join him. "You certainly bombed out of there fast."

"Yeah. I know," he replied sheepishly. "I—I mean, that place gave me the creeps. I can't stand seeing myself so close up like that."

She laughed. "You look perfectly okay close up." They started to walk across the carnival grounds, having to dodge excited kids, making their way past groups of teenagers lured from town and the beach by the discovery that the carnival had opened.

"I felt kind of strange in there too," April admitted, taking Gabri's arm. "All those mirrors and weird lights. My eyes started playing tricks on me. I thought I saw you—without any reflections!"

"Weird," Gabri said, smiling.

They walked past the game booths. She pulled him to a stop in front of a refreshment stand. "I want a Sno Cone," she said. "A blue one. How about you?"

Gabri made a disgusted face. "No, I don't think so. Nothing for me."

Pulling a dollar from her bag, she stepped into the line. "Didn't you ever wonder why there are no blue foods?" she asked. "I always eat blue Sno Cones," she continued, not giving him a chance to answer, "because they're about the only natural blue food found in nature."

She waited for him to laugh. When he didn't respond, she had to tell him that she'd just made a joke. He seemed suddenly distracted, as if he hadn't really heard anything she said.

They were walking past the kiddie rides, a small passenger train going round in a tiny circle, jet planes that rose up about six feet off the ground as they circled, and laughing at the excited little kids. April was enjoying her Sno Cone. "It doesn't taste blue," she said, offering Gabri a taste.

He declined, then, glancing at her face, smiled broadly. Blue lips. The ice had given April blue lips.

She looks dead, he thought. Dead already, and I haven't even sunk my fangs into her throat.

Her blue lips taunted him, teased him, tortured him.

I must get her alone, he thought, his mouth so dry, dry and powdery, dry as death.

I must try again.

And this time I must succeed.

"How about the Ferris wheel?" she asked, tossing the paper cup into a trash basket, wiping her blue lips with the back of her hand.

"Yes!" Gabri cried. Too quickly. Too enthusiastically.

She laughed, startled by his reaction. "You really like Ferris wheels? Don't they make you dizzy?"

"No," he replied, leading the way toward the Ferris wheel revolving at the front of the field near the parking lot. The line was short. They wouldn't have long to wait. "I love to be up high, to feel as if I'm flying."

"We should be able to see the ocean from the top," April said, picking up Gabri's enthusiasm. "And all of the town."

"When I was a little boy, I used to pretend that I could fly," Gabri said, fingering the tickets as the line moved forward a few feet. "I would spread my arms and soar over the treetops. The other kids made fun of me, but I didn't care. I pretended I could fly away from them."

"Funny," April said, "I can't picture you as a kid."

She didn't really mean it seriously, but he appeared stung by the remark. His frown lasted only a second, just long enough for April to catch the hurt in his eyes.

She started to say something, to apologize, but the Ferris wheel operator, a fat guy with long, oily hair, wearing a sweatshirt that came down only halfway over his stomach, motioned for them to step into the waiting car.

April leapt into the swaying car, then turned and helped pull Gabri in. He glanced at her uncertainly, then settled himself back against the plastic seat, still warm from the last occupants. The safety bar was slammed down over their thighs.

Then the car swayed harder and lifted up, traveling only a few yards until it came to an abrupt halt. Someone was being loaded into the car under theirs.

"Can't see much from here," April joked.

Gabri smiled, a strangely distant smile, as if his thoughts were once again far away.

April suddenly thought of Matt. No doubt he was slouched in his movie seat at that very moment, watching teenagers being hacked to bits and enjoying every blood-soaked minute of it.

And here she was with a new boy. A strange boy. A boy she realized she felt attracted to even though they had barely spoken.

"Do you have a girlfriend or anything?" she asked, the words popping out of her mouth before she had a chance to think about them. Maybe he's thinking about someone else, she thought. Maybe that's why he keeps drifting away, looking so thoughtful and serious.

Her question seemed to snap him out of his thoughts. "No, not really," he replied.

Their car swayed again, rocking back and forth. Then it was lifted to a higher position before abruptly stopping again.

The air was cooler up off the ground, April realized, turning her head to let the gentle breeze blow through her hair. Gazing up at the sky, she searched for the moon, but it was hidden behind a curtain of low clouds.

"I hope it isn't too dark to see the ocean," she said to Gabri, who was also staring up at the sky.

When we are at the very top, he thought, there will be time.

We will be too high for people to see into the car.

We will be too far away for anyone to wonder, to protest. Too far away for anyone to stop me.

When we stop at the very top, April will be helpless.

I will taste the nectar, taste deeply of the sweet, precious nectar without being interrupted.

He smiled at her. "I'm enjoying being with you," he said, raising his arm behind her on the seat back.

"I'm having fun too," April said as the car jolted, then floated up to the very top.

It suddenly became darker.

April leaned forward, resting her arms on the safety bar, and gazed out toward the ocean. The beach appeared as a silver ribbon. The rolling blue-black darkness behind it was the ocean.

"Wow," April said quietly. "What a view."

Now! Gabri's silent cry rang loudly in his mind. *Now!*

He turned her head and kissed her lips.

She started to pull back in surprise. But gazing into his wide, glowing eyes, she felt weak, drained of any power to resist.

Besides, why should she resist?

He kissed her chin.

Was she dizzy from the kisses? From the view? From being so high in this gently rocking cart?

I'm so dizzy, she thought, her head tilted back,

his face above hers now, his eyes glowing down into hers.

So dizzy and weak.

Please—kiss me again. "Kiss me again, Gabri," she heard herself whisper. "Please."

He kissed her again.

Then he sank his fangs deep into her throat.

When he removed them, dark ruby droplets clung to his smiling lips.

GOOSEBUMPS

Chapter 14

JUST AN ACCIDENT

Matt stretched and yawned. He made his way to the bedroom window and, blinking against the bright light, peered out. The sun was already high above the trees in a clear sky. His bedroom felt hot and sticky.

He yawned again, bumped into his dresser, opened a drawer, found a bathing suit, and sleepily stepped into it.

Padding heavily into the kitchen, brushing the hair out of his eyes with one hand, he found a note from his parents on the kitchen counter. They had gotten up early to go fishing with friends. Didn't want to disturb him. Wondered what time he had gotten in. Would see him later.

What time *did* I get in? Matt wondered.

He wasn't sure. After the triple feature, he, Ben,

and some other guys had headed to the carnival grounds to check it out. But the field was dark, the rides all shut down, the booths covered for the night.

It must have been well after midnight. Back in town, Matt met some friends who had been to the carnival. One of them started teasing him about April.

"What are you talking about?" Matt asked, confused.

"April was there all night. With another guy. A tall guy. Straight, black hair. You'd better watch out, Daniels." The boys walked off, snickering and making jokes at Matt's expense.

Gabri. She was there with Gabri, Matt realized.

As he made his way down Seabreeze Road, kicking clods of sandy dirt as he walked, he decided he'd better apologize to April. He probably shouldn't have spent the night with the guys, even though he had really wanted to see those movies badly.

He realized he hadn't spent much time with April since they'd arrived at Sandy Hollow. And now this townie with his dark, romantic eyes and slick smile was moving in on her.

He'd put a stop to it, Matt decided, sneaking into the cottage, hoping his parents wouldn't hear him come in. He'd call April first thing in the morning.

Now it wasn't exactly first thing in the morning. It was ten-thirty, to be exact. But he gulped down a glass of orange juice—too quickly, for it gave him a sharp pain between his eyes—and then dialed April's house.

The phone rang three times before someone picked it up. "Hello?" April's mother said.

"Hi, Mrs. Blair. It's me. Can I talk to April?"

"Oh. Hi, Matt. She's still asleep."

"Huh?" April was a morning person. She was usually up at dawn.

"The twins tried to rouse her for breakfast more than an hour ago," Mrs. Blair said. "She muttered something about not feeling well, said she felt like sleeping for weeks. That's not like her. I figured I'd better let her sleep."

"Yeah. Well . . ." Matt was surprised. He wanted to ask, "How late was she out with Gabri?" But instead he said, "Tell her I hope she feels better. If she wants to, she can meet me at the beach."

He hung up the phone, feeling troubled. He scratched the back of his neck. His skin felt all prickly. The air in the small kitchen was heavy and wet.

It's really going to be hot today, he thought. I've got to get to the beach.

He called Todd, who had also just pulled himself out of bed, and arranged to meet him at the beach. "Bring your Boogie board," he told him. "Maybe the surf will be good this morning."

But when he arrived at the beach, already crowded with morning sunbathers, several swimmers diving and darting through the low, blue-green waves, Todd was stretched out on a beach towel in the shade of a yellow- and white-striped beach umbrella.

"Hey—" Matt called.

"How's it going?" Todd asked sleepily.

"Where's your Boogie board?"

Todd raised his head and looked around. "Guess I forgot it."

Matt sighed impatiently and dropped his Boogie board to the sand. "What'd you do last night? See that girl?" He dropped onto his knees, then sat down on the Boogie board, the sun warm on his back.

"Yeah." Todd yawned loudly. "Jessica. We just walked around town. She wanted to go down to the beach, but I wasn't up to it. I went home early."

"Hey, man—you need a swim," Matt urged. "We both need something to wake us up this morning."

Todd didn't respond.

"Hey, Todd—come on, man."

Silence.

"Todd?"

Leaning over his friend, Matt saw that Todd had fallen asleep.

What's *with* this guy? Matt wondered. How can he conk out before eleven in the morning?

Todd uttered a sigh in his sleep and rolled onto his side.

What kind of suntan lotion is Todd using? Matt wondered, staring at his friend. He seems to be getting paler—not darker.

As darkness descended, Jessica tingled with excitement and felt almost alive. She could feel the renewed energy coursing through her body.

She swept her long hair back over her shoulders, allowing the soft breeze off the ocean to ruffle through it, and thought about the nectar.

So sweet and tart at the same time.

So rich and thick.

And thirst quenching.

The moon, which had begun as a pale, white disc, was growing bolder, beginning to gain its golden glow. Staring up at it, Jessica tried to remember her life.

What had she been like when she was sixteen—like Todd and his friends?

Did she summer at the beach? Did she have boyfriends?

Try to remember, Jessica, she urged herself. Try.

But she had no memories.

No memories of her real life.

Her childhood was gone. Her family was gone. Her teenage years—*all* her years—her *life* was gone.

Even her death was gone, she realized.

How did I die?

But of course she *hadn't* died.

And that was why her only memories were of her life as an Eternal One. Her only memories were those of the gray, twilight world she roamed in, floated in, soared in, shadowy memories of longing, of need, eternal need—of *thirst*.

Was that a tear rolling down her soft, pale cheek?

Was she actually *crying* for her past, for all that was lost to her? Crying for a life she hadn't a single memory of?

No. It was just the salty air, she told herself, brushing the wetness from her cheek, forcing her morbid thoughts away.

This was to be a night of triumph, after all.

A night of victory, and then of celebration.

A night of nectar. A night of renewal.

She saw Todd approaching along the shore. This is *your* night, Todd, she thought, all of her sadness lifting as he neared, and her tingling excitement returned.

This is your night, my poor, innocent, shy, not-so-very-smart Todd.

This is the night you become an Eternal One. The night you shed your boring, old life and soar into the dark sky.

He waved to her, and she stepped toward him, her bare feet light on the wet sand, moving out of the shadows of the rowboat dock. Behind her, the three rowboats tied to the dock bobbed like flat fish in the water, bumping gently against the wooden piles.

"Todd!" she called enthusiastically, running toward him, her short sundress lifting high on her long, slender legs as she ran.

"Hi," he said. Still shy. Still reluctant. "Nice night, huh?"

She took his arm. Kissed his cheek.

So near the precious nectar. So near.

Her pulse throbbed. She could feel it.

And she could feel her thirst.

One last sip. One little taste, Todd, and you're one of us. Forever.

"What did you do today?" she asked, locking her eyes on his.

"Went to the beach," he told her. "But I didn't swim or anything. I was feeling kind of lazy."

Wonder why, she thought dryly, holding on to his arm, staring into his eyes, letting her power do its work.

"You want to go to the carnival or something?" he asked, his voice quavering.

He's under my spell, she thought.

He's *mine*.

"It's so peaceful here on this end of the beach," she whispered, leaning against him, moonlight reflecting off her pale face, her bare shoulders. "And we're all alone."

He turned his eyes to the water, to the small, wooded island out beyond the rowboat dock. But she forced his eyes to return to hers.

"How about a kiss, Todd?"

She didn't wait for a reply. A faint smile began to spread on his lips as she moved her face forward and pressed her mouth to his.

He's mine. He's mine.

But what was that sound? That fluttering over the rush of the waves.

Was it just the rowboats bobbing against the dock?

No.

She pressed her lips against Todd's, sighing softly. And raised her eyes to the purple sky.

And saw the bat hovering low overhead.

Gabri! It must be Gabri! she realized.

He's come to ruin it for me. He's come to rob me of my victory.

No, Gabri, she thought, her pulse pounding as the wild, inhuman energy flowed through her.

No, Gabri. Not tonight.

You will not interfere tonight.

You are *too late*. The boy is *mine*.

The bat hovered lower.

Quick, quick! Jessica commanded herself.

Her fangs lowered, and her face pressed against Todd's throat, and she bit deeply.

Deeply.

And drank.

The bat fluttered low. Lower. But he was too late.

Too late.

The race was lost.

Jessica drank. More and more.

Then, as Todd uttered a loud moan, of pain, of helplessness, of ecstasy, Jessica pulled her face back.

The color faded from Todd's eyes as they rolled up into his head.

"No!" Jessica shrieked. "No! No! No! It was an accident! I—I don't believe I did this!"

Chapter 15

A DROWNING

Matt sat up in bed, pushing away the sweat-drenched sheets. He peered out the window, listening to the soft calls of birds in the nearby trees, announcing the dawn.

"I can't sleep," he said aloud, rubbing his eyes. "What time is it, anyway?"

Five thirty-five, the clock on the night table said.

He'd been tossing most of the night, his mind whirling with troubled thoughts.

Mostly he had been thinking about April.

He had tried her house when he got back from the beach in the afternoon, but the line was endlessly busy. Then he tried calling after dinner and her mom said April had gone out.

Probably with Gabri again, Matt thought unhappily.

I've got to talk to April. I thought we were going to have a great summer together.

Thinking about her had kept him up all night. Now, as the sky slowly brightened and the chirping of the birds grew louder, he decided there was no point in staying in bed.

An early jog on the beach might help to clear my mind, he thought, pulling on a pair of black spandex bicycle shorts and squeezing his feet into his running shoes.

He closed the cottage door silently behind him, stepping out into the morning air, still cool and dew laden. The salty-fish smell of the ocean invaded his nostrils as he began to jog past the other cottages to the dunes that led down to the ocean.

The lapping waves were still inky black under a pearl gray sky as Matt began his jog along the shore. Sea gulls scattered as he ran, squawking in shrill protest.

The beach was empty. All his. Not even one other early-morning jogger in sight.

Off on the brightening horizon, he could see the dark outlines of a ship. Some kind of barge. The image shimmered above the water, its outlines bending and shifting in the eerie morning light. Like some sort of ghost ship, not real.

Matt jogged slowly but steadily, past the dying embers of a small campfire someone hadn't fully doused, past a blackened, charred log the ocean had tossed up, past a pair of starfish dead and drying on the sand.

The spray felt cold and refreshing against his face as his sneakers crunched over wet sand. The gray of the sky was beginning to lift, like a pale curtain rising, revealing the crimson morning sunlight underneath. The ocean water brightened with the sky, reflecting its color.

This is really beautiful, Matt thought, jogging steadily, his forehead dotted with beads of sweat despite the cool air. He gazed ahead at the dark rock cliff that rose up at the water's edge beyond the dunes.

As he approached the cliff, the sand beneath his shoes becoming pebbly, then harder, he looked to the small rowboat dock that jutted out in the shadow of the cliff.

Something appeared to be floating in the water beside the dock.

Was it a small boat of some kind? He was too far away to see clearly.

As he drew closer, crimson sunlight rippling along the water's edge, he could see it clearer, something dark, pretty large, bobbing beside one of the rowboats.

Has a whale lost its way and trapped itself near shore? He dismissed that idea as he drew closer, and was better able to judge the size.

He stopped just before the dock, his chest heaving from the effort of his long run. Wiping away the perspiration from his forehead with his arm, he turned his eyes to the water.

And his breath caught in his throat.

It was a person.

Bobbing like a rowboat.

Bobbing facedown.

Arms floating out at its sides stiffly, so stiffly.

And before he even realized it, Matt was in the water, cold around his ankles, over his sneakers, which he hadn't thought to remove.

He hadn't thought.

He hadn't thought he'd find a person.

He hadn't thought *anything*.

And he was tugging the person by the shoulders, the water up over his waist. Pulling hard now. But the person—the body—the person—was so *heavy*.

The water felt so cold, swirling about his hot body. Matt gasped for breath, his chest heaving.

Are you breathing?

Please be breathing!

But, no—how could he be breathing?

It was a he. Yes. A he. But Matt still hadn't been able to lift his face from the water.

How could he be breathing with his face still in the water? With his arms stretched out so stiffly?

What was he wearing? Only undershorts?

His skin so white and smooth, like some kind of sea creature.

Only sea creatures can breathe in the water.

And this person wasn't breathing, couldn't be breathing.

Panting loudly, Matt heaved his heavy cargo onto the shore. Pushing the wet, matted hair back from his forehead, Matt stood for a moment, hands on hips, leaning forward, breathing, breathing deeply, waiting for his heart to stop racing.

And then he bent over the person—the body—turned it with great effort onto its back.

And screamed: "Todd!

"Todd! How? How, Todd?"

With dreadful clarity, his friend came into sudden focus. His nearly nude body was covered with gashes and cuts from banging against the rocks around the rowboat dock.

So many cuts.

So many cuts, his blood appeared to be completely drained.

"How, Todd? How?"

So many cuts, all over his face and neck.

"No. It can't be Todd. It *can't* be."

So many cuts.

So many cuts, it made no sense.

How did Todd drown?

Why would he swim way out here, so far from everyone?

Did he drown farther up the beach where everyone hangs out? Was his body carried here by the current?

His body?

How could Todd be just a body now?

How could he no longer be Todd?

Matt sank to his knees, his mind swirling faster than the ocean waters.

He closed his eyes, but the vision of his drowned friend, his skin so white except for the cuts, the cuts, the cuts, stayed with him.

Todd wasn't a strong swimmer.

Why would he brave the undertow at night?

Todd knew how powerful the undertow was, how unpredictable, how deadly.

So why did he go swimming?

"Why, Todd?" Matt cried, opening his eyes, raising his face to the orange, rising sun.

Several minutes later two fishermen, tackle boxes and fishing rods in hand, came upon Matt, still on his knees, still huddled over his friend's body, still asking the question, "Why, Todd? Why?"

Chapter 16

A NEW VICTIM

*B*ats fluttered and swooped above the trees of the small island, darting shadows against the charcoal sky. Beneath the shelter of the trees stood shingled beach houses, long deserted by their human inhabitants.

Bats had claimed the island years before. Bats and the Eternal Ones, the ones who could transform themselves, become bats when the need arose.

The island was reachable only by boat, and this discouraged most people from building on it. Those who had built summer houses were driven away by the bats, murdered by those masquerading as bats, or had given up their nectar and had become Eternals themselves.

Now, Gabri waited in a darkened house. He had claimed part of the house as his own, having spread the ancient burial dirt on the floorboards and placed the carefully polished, dark wood coffin against the eastern wall, the safe wall.

Leaning heavily against the window frame, he stared out through the open window at the diving bats that the moonlight revealed.

Gabri sighed, unable to keep a pleased smile from spreading across his face. The air was warm and heavy, the way he liked it. The flutter of bat wings provided a pleasant background for his thoughts.

Pleasant thoughts.

Thoughts of how he had ruined Jessica's chances to win the bet. Thoughts of April, of fresh nectar.

He had sampled the nectar so gingerly, so carefully. His thirst was barely slaked.

But the summer was young.

He had reason to be patient.

Poor, impatient Jessica.

He was thinking of her as the bat floated down to the window. He pulled his head back as the creature, screeching like a fire alarm, buzzed by his face. It landed lightly on the floor and began to whir about, faster and faster, until it appeared as only a shadowy whirlwind.

A few seconds later Jessica emerged from the whirlwind, ruby droplets of blood still clinging to her full lips. She angrily tossed back her mane of hair and advanced on Gabri. "Wipe that disgusting smile off your face."

Gabri made no attempt to change his expression.

"What's the matter, Jessica? A little too much to drink?" He snickered at perhaps the only joke he had ever made.

Jessica raised her hands and lurched forward as if to attack him, groaning in anger. He stood his ground, his features narrowing. "Calm down. What's the big deal? You're a loser, that's all."

She glared at him, balling her hands into fists, too overcome by anger to speak.

"At least you're not thirsty," he said.

"Shut up, Gabri," she snarled. "Just shut up." She crossed her arms tightly in front of her chest, shuddering with anger, her teeth clenched, her face suddenly old, as if her anger were revealing her years.

He stood calmly at the window as she paced, enjoying her anger, enjoying her defeat, his victory. "Don't be a poor loser," he said softly as bats fluttered and screeched outside the window.

"I'm *not* a loser!" Jessica declared, stopping inches in front of him. "You're a cheater, Gabri. You play a dirty game."

His dark eyes widened in mock innocence. "Me? What did I do?"

"First you bit the girl to distract Todd," she reminded him, her face nearly in his, neither of them willing to back up. "Then you interrupt us, you fly overhead, you get me nervous and cause me to accidentally bite Todd too deeply."

He laughed. "I made you nervous?"

"Stop laughing!" she screamed. "I *killed* that

123

boy—for no reason! Just because you were determined to win our bet."

"At least you had your fill of the nectar," Gabri replied with a sneer. "What are you complaining about, Jessica?"

"It wasn't part of the bet, Gabri."

"Stop being a sore loser," he snapped, suddenly impatient, pushing himself away from the window. "All's fair in love and war, you know."

"I'm not a loser. *You're* going to be the loser," she insisted vehemently, following him, her coppery hair flowing behind her as she moved.

He laughed scornfully. "How can *I* lose? I have only two more encounters with April to go, two more tastes, and I will win." He walked to the coffin against the wall and, seeing the sky begin to brighten as dawn approached, pulled open the lid.

"But my victim—" she started.

"Your unfortunate victim is dead," Gabri said with a sneer. "Your clumsiness killed him. You must concede defeat."

"No way," Jessica insisted, following him to his coffin. "I am not defeated. I am still going to win. I will simply choose a new victim."

Gabri began to lower himself into the coffin. "A new victim? Get serious."

"I am serious," Jessica said, finally calm, finally rid of her anger.

She had an idea, an idea that was restoring her hope as it vanquished her fury.

"I am very serious, Gabri," she told him as she slowly lowered the coffin lid over his reclining figure. "Todd's friend Matt will be my victim. He will do nicely. In fact . . ." She smiled for the first time that night, letting him see her smile before she let the lid fall. "In fact—Matt will be easy prey."

PART TWO

LAST KISS

Chapter 17

VAMPIRES!

*F*our nights later, tossing in bed, his sheets tangled, his blanket in a heap on the floor, Matt dreamed about Todd.

He saw a broad, sandy stretch of beach, golden under a bright sun. High waves rose majestically at the shore, capped with white froth, rose and then fell onto the gleaming sand.

Todd appeared, running barefoot at full speed. He was wearing baggy black swim trunks. His footsteps made no sound as he moved across the beach.

Matt struggled to see Todd's face as Todd, running faster and faster, came toward him. But, although the beach shimmered in sunshine, Todd's face was blanketed in shadow.

Please, Matt thought, watching his friend lean

forward as he ran, the tall waves thundering behind him, please let me see your face, Todd.

And then Todd came into clear view.

And his face was twisted in horror, his eyes bulging, his mouth locked open in a relentless, silent scream.

The sky darkened, grew black.

The blackness followed Todd, moving toward him, moving faster than Todd could run.

At first the blackness seemed like a funnel-shaped cloud blocking the sun.

Todd was still in the sunlight, but the black cloud was gaining, about to swallow him up.

And then Matt saw that the darkness wasn't a cloud at all. It was made up of thousands of moving creatures.

His vision cleared and he saw the black and purple wings, heard the shrill chittering, saw the dark heads bowed low in flight.

The black shadow chasing Todd was a cloud of *bats*.

Thousands and thousands of bats, fluttering, flapping, swooping together, blocking the sunlight as they moved, shadowing the beach, chattering and shrieking until the ocean's thunder faded.

Running harder, sweat pouring down his forehead, Todd closed his eyes. But his mouth remained open.

Run, Todd—run! Matt urged.

But the cloud of bats swooped over Todd. He toppled to the sand, first on his knees, then facedown. And the bats descended over him like nightfall.

And everything went black.

Matt sat straight up in bed, relieved to see his room, relieved to see gray morning light through the bedroom window.

He stood up, half awake, half in his dreamlike state.

The shrill cries of the bats stayed with him as he made his way uncertainly across the floor to the window. The cloud of bats. The blackness descending over the beach, over Todd.

Leaning heavily on the windowsill, wanting to step out of the dream, wanting to escape from its frightening hold, but not wanting to forget it, Matt shook his head hard.

He realized he had awakened from the dream with a word on his lips.

Say it. Say the word, he urged himself.

And so he said it: *"Vampires."*

The dream was trying to tell him, trying to show him.

Matt knew it.

Matt knew how Todd had died.

The bats on the beach. The bats that lived on that small island off the shore.

The bat that had attacked that girl.

Vampires.

The bats were vampires.

The dream had revealed the truth to him.

Wide awake now, he hurriedly pulled on a pair of

wrinkled tennis shorts, picked up the T-shirt he had worn the day before, pulled it over his head, and headed for the back door without bothering to brush his teeth or hair.

"Hey—" his dad called to him from the breakfast table as Matt rushed through the kitchen.

But Matt was already out the screen door, the door slamming behind him. "Gotta go!" he called back and began jogging to April's house.

The sky was gray, the air tinged with a wet chill. The sandy road was wet beneath his sneakers. He realized it must have rained the night before.

He hadn't heard the rain. The dream had held him too tightly, first the thunder of the waves, then the frightening siren cries of the bats.

The vampires.

He had to tell April. He had to tell her that he had learned the truth.

Despite the sunshine and blue skies, the four days since Todd's death had passed in a gray fog of gloom and shadows.

The pictures all seemed to have faded in Matt's mind. Only the sounds remained. The anguished cries of Todd's parents. The murmurs of the police. The frightened, hushed conversations of kids on the beach and in town.

Matt had seen April only once in the four days. They tried to talk as if everything were normal, but neither of them could manage it. Then they tried to talk about Todd. But that was impossible too.

Matt had left her to go wander alone on the

beach, still wondering what had happened that night, why Todd had decided to go swimming, how Todd had died.

The town coroner had called it an accidental drowning.

But it didn't make sense to Matt—until the dream. Until he woke up with the answer on his lips.

And now he had to tell April.

Approaching the back of her summer house, a small white clapboard cottage with a wide sundeck that was cluttered with outdoor chairs and an umbrella table, he could see April through the kitchen window.

He leapt onto the deck and hurried to the back door, calling inside. April looked up, startled, from the table. Her mother was just clearing the breakfast dishes. The twins came racing to open the screen door, each calling, "I'll get it! I'll get it!"

Matt greeted everyone, still trying to catch his breath from the long jog from his house. "Have you had breakfast?" Mrs. Blair asked, pushing up the sleeves of the man's shirt she wore over her bathing suit. "There's still some pancake batter left."

"No thanks," Matt said, his eyes on April. She looked so pale and frail in the gray light filtering in through the glass windows. "I—wanted to talk to April."

"Play with me instead!" Courtney demanded.

"No—me!" Whitney cried.

April stood up and gently brushed both girls

aside. "Matt and I are going out on the deck," she said, giving Matt a faint smile as she led the way outside.

Matt followed her onto the deck, eager to tell her what he had figured out. The ocean air still carried a chill; the overcast sky was low and gray.

April leaned against the deck railing and stared out at the trees. Matt stepped beside her, wiping cold perspiration from his forehead with the hem of his T-shirt.

The T-shirt smelled, he discovered. And he suddenly remembered that he was in such a hurry to talk to April, he hadn't even brushed his hair.

I must look pretty gross, he thought. But he shoved these thoughts away, determined to share his new knowledge with her.

"How ya doing?" she asked somewhat shyly, staring out at the trees, dark under the low, hazy sky.

"Okay. I mean, not great. But okay."

"Me too," she said softly.

"I have to tell you something," he said impatiently, wishing she'd turn around and face him. "Something important. I mean . . ."

Should he just blurt it out?

She turned, curious. "I'm so sleepy," she said. "Guess it's all this fresh air."

"Listen, April, I want to tell you this. I know how Todd died."

Her eyes narrowed. Her pale face seemed to lose

even more color. "We know how he died, Matt," she said, her voice a whisper. "He drowned."

"Listen to me, April—please," Matt pleaded, putting an arm on the shoulder of the oversize blue T-shirt that stretched nearly down to her knees. "Please?"

She didn't reply, just stared into his eyes.

"This idea came to me in a dream," he said, speaking rapidly, urgently, his hand still on her slender shoulder, "but I know it's real."

There was no way to say it slowly, to introduce the idea gently, he decided. He had to get it out, say what was on his mind.

"Todd was killed by a vampire."

"Huh?" She pulled away from him, raised her hands as if shielding herself from this idea.

"Vampires," he repeated. "You know all the bats that fly over the beach? They must be vampires. A girl was attacked by a bat a few nights before Todd died. The bat bit her throat. And Todd—"

"Matt—this is a very dumb joke," April said heatedly, crossing her arms. "I don't get it at all."

Matt started to reply, but the tiny red marks on April's throat caught his eye. He gasped, staring hard at them.

Wild thoughts careened through his mind. Crazy thoughts.

Am I seeing things? Is it just a mosquito bite?

Gabri's face floated through his thoughts. April and Gabri. April and Gabri.

He pictured the two of them together.

Is it possible? Is it possible that Gabri is a vampire?

Or am I cracking up?

"I had this dream, see," he continued, his eyes locked on April's throat, his mind whirring excitedly. "Todd was running, and—"

"Stop, Matt!" April exploded. "Just stop it!"

"I know I'm right!" he insisted, ignoring her angry plea. "It makes sense, April. All the bats. And Todd—he had a cut on his neck. I remember—"

"Matt—I mean it," April said, her features tight with anger. "Shut up. Just shut up."

"But, April—"

What had he done wrong? What had he said wrong? Why wouldn't she listen to him, at least give him a chance to explain?

"Grow up, Matt," she said, her green eyes flashing angrily. "Grow up. Your best friend is dead, and all you can think about is some horror movie!"

"No—" he cried.

But she wouldn't let him continue. "I've got news for you," she cried heatedly, "life is real."

"I know. But—"

"Life is real, Matt. It isn't a dumb horror movie." There were tears in the corners of her eyes now.

Oh, no, he thought, feeling his heart sink. I didn't want to make her cry. Haven't we all cried enough this week?

"Todd is dead, and it's impossible to explain, impossible to accept," April said, forcing back the tears, trying to keep from losing control. "But blaming it on vampires like a—like a *child* isn't going to help anyone."

"But, April—" He didn't know what he was going to say. He couldn't take his eyes off the small bruise on her throat.

"Gabri is a vampire," he muttered. He didn't even realize he was talking, didn't hear the words as they came out, didn't mean for April to hear.

Wiping away the teardrops that stained her pale cheeks, she glared at him furiously. "Are you totally losing it, Matt?" she screamed. "Go away! Just go away from me!" She spun angrily and moved toward the house.

He started to follow, but she pushed him back, pressing her fists against his broad shoulders.

"I mean it. Go away. I don't want to see you again! Don't call me—and don't come over!"

"What's going on out there?" one of the twins called, poking her golden head out the door.

"Are they fighting?" the other one asked from inside. "Let me see!"

They both clamored noisily out the door as April pushed past them into the house, sobbing loudly.

Matt sighed miserably and, without looking back, stepped off the deck and headed back to the road. Two rabbits hopped excitedly across his path, but Matt didn't notice.

It started to rain, a few large drops, a sprinkle at first, and then after a few seconds a hard, steady downpour.

Trudging slowly, his head down, Matt didn't react to the rain. His thoughts weighed heavier on him than any downpour.

Of course April is right, he told himself, kicking up clumps of mud with his sneakers. His hair fell down over his forehead. His wet, fragrant T-shirt clung to his back.

Of course she's right. How could I run over there talking about vampires? I really must have been totally off my nut.

Vampires!

Of *course* she thought I was a jerk. And she's right.

Gabri isn't a vampire.

I'm just jealous. And upset.

And feeling sorry for myself.

Vampires . . .

I'd laugh myself—if I didn't feel so much like crying.

How did I ever get such a dumb thing in my head? And how could I be so crazed that I took it seriously?

He sighed loudly, shaking his fists at the trees as they bent under the weight of the falling rain. He wished he could sink into the mud, sink down over his head, and never return.

I've made a total fool of myself, he thought, shaking his head miserably, shivering as a hard gust of wind swept cold rain down the back of his shirt.

I've made a total fool of myself. And I've lost April for good.

"So what did you do in the rain all day?" Ben asked, leading the way through the high grass, over the dune.

The grass, still wet from the day's rain, tickled Matt's ankles as he walked, and he wished he'd worn jeans instead of shorts. "Not much," he muttered to his friend.

Actually, he had spent most of the day staring out of the living-room window at the rain, pacing back and forth, rolling Todd's plastic butane lighter around in his hand, and thinking about his dream, and how stupid he'd been to run right over to April's without stopping to think.

He fingered the lighter now as he made his way over the dunes with Ben. The lighter was somehow comforting, his only memento of Todd.

"The sand is dry already," Ben said, kicking at it with the toe of a sandal. "Isn't that amazing? It rained all day, and the sand completely soaked up the water."

Matt looked toward the ocean. The clouds had finally parted as evening arrived. The night sky was nearly clear, the moon a pale circle over the ocean horizon.

"I did a really stupid thing this morning," he blurted out.

"So what else is new?" Ben joked, bending to pull

a long piece of dune grass up and stick it in his mouth.

"No. This was really stupid," Matt insisted. In a few sentences, keeping his eyes on the sand, he told Ben about his dream and his conversation with April. "It was a dumb move," he concluded sadly.

Ben chewed thoughtfully on the long piece of grass. *"Dumb* is a good word for it," he agreed, shaking his head. *"Stupid* is even better. I might even be tempted to use *idiotic."*

"You know, I didn't tell you about it so you could make jokes!" Matt snapped angrily.

Why *did* I tell Ben? he wondered.

Did I expect him to jump up, slap me on the back, and say, "You're right, Matt! Those bats *are* vampires!"

I guess I just needed to confide in someone.

"Sorry," Ben said quickly. "Really. You must feel like a jerk already, right?"

"Some apology," Matt muttered.

A bat swooped down low just ahead of them, a dark, fleeting shadow across the beach. Matt looked up again and saw two bats hovering over the next dune.

"In science class last year we learned that bats are good," Ben said, slurring his words because of the long stem of grass he was chewing. "They're really needed for ecological balance, you know. They eat insects. And bat guano is a really important fertilizer."

"Bat guano to you too," Matt muttered bitterly. "Thanks for the science lesson."

"I don't blame you for being in a bad mood," Ben said sympathetically. "I still feel creeped out about Todd too. And then having that guy move in on your girl—"

"I don't want to talk about it anymore," Matt snapped, surprising himself with his own vehemence. "Really."

"Hey—I'm heading to Swanny's," Ben said, obviously eager to end the conversation. "You coming?"

Matt shook his head. "Think I'll keep walking," he replied glumly. "Maybe I'll catch you later."

Ben gave him a little wave as he headed off. "Cheer up," he called back. "It'll only get worse." He didn't even bother to laugh at his own dumb joke, just hurried toward town.

What a goof, Matt thought. With his science facts and ancient, dumb jokes, Ben usually cheered Matt up—but not tonight.

He made his way over the dune. Then seeing a group of kids he knew on the beach, he turned, eager not to be seen, and began to walk quickly in the opposite direction, his eyes on the stone cliff, a black silhouette against the clear night sky.

He found himself thinking of ways to apologize to April. But none of them seemed right. He couldn't imagine himself saying them.

As he walked over the sand, he tried to think of

how he could ask her to go out with him again, how he could ask her to stop seeing Gabri. But that seemed impossible too.

Shaking his head, he tried to push all of those thoughts from his mind, tried to let the steady rush of the waves drown out all of his thinking.

He stopped short as something caught his eye up ahead.

Something huddled low and dark on a high dune.

Low and dark and still.

"Oh, no," he uttered aloud, staring hard at it.

What is that? Another body?

Chapter 18

ANOTHER ACCIDENT FOR JESSICA

*F*rozen in horror, Matt stared across the low, dark dune. His breath burst out in loud gasps. He had the urge to turn and run, but knew he had to see what was huddled there on the sand.

Walking unsteadily, trying to focus his eyes in the darkness, he made his way to the dune. When he saw her there, sitting in black tights and a long-sleeved black top, her legs pulled up, her arms encircling her knees, her head bowed, he stopped in surprise.

"Jessica?"

She didn't respond.

"Jessica?" he repeated more loudly, taking a hesitant step toward her. He stood over her now, staring down at her mane of red hair.

"Hey—Jessica?"

He saw for the first time that her shoulders were trembling.

And when she finally lifted her face up to him, he saw the tear-soaked cheeks, the wet eyes, her quivering chin, and realized that she'd been crying.

"Sorry," Matt said, and took a step back. He felt awkward, overcome by embarrassment. "Sorry," he repeated. He didn't know what to say.

She blinked several times. It seemed to take her a while to recognize him. She seemed confused, as if she were so deep in her thoughts, so deep in her sadness, that there was no room in her memory for someone from the outside world.

Then she forced a wet smile, closing her eyes and raising both hands to wipe the tear tracks from her cheeks.

"I—I didn't know it was you," Matt stammered, trying to decide what to do with his hands. Finally, he just lowered them to his sides. "Are you okay?"

"I guess," she replied, her voice muffled in her throat. She sighed, and added, "I don't know. I can't seem to stop crying."

"About Todd?" Matt asked, and then felt like a fool. Of *course* she was crying about Todd. "I mean—"

"I just keep thinking I'm going to run into him on the beach or in town," Jessica said, the words pouring out. "I can't believe it. I can't believe I was the last person to see him. I can't believe any of it, you know? I mean, I've never known anyone who died. Never."

"Yeah," Matt said quietly, turning his eyes to the water. "It *is* unbelievable. He was my best friend, you know."

She didn't reply. Shaking her head sadly, she pulled herself to her feet and brushed away the sand that clung to her black tights. Then she stepped closer to Matt, close enough that he could smell her perfume, tangy and pungent even in the heavy sea air.

"I knew him for such a short time," Jessica said, allowing a single tear to descend down her cheek. "But I felt so close to Todd."

"He was a good guy," Matt said, staring into her hypnotic eyes, feeling guilty for thinking about how good-looking Jessica was while talking about his dead buddy.

The ocean wind seemed to circle them, to draw them together.

Matt felt strangely dizzy. Was it her perfume? Was it the swirling wind? His sadness?

"I don't understand why Todd tried to swim so late at night," Matt said, unable to release his eyes from her stare.

"I don't either," she said softly. "He teased me about going for a swim. You know, taking off our clothes and jumping in. I knew he was just joking. At least, I thought he was joking."

"Weird," Matt replied, shaking his head, trying to shake away the dizziness. "Todd wasn't much of a daredevil. He was pretty timid, you know?"

"I know," she said, turning her gaze beyond

Matt, her eyes surveying the nearly deserted beach. "That's why I thought he was joking about skinny-dipping so late at night. When he dropped me off at my cottage, I was sure he was going to go straight home."

"Weird," Matt repeated, his head spinning.

"The next morning, when I heard—" Jessica started. But her voice caught, and instead of words, she uttered a pained cry.

Without thinking about it, Matt put an arm around her trembling shoulders to comfort her. She sobbed silently for a moment, then smiled up at him.

Her perfume was so strong, so sweet, so intoxicating, it seemed to penetrate to his brain.

"Did you cry too?" she asked as they started to walk together across the sand, his arm still around her shoulders. She felt so warm and . . . fragile, he thought.

"Yeah," he admitted. "I went a little berserk, I think, when I found him. I mean, I sort of lost track of what happened. Some fishermen found me with him. I guess I was a little out of my head."

"I haven't stopped crying," she said softly, closing her eyes and leaning against him. "You're the first person I've been able to talk to."

She rested her head on his shoulder, for the briefest moment. He felt her soft hair brush his cheek and felt a shiver of excitement run down his body.

I wonder what she'd do if I kissed her, Matt thought.

A wave of guilt swept over him. Here we are talking about Todd. Here she is sharing her sadness with me, confiding in me, trusting me—and all I can think about is kissing her.

She smiled at him, the sadness fading from her pale face.

To Matt's surprise, her smile was a knowing smile, as if she knew what he was thinking, as if she shared his thoughts.

"Should I . . . uh . . . walk you home?" he asked, his arm sliding down around her slender waist.

Again, her hair brushed his face as she turned to gaze into his eyes. "No. Let's keep going," she suggested in a whisper, so quietly he had to lean closer to hear. She pointed toward the rocks that led up to the steep, black cliff. "Let's just keep going and going and going, Matt," she whispered. "You're making me feel better. You really are."

"I'm glad," he replied.

Suddenly she pulled away from him and started jogging toward the cliff, taking long, steady strides.

Startled, he immediately missed her touch, missed her warmth, missed the feel of her under his arm. "Hey—wait up!" he called.

Without slowing, she turned back to him, a mysterious smile on her face.

"Jessica—wait up!" he repeated, and began running over the beach, following her as the sand gave way to smooth rock, following her up, up toward the cliff ledge, the water crashing noisily below, crashing like his heartbeat, louder, faster, harder.

"Come on—stop!" he called, running at full speed now, staring at her hair that flew behind her like a proud pennant.

Her laughter floated back to him on the swirling wind.

They were both high above the beach now, running across the smooth, flat cliff ledge.

"Hey—slow down!" he warned, breathing hard.

He saw her expression change as she neared the cliff edge, saw her mouth open wide with fear and surprise.

She tried to stop.

But her sneakers slid on the slippery slick stone surface.

She raised her hands as if to grab on to something. But there was nothing to grab on to.

"Jessica—no!" Matt cried.

But his words couldn't stop her, either.

She slid right off the edge of the cliff.

He heard her terrified scream as she went over the side.

Saw her arms flail the air as she began to drop.

Then silence.

Then he was alone up there.

All alone.

Chapter 19

MATT'S
MOONLIGHT KISSES

Without realizing it, Matt was at the cliff edge too, on his hands and knees, peering down into the swirling blackness, weighted down by his dread, not even breathing, holding his breath, staring into the rolling, twisting waters.

She's dead too, he realized.

She has fallen to her death.

Frozen by his fears, by the thought of what he knew he would find, Matt stared down into the waters, crashing against the wall of rocks.

And saw Jessica smiling up at him, standing near the shore, waist-deep in the water, her hair catching the bright moonlight.

"Huh? Jessica?" he managed to utter, surprised that he had any voice at all.

She waved up at him, tossing her head back.

149

Then she motioned for him to come down, to join her.

"You're okay?" he called.

She couldn't hear him way down there. She motioned again for him to come down.

But he couldn't stop staring at her.

How had she survived that fall? he wondered, feeling his heartbeat return to normal, feeling the heavy dread lift from his body.

How did she keep herself from crashing against the rocks?

How did she do it?

He was on his feet now, waving back at her.

So happy. So happy she was alive. So happy that he felt like spreading his arms and taking off, flying off the cliff edge and floating down to her.

But he turned and carefully made his way across the flat stone ledge. The rocky pathway down was steep and slippery, but he ran eagerly, stumbling, kicking stones, sending them scuttling down in small avalanches.

"Jessica—you're okay!"

She still couldn't hear him over the wind and the waves.

Standing on the pebbly shore now, she smiled at him, hair aflame in the bright moonlight, arms at her sides as if patiently waiting for him.

"Hey—you scared me!" he cried, sneakers splashing in puddled crevices in the rock-strewn sand. "You really scared me!"

She didn't reply.

She threw her arms around his shoulders and pulled his face to hers.

The perfume. It seemed to float around him, to hold him, to draw him near.

She felt warm and cold at the same time, wet from the ocean waters, yet her lips were so dry, hot and dry.

Before Matt could take a breath, before he even realized what was happening, she was kissing his mouth, kissing his eyes, kissing his chin.

Kissing him with such surprising passion.

So hot and so cold at the same time.

The tangy perfume, the hot, dry lips, the brush of her hair, the warmth of her face—it all overwhelmed Matt.

The kisses. The kisses.

He struggled to respond.

But he found himself sinking—willingly, so willingly—into dizzying, spinning darkness.

Chapter 20

VISITORS
IN THE NIGHT

Gabri rose slowly from his coffin, into the blue evening. The dirt that formed his mattress, precious native soil, all that was left of his homeland, of his own true time, clung to his clothing, and he brushed it off wearily.

Just waking, his face revealed the centuries. It took effort to compose himself, to soften the ravages of time; effort to make himself young again, to smooth his features, to bring the spark of life to his eyes, to lift himself through the pain, the ancient pain that swept over him every day as he slept his unnatural sleep.

He groaned and smoothed back his dark hair, practiced motions, so much harder without a mirror.

So much harder to summon the youthful face without a mirror.

Yet somehow, it was much easier to continue the evil, endless journey of a vampire without having to look at oneself, without having to see what one has become.

"Well, well. You're very philosophical today, Gabri," he said aloud, speaking to shifting shadows on the beach-house wall.

A quiet snicker made him spin around. A soft cry of surprise escaped his lips. "Jessica!"

Her jumpsuit matched the blue of the night. Standing just inside the window, her billowing hair caught the pale light of the rising moon.

At first she seemed to him part of the evening, a shadow stepping out of shadows. But as her eyes lit up, the rest of her appeared to take shape, to come alive. Her laugh sent a dry shiver down Gabri's back.

"Who invited *you?*" he snapped.

"I was in the neighborhood," she joked.

"What do you want?" he asked impatiently, his expression revealing the sourness he felt, the sourness of her unwelcome intrusion, the sourness of waking up after so many long centuries, of rising up from the dirt one more time to fly and prowl.

"You're not very friendly tonight," she said, approaching him slowly, a smug smile crossing her face. "What's wrong, Gabri? Not succeeding as well as you planned with the little blonde?"

"I'm succeeding better than you are," he replied coldly.

Thoughts of April, of the nectar, the sweet taste

of nectar, warmed him. "At least I haven't killed anyone."

"That's no problem," she said with a nonchalant shrug of her slender shoulders. "No problem at all. You don't think I'd let a little thing like that stand in the way of my winning our bet, do you?"

He uttered an unpleasant curse. "You cannot win. April is a willing victim."

"Ha!" Jessica cried nastily, crossing her arms. "What did you do? Sneak up from behind and bite her back?"

"No need to sneak," Gabri replied. "I have won her affections. She has broken off with that boyfriend of hers."

"What?" For a brief moment Jessica's eyes revealed surprise.

"She is no longer seeing Matt. She is with me now." The smile that crossed his face was triumphant and leering.

"That's a victory for *me*—not you," Jessica said, recovering quickly.

"What do you mean?"

"By splitting up April and Matt, you've made it easier for me to conquer Matt," she told him.

He shook his head, brushing back his hair once again, smoothing the lines from his cheeks with both palms. "Dream on, Jessica," he said dryly. "You can stand here and brag about what you're going to do for the rest of eternity, but April will be an Eternal One by the end of the week."

"I'm not the one who's bragging—" she started.

He pushed past her toward the shadows near the window. And as she turned to face him, the shadows began to whirl, a dark dust storm.

The dust cleared. Gabri emerged in bat form. "I must fly to her now!" he rasped, and took off through the open window, soaring until he disappeared into the darkening sky.

"What a cornball idiot," she muttered aloud. Reaching into his coffin, she grabbed up a handful of dirt, the precious dirt that helped maintain Gabri, and tossed it angrily to the floor.

Courtney jumped on Gabri's shoulders. Whitney grabbed him around the waist. Giggling loudly, they pulled him to the deck and climbed on him.

"No! No!" he cried helplessly, laughing and squirming, trying to unseat them, causing them to hold on even tighter.

"Girls—give Gabri a break!" Mrs. Blair cried, shaking her head.

"It's okay. I can handle them," Gabri boasted. *"Owww!"*

His words caused the two girls to bounce even harder on his back.

"Come on, girls," Mr. Blair pleaded, looking up from the newspaper. "Gabri isn't a carnival ride, you know."

"Yes, he is," Whitney replied.

"He's a roller coaster," Courtney said. "Wheeeee!"

"Ow!" Gabri cried, laughing through his pretend pain, slapping the deck floorboards like a wrestler.

Finally April appeared from the house. She was wearing snug-fitting white leggings, and a black T-shirt under a bright banana yellow shirt tied in a knot at her waist. "What's going on?" she cried.

"You look very nice," her mother said approvingly, having to shout over the twins' squeals.

"But what are Courtney and Whitney doing?" April repeated.

"They've really taken to Gabri," her mother replied in a confidential whisper.

"That's because he lets them do whatever they want!" April said, amused by the spectacle of seeing a grown teenager helpless beneath two tiny girls.

"Hellllllp!" Gabri moaned.

April came to his rescue, grabbing an arm of each sister and pulling the protesting girls off. "Gabri and I have to go," she told them.

"But the ride isn't over," Whitney said grumpily, making a move back to Gabri, who was struggling to get to his feet. She caught him around the knees. He grabbed the deck railing to keep from falling.

"That's enough!" Mr. Blair called firmly. "I mean it, Whitney."

She ignored him, of course, and continued trying to tackle Gabri, who held on to the wooden railing for dear life.

It took another ten minutes to pull the girls

away—and convince them to stay away. April's parents kept apologizing, but Gabri insisted he'd had a great time. "Next time, I'll outwrestle you both!" he boasted to the twins. Then he said good night to everyone and he and April stepped off the deck and began to follow the sandy path that led past other beach houses to town.

"My sisters really like you," April said.

"Because they can beat me up," Gabri said.

"My parents think you're really nice too," she added, her eyes on the path.

"Your parents have good taste," he said, smiling.

"Oh. Look. I almost forgot to show you," April said, stopping suddenly.

"What is it?"

"My dad got me an early birthday present," she replied, her hand searching under the black T-shirt. "My birthday isn't until next month, but Dad can never wait."

The yellow shirt she had on top seemed to shimmer in the moonlight. Gabri stared, following her hand as it found the chain she was wearing around her neck.

"Look," April said, and raised the small, shiny pendant for him to see. "It's a silver cross. Isn't it elegant?"

The cross caught the moonlight and glowed, the light catching the horror on Gabri's face.

Gabri took a step back and tried to soften his expression before April noticed.

His thoughts churned. The light of the cross had burned him as if it were a searing flame.

"Very beautiful," he managed to say.

What am I to do? he thought, suddenly in a panic. I dare not come close, I dare not puncture her throat, I cannot taste the nectar while she wears that cross.

What to do? What to *do?*

Its simple power could blind him forever, its light could burn his already-dry flesh; it could consume him in flames.

What to do? What to do?

Then, as April replaced the cross, trying to tuck it back under the shirt, it slipped out of her hand. "Oh!"

Gabri saw it hit the sand.

April bent down quickly, her hands searching the ground. She pulled it back up, a frown on her face. "The clasp is a little loose," she said, squeezing the cross in her hand. She turned to him. "Would you help me put it back on?"

"Okay." He stepped behind her so she wouldn't see his hands trembling.

With the cross at her throat, she raised the ends of the chain behind her neck. "Just clasp it for me."

"No problem," he said softly, being careful not to let his eyes rest on the cross. He took the ends of the delicate chain and pressed them together.

He pretended to have difficulty, then pretended to succeed in closing the clasp.

"It should hold," he told her.

But he had deliberately left the chain unclasped.

"Thank you," she said, turning to flash him a grateful smile.

He smiled back, careful not to glance at the cross, gleaming just below her throat. "It's very pretty," he said, a cold tremor coursing down his back from the thought of it.

They made their way toward town, walking slowly past rows of beach cottages, all of their windows glowing with orange and yellow light.

As the houses gave way to a field of tall grass, Gabri saw the unclasped cross slip off and silently fall to the ground.

They kept walking.

April hadn't noticed.

Gabri smiled at her, unable to conceal his joy and relief.

Happily, so happily, eager for what was about to happen, he put his arm around her shoulders and drew her close.

Later that same night Matt arrived home from his date with Jessica. He stopped at the back door, closed his burning eyes, and pressed his feverish forehead against the cool glass.

I'm so tired, he thought.

So tired, it seemed an impossible effort to pull open the door and get into his bed.

It couldn't be that late, Matt thought, opening his

eyes and pushing himself with great effort away from the doorway. The moon was still high in the sky. The air was cold and heavy with dew.

He coughed.

His throat ached.

Hope I'm not getting sick.

To his surprise, his night with Jessica was already fogged in his memory.

Where had they gone? What had they done?

He remembered the dark beach. He remembered her mouth, her lips, her kisses.

He remembered the pain. The sweet pain.

Pain?

No.

Couldn't be pain.

I'm too tired to remember, he told himself.

I'm just . . . so . . . tired.

Somehow he pulled open the door. Silently he moved across the squeaking floorboards, through the dark kitchen, through the short, narrow hallway, past his parents' room.

Silence.

To his room.

So tired. So weary. It took such effort to push open the door. He felt so heavy. His *clothes* felt so heavy.

His *hair* felt so heavy on his head.

He was breathing hard from the exertion of walking.

He had to get undressed, out of the heavy clothes that were weighing him down.

He had to get to bed, to sleep.

Had to sleep away this weariness.

Sleep away the aching of his throat.

But where was he?

Why was everything tilting and swaying?

Just tired. Just . . . so . . . tired.

Jessica, he thought, picturing her pale, dramatic face; picturing the flowing red hair, the burning eyes.

Jessica, why am I so tired?

What did we do, Jessica? What did we do?

He forced himself not to think about her. If he started to think about Jessica, he'd never get to sleep.

First, I have to get undressed, he decided, struggling to clear his mind.

The familiar furniture in his room was a blur of shadows.

A blur. A blur among blurs.

But suddenly, one of the blurs came into solid focus.

Matt blinked. Once. Twice.

Someone was sitting on his bed, sitting in the dark room, his back to Matt.

He blinked again, willing the image away. But it wouldn't leave.

It was really there.

Someone was on his bed.

Gripped with fear, Matt stared at the unmoving form.

Who was it?

Who was in his room at this hour?

How did he get in?

"Hey—" Matt uttered in a whisper. "Hey—"

Holding his breath, summoning his courage, struggling to clear his head, he reached out and tapped the person on the shoulder.

As Matt touched him, the dark figure slowly turned.

His face came into view.

And Matt began to scream.

Chapter 21

"BUT—YOU'RE DEAD!"

Pressing both hands over his mouth to muffle his shrieks, Matt backed away from the bed.

He bumped into his dresser, sending a stab of pain down his back.

Ignoring it, he gaped in horror at the somber-faced figure, hunched on his bed, staring back at him across the room.

Slowly, gulping for air, Matt lowered his hands.

"Todd—" he cried, his voice escaping his throat in a hoarse whisper. "Todd—you're *dead!*"

The figure, hands resting on the knees of his black slacks, leaned forward slowly, and his face edged out of the shadows into the square of pale moonlight from the window.

"Todd—" Matt repeated, his back pressed hard against the dresser.

Todd's face appeared in the light, green and swollen. His eyes were open but had sunk back in his head. Encircled by pus, the pupils were solid white.

A tear in the flesh of one cheek allowed the skin to sag like a pocket. When Todd finally opened his mouth to speak, his jaws grating as they opened like a squeaking, rusty door, Matt saw that several teeth were missing.

"Hi, Matt."

The voice was like wind, a rush of air.

"No!" A wave of fear nearly brought Matt to his knees. He turned and gripped the dresser top to keep himself upright.

"No!"

"Yesssssssss," the creature on the bed hissed.

The curtains on the window appeared to billow up in response.

"Yessssss," Todd repeated as if testing his own breathless voice. And again the curtains flapped in reply.

This isn't a dream, Matt realized, feeling the knob on the dresser drawer press into his back.

How many times had he dreamed about Todd since that terrible morning when he had discovered him bobbing in the water, cut and lifeless?

How many times had Todd returned to invade Matt's dreams?

But this was no dream.

Todd—dead Todd—sat on Matt's bed, his sunken egg-white eyes staring up at Matt, his sagging, ripped face testifying to his death.

"Todd—you're dead," Matt repeated.

The thought formed a barrier to any other words. He couldn't get past it.

"You're dead."

"I'm not dead at night," Todd whispered, leaning closer to make himself heard.

The curtains blew out the window, as if being sucked out by some invisible force.

"I'm not dead at night," Todd repeated breathlessly. "At night I'm caught between life and death."

Todd's head angled to one side, dropping nearly to his shoulder, as if holding it up were a strain.

"No!" Matt cried, closing his eyes, unable to continue staring at this hideous, distorted form of his old friend.

When he opened his eyes, he gasped in horror.

Todd had risen up off the bed.

"No—please!" Matt cried, trying to back away, but he was trapped against the dresser.

Todd moved forward quickly, seeming to float across the room. He reached out and grabbed Matt by the shoulders.

His grip was hard as bone.

The blank white eyes, so deep in their red, pus-filled sockets, stared into Matt's eyes as if accusing him.

"Todd—no!"

But Todd's grip tightened.

An odor of decay filled Matt's nostrils.

He tried to hold his breath, but his chest was heaving.

The foul odor encircled him, closed in on him, until he uttered a strangled cry. He almost suffocated under the power of the fetid smell.

Still Todd gripped his shoulders, his white eyes staring blindly into Matt's, hovering over Matt, floating above him in the dark room, imprisoning Matt, cornering him, paralyzing him with the odor of decay, the smell of death.

"Todd—what are you doing?" Matt managed to cry out in a terrified voice he didn't recognize. "What are you doing?"

Chapter 22

WARNING FROM THE GRAVE

"*I*—I came to warn you," Todd whispered, the words escaping hesitantly in small bursts of foul breath.

"Huh?"

Matt closed his eyes, tried to keep down the waves of nausea.

Todd loosened his grip but didn't back away.

"I came to warn you," he repeated, tilting his head till it rested on his shoulder. Matt opened his eyes to see a foot-long tear in the flesh of Todd's neck.

"Vampires," Todd whispered.

"Yes," Matt agreed, nodding solemnly. Everything was spinning, spinning so fast. He had to close his eyes again.

If only he could escape from the smell, so putrid, so sour, so sickening, so suffocating.

"They're vampires, Matt," Todd warned, reaching out to Matt as he floated backward.

"I know," Matt whispered, his eyes closed. "I know, Todd."

"Lissssssssssten," Todd hissed, suddenly sounding far away. "Lisssssssten, Matt. I came to warn you. They're vampires."

"I know, Todd. I *know!*" Matt cried with a loud sob. His eyes were shut tight. He tried not to inhale. The smell was so powerful, so disgusting.

"I know, Todd," he repeated weakly. "But I'm so tired."

Silence.

Matt kept his eyes shut.

"I'm so tired, Todd. Really. I'm just so—tired."

Silence.

"I'm sorry, Todd. I'm really sorry. But I'm very, very tired now. I'm just . . . too . . . tired."

Matt swam slowly to consciousness and, one eye open, peered at the window. A wash of gray morning light filled the room.

He groaned and tried to open his other eye, then gave up and closed them both.

He didn't remember falling asleep. He didn't remember sleeping.

He only remembered the dream.

Am I ever going to stop dreaming about Todd? he wondered, yawning, stretching his legs over the bedcovers.

"Hey—"

He pulled himself up and, squinting, looked down.

He was still dressed. Still wearing the denim cutoffs and blue long-sleeved polo shirt he had worn with Jessica.

"Ohh," he groaned, seeing that his sneakers, caked with wet sand, were still on his feet.

The bedspread was streaked with sand. He must have just fallen onto his bed, unconscious.

Reaching for his alarm clock, he knocked his Walkman onto the floor. It hit with a loud *clunk* and bounced. It was only seven-fifteen. Still early.

What was that smell in his nostrils?

That sour smell?

It was in his throat too. It seemed to be on his skin.

Had he thrown up without realizing it?

Still squinting and struggling to wake up, Matt pulled himself to his feet and looked about unsteadily.

Bits of the dream flashed into his mind.

It had been a terrifying dream. So real.

So real the foul aroma had stayed with him.

He stumbled to the mirror over the dresser and grabbed the dresser top for support.

Even though he had slept for hours, he didn't feel at all rested or refreshed.

In fact, he had never felt this tired in all his life.

Must be sick, he thought, the foul odor clinging to his nostrils.

He bumped the Kleenex box onto the floor.

Not bothering to pick it up, he peered into the mirror.

And saw the dark pinprick bruises on his throat.

And knew it wasn't a dream.

"Todd was here," he said aloud, his voice hoarse and sleep clogged.

"Todd came back to warn me."

He leaned forward, pressing himself against the wooden dresser to get a better look.

Tiny, round pinpricks. The color of red plums.

A tiny bruise.

Where Jessica had drunk.

Jessica.

She was a vampire.

Todd had come to warn him about Jessica.

She had given him the same kind of throat wound as—April had.

Staring into the mirror, Matt knew he had been right. Gabri was a vampire too.

Todd had come to warn him.

He raised two fingers to his throat and gently, reluctantly touched the bruise.

Touching the spot gave him a chill of pleasure.

Those kisses. Those lips. So wet against his throat, so warm.

He pressed the spot lightly and received another chill.

It wasn't a dream. Todd was here.

And *now* what can I do? What *should* I do?

He realized his legs were trembling. He felt so weak, so completely exhausted.

Dizzily, he made his way back to the bed. He sat down heavily and tried to pull off his sneakers.

But the effort was too much for him.

I've got to do something—got to warn April.

Sighing, he toppled onto his back, his arms dropping weakly over the sides of the bed.

"Got to warn April," he whispered, struggling to open his eyes. "Got to save us. . . ."

Then he was asleep again. Not a normal sleep, but a deep unconsciousness. A dreamless darkness.

He was awakened some time later by hands shaking him roughly.

"Todd?" he cried, sitting up straight. "Todd? You're back?"

Chapter 23

A STARING MATCH

"Huh? Todd?" Matt muttered, struggling to consciousness. He felt as if he were at the bottom of the ocean, trying to push himself up, up through the heavy swirl of waves.

It wasn't Todd shaking him. It was his dad.

"Hey—wake up! Lazy bum!" Mr. Daniels called with mock anger.

"Huh? What time is it?" Matt stared into the bright, golden sunshine flooding into the room through the open curtains.

"We let you sleep till ten," his father said, pointing to the bed-table clock. "But we all have to go. Come on. Get dressed. You can eat breakfast on the way to the pier."

"Whoa." Matt tentatively placed his feet on the floor. "Am I forgetting something here?" He squinted at his father, still unable to open both eyes at the same time.

"We're going deep-sea fishing, remember? On Dr. Miller's boat?" Mr. Daniels gave Matt's shoulder a playful shove. "Hurry it up, you bum." He started toward the door.

"I can't," Matt called to him, sinking back onto his pillow.

His father turned at the doorway, a concerned expression on his handsome face. "What's wrong? You sick?"

"Yes," Matt answered quickly. "No. I mean, I don't know."

"What's your problem, Matt?" Mr. Daniels took two steps back into the room, pulling down one sleeve of his white V-necked sweater.

"I'm just so tired, Dad," Matt said, not lifting his head from the pillow. "Maybe I *am* coming down with something."

"You look really pale," his dad said, squinting at him. "Maybe you *need* a day out on a boat in the sun."

"I'm—too tired," Matt told him. "I think I'll just stay home and try to get over this."

Mr. Daniels glanced at the clock. "Well, okay," he said hesitantly. "Your mom and I are really late. Sure you'll be okay?"

Matt nodded yes. "Tell the Millers I'm sorry."

His father turned and started to leave. He stopped again at the doorway and sniffed the air. "What's that odd smell?" he asked, making a face.

It's just my dead friend, Matt thought darkly. Just my dead friend come back to warn me that I've been going out with a vampire. Nothing to worry about, Dad.

"I don't know. It's coming from outside, I think," Matt said, yawning.

Still sniffing, Mr. Daniels gave a quick, regretful wave and disappeared out the door. A few minutes later Matt heard the back door slam. Then he heard the car start up and pull away.

Alone in the house, he forced himself up.

The terror of the night before swept over him, and he knew he'd vomit. Choking it back, he staggered to the bathroom and leaned over the bowl.

He had dry heaves until his stomach ached. His head spinning, beads of cold perspiration covering his pale forehead, Matt sat on the cool tile floor and waited to feel better.

After a minute or so his stomach seemed to unknot and the bathroom walls stopped whirring about.

No time to lose, he told himself.

I've got to warn April. I've got to.

She's *got* to believe me this time.

I'll show her the bruises on our throats. I'll tell her about Todd.

She's got to believe me. I'll *force* her to believe me!

He brushed his teeth, threw cold water over his burning face, pulled on a bathing suit, and, still feeling shaky, made his way to the phone in the kitchen.

He pushed April's number and listened impatiently to the ringing. Once. Twice.

He let it ring ten times.

No one was home.

"April, *please!*" he pleaded out loud. "I've *got* to talk to you."

He stood there for the longest time, leaning against the counter, the steady ring of the phone in his ear, waiting, waiting for her voice.

"April—*please.*"

But no one heard his plea.

After a quick breakfast, Matt tried calling April's house again. Still no reply.

Feeling a little more energetic, he walked to town and searched for her there. It was a humid day, the temperature in the nineties, unusually hot for this beach community. The walk to town tired Matt. He searched Main Street and, not finding her, headed for the beach.

No sign of her there, either.

He spent the afternoon lying on the couch in his living room, getting up every few minutes to phone April's house, letting the phone ring and ring. No one picked up.

That evening he eagerly headed to town to renew his search.

"Yo—Matt!" a familiar voice called as Matt

headed along Seabreeze Road, the sandy path to town.

He turned to see Ben, dressed in ragged denim cutoffs and a faded Def Leppard T-shirt, running to catch up with him. "How's it going?" Ben asked, puffing from his short run.

"Okay," Matt replied without slowing his pace.

The sun was lowering behind the trees, but the air was still hot and humid. Matt felt prickly all over and heavy, as if he weighed a thousand pounds.

"I looked for you at the beach," Ben said, struggling to keep up with Matt's long strides. "It was so hot, I thought you'd be there. The surf was excellent."

"I can't believe you left the nice cool arcade to go to the beach," Matt said dryly.

"It was closed," Ben admitted, chuckling. "They were fixing the machines or something."

"I wasn't feeling well," Matt said. He really didn't want to get into a big explanation with Ben. Intent on finding April and telling her the peril they were in, he wished he hadn't run into Ben.

"Yeah. You don't look too great," Ben said, studying Matt's face.

"What do you mean?" Matt asked defensively.

"You're kind of pale," Ben replied. A sly grin replaced his concerned expression. "Must be vampires, huh?" he teased, remembering his previous conversation when Matt explained how he'd made a complete fool of himself with April.

"Huh?" Matt stopped on the path to gape at his friend.

"You've been hanging out with vampires again, huh?" Ben said, repeating his joke. "Has that great-looking redhead been sucking your neck?"

"I just have a virus or something," Matt said brusquely.

"Hey—it was a joke," Ben snapped, his smile fading. "What's your problem, Daniels?"

Matt started walking again without replying.

They walked along the path in silence for a while. The rows of houses gave way to the broad, grassy field that bordered the town. The sky grew gradually darker, as if someone were turning down a lamp.

"You want to go to the carnival tonight?" Ben asked. "A bunch of guys are going to check out the arcade, then head over there after dark."

"Maybe," Matt said without enthusiasm. He stopped again. "Hey—there's April."

She was several yards up the road, her head down, walking slowly as if searching for something. "Hey—April!" Matt shouted.

"Catch you later," Ben said, and, giving April a brief hello, headed past her toward town.

"April—hi!" Matt called, running to catch up to her.

She stopped and raised her head. She didn't smile. "Oh, it's you. Hi."

Not much of a greeting, he realized. But he didn't care. He had to talk to her. He had to tell her what was going on.

She stared at him impatiently, her face pale in the fading light, her eyes tired. Even in the descending darkness, he could see the two puncture marks on her throat.

"I've got to talk to you," he said breathlessly. "I really—"

She raised a hand to cut him off. "I really don't have much time. I'm meeting Gabri in a few minutes. But I'm trying—"

"That's what I want to talk to you about," he cried, interrupting her. "Look at you. Look at your throat. Look at my throat." He tilted his head so she could see his neck clearly.

"Matt—" she began, her anger rising immediately. "Don't start." She turned her head, unwilling to examine his neck.

"Just give me one minute," he pleaded, putting a hand on her shoulder. "One minute—okay?"

She considered it for a long moment. "Okay. One minute. But if you start in with that vampire stuff again, your time is up."

"But that's what I want to tell you, April," he said, not meaning to sound as if he were whining, but too eager, too excited, too desperate, to keep his voice down. "Gabri is a vampire. I know it. So is Jessica. They're both vampires."

"Good-bye, Matt," April said coldly, rolling her

eyes and motioning with both hands for him to leave.

"April—listen."

"No!" she shouted. "Go away."

"But Todd told me—"

She gasped, and her head snapped back, as if she'd been slapped. "Huh?"

"Last night. Todd told me—"

"Matt, you need help," she said softly, her tone growing more sympathetic. "We were all upset about . . . what happened to Todd. But you're really mixed up or something. You've got to get help."

"No, I don't," he insisted, unable to keep his frustration from his voice. "I know I'm right, April. It sounds crazy—"

"Yes, it does," she said, nodding, her eyes locked on his as if trying to determine how crazy he had become.

"But I know I'm right. If you'd only listen to me," he begged.

"I can't now," she said softly. "I'm looking for something and—"

"What? What are you looking for?" he demanded.

She lowered her head again and resumed walking slowly, sliding her sandals over the sand as she moved, her eyes darting over the ground. "It's a silver cross. I was walking with Gabri last night, and the clasp was loose. It must have fallen off. I'm trying to retrace our steps."

"A silver cross?" Matt asked excitedly. "And you showed it to Gabri? Did he raise his hands to protect his eyes? Did he cringe away from it? That would *prove* he's a vampire! He did—*didn't* he, April! He cringed away from it."

He moved in front of her on the path, studying her face, eager for her reply. Finally he might have some proof to back up his claim about Gabri.

"Why are you acting like such a jerk?" April asked, frowning. "As a matter of fact, I showed the cross to Gabri—and he liked it."

"He didn't try to hide from it?" Matt demanded.

"No. He wasn't afraid of it, Matt. In fact, he helped me with the clasp."

They stared at each other in silence for a moment, the sun dipping lower, the sky darkening to a rosy purple.

"I guess that's the end of your theory," April said curtly.

"No, it isn't," Matt insisted, following behind her as she continued her search. "Have you been feeling tired and weak lately?"

"I'm not going to answer any more stupid questions," she said without turning around.

"Have you ever seen Gabri in the daytime? Has he ever told you where he works during the day? Have you ever visited him there? Don't you wonder why he didn't have pizza that first night when all the rest of us did?"

She turned angrily, balling her hands into tight fists at her sides. "Matt, you're really unbalanced."

"Answer the questions, April," he insisted.

"You're being so stupid. I really want you to go away."

"No, April. I won't. Not until you listen to me."

"Go away, Matt," she repeated louder, and then she lost her temper and screamed, "Go away! I *mean* it! Go away!"

Unwilling to give up, Matt reached for her shoulder.

She pulled away.

A dark shadow appeared on the path, darker than the sky.

"Hey—" Matt cried in surprise as Gabri stepped up beside April, his eyes on Matt. He was wearing black denim jeans and a dark, long-sleeved pullover, despite the heat of the night.

"What's going on?" he asked April softly, keeping his gaze leveled on Matt. "Trouble?"

Matt, staring back at Gabri, felt the fear begin to knot his stomach, felt an icy chill course through his entire body.

"No. No trouble," April replied uncertainly.

Matt stepped back, lowering his arms to his sides. He felt the power of Gabri's eyes, burning into him, searing like a laser light.

"No trouble," April repeated as Gabri continued to challenge Matt with his eyes. "We were just talking."

Gabri released Matt from his stare and turned to April, a smile crossing his face. "Were you talking about me? My ears were burning."

"As a matter of fact, we were," April said, and took Gabri's arm. They started walking away, chatting comfortably.

Matt stood motionless, watching them leave, still feeling the heat of Gabri's eyes.

April glanced back once to see if Matt was following. Gabri never turned around.

I know I'm right, Matt told himself, watching until they disappeared around a bend in the path.

I'm going to prove it to April.

I have to save her life.

And suddenly, in a flash of inspiration, he knew how.

Chapter 24

SAY "CHEESE"

"Where are you going with that camera?" Mr. Daniels called from the living room.

Matt stopped at the door. "Oh, hi, Dad. I didn't know you guys were back." He swung the camera case over his shoulder and stepped back into the room. "Okay if I borrow this?"

"Do I have a choice?" Mr. Daniels asked sarcastically. He gestured with his hand. "Go ahead. Be my guest."

"There are these really neat birds on the beach at night," Matt lied. "I want to see if I can get snapshots of them."

His father lowered the book to his lap and eyed Matt cynically. "Since when are *you* interested in birds?"

Matt shrugged. "These were really neat. I don't

know what they are. They chased all the terns and sea gulls away."

He felt bad about lying to his father. But there was no way he could have told the truth—"I'm going to take pictures of a boy April is dating, and when the boy doesn't show up in the pictures, it'll prove he's a vampire."

No way his dad would buy that one.

Who *would*?

"There's very fast film in there," Mr. Daniels said, setting down the book and walking over to Matt. "The only difficult thing about shooting at night with this camera is the focusing. Here. Let me show you."

Matt was eager to get to the carnival, but he couldn't just run out the door. He stood patiently while his father removed the camera from the case and showed him the best way to focus in the dark and the best shutter settings.

"Be careful with it," Mr. Daniels warned as Matt hurriedly pushed open the door, fastening the camera case as he walked. "I spent a fortune on that camera. Glad someone's getting some use out of it."

Matt called good night. "I'll get very good use out of it," he muttered to himself. "I'm going to trap a vampire with it."

His plan was to snap an entire roll of Gabri and April at the carnival. When Gabri came up invisible in every shot, April would *have* to believe Matt.

The proof that Gabri was a vampire would be right there.

Half jogging, half walking, he made his way to the carnival grounds. Stepping into the white light of the powerful spotlights, his eyes surveying the spinning, whirling, toppling rides, his ears filled with delighted squeals and shrieks, Matt suddenly remembered that he had arranged to meet Jessica at the beach.

Too bad, he thought bitterly.

Maybe when I don't show up, she'll take the hint. Maybe she'll realize that I've caught on, that I know what she is and what she's been doing to me.

He raised a hand to his throat and felt a warm pang.

Jessica is so beautiful, he thought. So exciting.

He could suddenly smell the fragrance of her perfume, so sweet, so sharp.

The carnival appeared to melt in a blur of white light. He felt drawn away, drawn to the beach, drawn to—her.

To her soft red hair. To her dark lips.

No!

Gripping the camera case with both hands, he strode purposefully past the Ferris wheel, his eyes searching the crowd. A group of little kids came running past, eager to get to the next ride, and nearly knocked him over.

He grabbed on to a pole to regain his balance. He checked the camera. It seemed okay.

After a short search, he spotted April and Gabri holding hands, in line for the Ferris wheel.

Quickly, his hands shaking with excitement, Matt pulled off the leather camera case, letting it hang around his neck, and raised the camera to his eye.

Someone stepped in front of him, blocking the view as he clicked the first shot. "Sorry," a woman's voice called, already several yards away.

Keeping to the side of a refreshment booth, Matt moved a few feet closer and snapped again. And again.

He refocused, moved a little closer, made sure the light was right, and snapped again, making sure that both April and Gabri were in the frame.

April looked up. Matt ducked back against the side of the booth.

Had she spotted him?

He watched her intently, poking his head out gingerly from beside the wall of the booth.

No. She turned back to Gabri.

He didn't want to be seen. Gabri, he knew, would immediately guess what Matt was up to. Matt shuddered. There was no telling what Gabri might do to keep Matt from getting his proof.

He waited out of sight until he saw them board the Ferris wheel. Using the built-in zoom lens, he snapped them sitting side by side in the metal car.

He followed them after their ride as they made their way along the row of game booths. Trailing behind, keeping on the other side of the wide aisle, Matt clicked snapshot after snapshot.

He tried to ignore how close they seemed, how happy April appeared to be with Gabri, how comfortable they seemed with each other. All that would change, he kept assuring himself, as soon as his pictures proved the truth about Gabri.

With just a few shots left on the film, he stepped into the center of the crowded aisle as April and Gabri stopped to watch the carousel. April turned suddenly and spotted him.

At first, she pretended she didn't recognize him. Then, knowing that Matt was watching, she turned back to Gabri, put her arm around him affectionately, and kissed him on the cheek.

That's okay, April, Matt thought glumly, replacing the camera in its case. You'll feel differently when I show you the truth.

You'll feel differently after I've saved your life.

He didn't blame her for being angry at him. He'd given her no reason to believe him.

But now he had the reason right in his hands.

He had to get the pictures developed as quickly as possible. He had to show them to her as quickly as possible. Watching April snuggle up against Gabri, their fingers entwined, leaning against each other as the carousel spun behind them, Matt knew he had to hurry.

Holding the camera tightly with both hands, he turned and ran from the carnival field. Someone called to him—Ben, probably—but he didn't stop or turn around.

He crossed the parking lot, cutting through the rows of cars, and jogged onto Main Street. The one-hour film-developing store was just a block away, on the corner of Dune Lane.

One hour, Matt thought, his excitement driving him on as he made his way through the couples and small groups of people strolling along Main Street.

Just one hour and this nightmare will be over.

He called back an apology to a middle-aged man holding a double-dip ice-cream cone he had accidentally run into, then bounded across Dune Lane without stopping at the corner to check for traffic.

A blue station wagon squealed to a halt at the corner. The driver yelled something at Matt.

One hour is all Matt heard.

One hour to get my photos. One hour to get my proof.

He grabbed the doorknob on the store's front door, turned it, and pulled hard.

It took him several seconds to realize that the film-developing store was dark and closed.

Chapter 25

TOO LATE

Matt's alarm went off at eight the next morning. His first waking thought was of April. And the film.

I've got to save April. I've got to show her the pictures. The proof.

He pulled on some clothes, slugged down a glass of orange juice, and hurried out of the house before his parents had even awakened. As he jogged to town, he kept one hand in his jeans pocket, wrapped tightly around the plastic canister of film.

A fog had rolled in off the ocean during the night. It slowly lifting as Matt arrived on Main Street, but the sky was still overcast, the air cool, and patches of mist floated among the low buildings.

Like most of the shops in Sandy Hollow, the film-developing store didn't open till ten. Matt wandered back and forth along the nearly deserted street, his hand still wrapped protectively around the roll of film in his pocket. He didn't stop to look in store windows. He kept walking, pacing impatiently, checking his watch every five minutes.

As he paced back and forth along the street, he had the troubling feeling that Gabri might pop up suddenly, force him behind one of the stores, and steal the film from him, steal away his proof.

But, of course, that was foolish. Gabri would never appear in the daylight.

Seeing that it was still only nine-thirty, Matt took a seat at the counter in the Seabreeze Coffee Shop and ordered a cup of coffee. He hated the taste of coffee, but he had to do something to kill the next half hour. Filling the cup up to the brim with milk, he sipped it slowly, wondering why people liked the bitter taste so much, his eyes on the neon-circled wall clock behind the counter.

He was back at the film-developing store at five to ten, just as the manager, a young man with spiked red hair and a green emeraldlike stud in one ear, was unlocking the door. "Morning," he said warily, studying Matt before letting him into the store. "You're here bright and early."

Matt pulled the plastic film canister from his pocket and set it down on the glass counter. "I—I have this film," he stammered. "I mean, I'm kind of in a hurry."

The manager removed a container of coffee from a paper bag and slowly pulled off the plastic lid, eyeing Matt. "It'll take me a little while to get the machine up and running," he said, yawning.

"But can I have the prints in an hour?" Matt asked eagerly.

The young man shook his head. "Come back around eleven-thirty." He wrote down Matt's name and local phone number. "We have a special this week on a second set of prints. Half price for a second set of three-by-fives."

"No thanks," Matt replied. "Eleven-thirty? They'll be ready?"

The young man nodded. "These must be some pretty hot photos," he said, leering at Matt. "Maybe I'll want to make a set for myself." He laughed loudly to show that he was joking. But Matt turned and hurried out without cracking a smile.

Back on Main Street, he thought of April. I should call her, he thought, and find out where she's going to be at eleven-thirty.

He began to search for a pay phone, then changed his mind.

I'd better wait till I have the proof in my hands, till I have the snapshots showing April and no Gabri.

She probably wouldn't talk to me on the phone anyway.

Too nervous to hang around town for the next hour and a half, Matt headed to the beach. The fog was still low, forming a heavy gray cloud that hovered over the ocean, darkening the sand and keeping sunbathers away.

He walked along the dunes for a while, trying to will time to move faster.

He was back at the developing store at eleven-twenty. The young man greeted him with an apologetic smile. "Sorry."

"Huh?" Matt didn't grasp his meaning. "Sorry? Am I too early? You don't have my prints?"

"Yes to both questions," the store manager replied, scratching his heavily slicked spiky red hair. "The machine is down."

"What do you mean?" Matt asked shrilly, his heart pounding.

"It's just a gear. I called the other store at Newton's Cove for a replacement."

"But when will you have it?" Matt demanded.

The young man shrugged. "I'm open till seven tonight. Come back around then, just to be safe." He picked up a local newspaper from the folding chair behind the counter. "I'll have them for you at seven. No problem."

Somehow Matt managed to pass the time. The sun never did come out. The afternoon sky brightened to a white glare, but the air continued to carry a damp chill.

He dozed off in the afternoon, sleeping fitfully, images of Jessica floating in his mind.

Those kisses. Those soft, wet kisses.

He awoke, frightened.

He had to resist Jessica, even in his dreams.

Evening was only a little darker than the day had been. He pulled on a clean T-shirt, brushed his hair, checked his wallet, and headed out of the house.

What a wasted day, he thought glumly.

Well, it wouldn't be a waste if the pictures came out the way he was sure they would. It wouldn't be a waste if April finally believed him, if he could convince her never to see Gabri again.

"Hey—there you are," the manager of the film-developing store said, grinning as Matt rushed into the store at a few minutes before seven.

Matt didn't bother with any polite greeting. "Have you got 'em?"

The young man nodded and plopped a fat envelope of photos onto the counter. "That's some camera," he said, whistling. "What kind is it?"

"I don't know," Matt said, closing his hand over the envelope of pictures. "It's my dad's. The pictures came out?"

"Yeah. They're good and clear. Considering the lighting. Some are a little out of focus."

Enough chitchat, Matt thought impatiently. "How much?" he asked, reaching for his wallet with a trembling hand.

A few seconds later he bolted through the door and around the corner to the back of the store. Leaning against the painted shingle wall, he pulled the stack of glossy photos from the envelope.

I've got to be right, he thought, offering up a silent prayer, his stomach knotted, his entire body tensed in anticipation.

I've *got* to be right.

Focusing in the dim light, he flipped slowly through the snapshots.

They were all pretty grainy, some more out of focus than others.

But, yes.

Yes, yes, yes!

Matt was right.

There was April in photo after photo, smiling at an invisible companion, holding hands with an invisible companion, arm in arm with an invisible companion.

Seated in the Ferris wheel car beside an invisible *vampire*.

The thrill of it, the *horror* of it, struck Matt all at once.

Nearly dropping the photographs, he fell back against the building wall, gasping for breath.

It took nearly a minute to recover. Even though it was only a little past seven, the heavy clouds overhead made it as dark as midnight. Gabri, he knew, would once again be on the prowl.

April, I'm coming, he thought, carefully slipping the envelope of snapshots into his back pocket.

I'm coming to save you from him.

Please be there, April.

You'll *have* to believe me this time. So please be there.

He tried calling her house from the pay phone on the corner. No answer.

He searched the town for her, starting at the movie theater at the south end, studying the faces of the people lining up for the first show, then crossing Dune Lane to Swanny's. She wasn't in the ice-cream parlor or the arcade next door.

Please be there, April. Please.

He made his way to the end of the street, crossed over, and hurried along the other side, poking his head into restaurants and clothing shops, his eyes surveying each couple, each person, each group of people who passed.

April—please. Where are you?

He searched the town for nearly an hour without success. He checked his watch. Nearly eight-fifteen.

Shoving the photos in his back pocket, he decided to try the beach.

Jogging along Seabreeze Road, the ocean wind in his face, he could feel his tension tighten his muscles, feel his fear knot his stomach. Tears of cold perspiration ran down his cheeks. His legs felt as if they weighed a thousand pounds.

But he had to find her. He had to show her the danger she was in.

The beach shimmered silvery blue in the darkening twilight. Low waves caught the last moments of sunlight, red streaks on the rolling, dark green surface.

April—please be there. Please.

The beach was dotted with people, enjoying the last moments of evening light. As Matt made his way across the dunes toward the water, the sun dropped away, the air immediately grew colder, the sky darkened as if someone had turned off a light.

Twice he thought he saw her.

The girls were blond and thin and carried themselves like April.

But they weren't April.

They turned to stare at him, startled by his intensity, by the desperation of his gaze, the heaviness of his breathing as he continued his frantic search.

Before Matt realized it, he was nearly to the rowboat dock at the edge of the beach where the tall rock cliff jutted into the water. Three rowboats bobbed there, bumping against the dock.

April—where are you? Where?

There were very few people here. He knew he should turn back.

He was breathing so loudly, thinking so hard, his sneakers crunching over the pebbly sand, he didn't hear the voice until it called for the third time.

"Matt! Hey—Matt! Stop!"

"Jessica!"

He stopped and crouched over, resting his hands on his knees, gasping, struggling to catch his breath.

"Matt—were you looking for me?"

Her hair floated behind her, carried by the wind, as she ran to him, her eyes aglow, her pale skin almost ghostly in the early moonlight, her lips curled in a warm, inviting smile.

"Were you looking for me? Here I am."

She spoke so softly, so tenderly, her voice nearly a whisper on the wind.

"I missed you yesterday, honey."

Her eyes found his. He stared at her mouth. He remembered the kisses. The wonderful kisses.

Her eyes seemed to draw him near, to pull him to her.

"I missed you so much, Matt. Where were you, honey?"

She moved closer until she was almost touching him. Her eyes stayed on his, holding him as if in a spell, holding him prisoner as she moved even closer.

And he hungered for one kiss.

Just one.

He stood up, still breathing hard.

Just one kiss, he thought.

And then over her shoulder he saw something.

His eyes broke the spell—and he saw someone.

Someone at the tiny dock. Someone climbing into one of the rowboats.

Someone helping someone into the rowboat as it bobbed unsteadily on the rolling waves.

April!

Gabri was helping April into the narrow boat.

No!

Jessica put her arms around Matt's shoulders. Her perfume invaded his nostrils. He inhaled deeply, unable to resist it.

April was sitting in the rowboat now. Gabri was taking the oars.

No!

Jessica pulled Matt to her. Dizzy from the perfume, he peered over her shoulder as Gabri began to row and the rowboat slid away from the dock.

"I missed you yesterday, Matt," she whispered, lowering her head and pressing her lips against his earlobe.

The rowboat moved easily from the dock, Gabri rowing steadily, effortlessly.

Just one kiss, Matt thought, drowning in the perfume.

Just one.

The rowboat was disappearing into the darkness, heading toward the tiny island offshore.

April. April and Gabri. Rowing away.

Rowing away forever.

"No!" Matt screamed aloud, and pushed away from Jessica, pushed her hard. Her mouth opening wide in astonishment, she staggered back, and Matt made his escape.

"Matt—come back!" she called after him.

But he was running to the dock now, away from her eyes, away from the perfume, away from her powers. Running, running full out, his sneakers sliding over the sand, panting loudly, eyes on the dock where two remaining rowboats bobbed in the water.

The photos dropped from his back pocket as he ran. He hesitated for only a moment, then kept running.

No time for photos now. No time for accusations and proof.

Gabri was rowing April away, rowing April to the mysterious, wooded island where all the bats lived.

No time. No time. No time.

Matt ran onto the dock and didn't stop until he reached the end. "April!" he called, cupping his hands around his mouth, trying to shout over the ocean wind.

"April! April!" he called.

She didn't turn around. She didn't hear him.

The rowboat was a dark silhouette now, shimmering ghostlike as it moved into the blackness.

"I'm too late," Matt whispered to himself.

Chapter 26

FLUTTERING

Seconds. It took precious seconds to untie one of the rowboats from the dock.

Then more precious seconds to leap inside the bobbing boat, to grab up the oars.

Tick tick tick. The seconds were passing.

He could hear Jessica now, close behind, calling to him, begging him to come back. He turned for a second and saw her running toward the dock, seeming to glide over the sand. But in the next second, he was hunkered low, pulling the oars, pulling away from the shore, Jessica's calls fading behind the wind.

The incoming current was stronger than Matt had imagined. Each time he rowed, leaning forward and pulling his arms back with all his strength, the boat seemed to lurch forward a foot, and slide back two.

Puddled water on the floor of the small rowboat rolled over his sneakers, soaking his socks. Salty spray off the waves forced him to close his eyes.

I'm too late, he thought. Too late. Too late.

But he knew he couldn't give up.

Where was April's boat?

Probably already at the island.

Matt squinted toward the black island silhouette ahead of him, low in the water like an enormous sea creature waiting to swallow him up. He couldn't see April's boat.

Turning his eyes to the sky, he saw the flickering forms of bats hovering over the island. And as he drew closer, the fluttering of their wings drowned out the rush of the water, the wind, drowned out all other sounds, even the sounds of his own breathing.

There were hundreds and hundreds of bats, he saw, fluttering noisily, swooping and darting over the trees, filling the sky, buzzing and chittering, nearly as thick as a swarm of bees.

Drawing near to the island, Matt spotted a small dock tucked into the tree-laden shore. A rowboat— April's rowboat—bobbed at one side.

Empty.

He pulled his boat to the dock, leapt out without bothering to tie the boat up, and looked around. A narrow dirt path curved through the trees.

Matt had started down the path when he realized he was carrying one of the oars. My only weapon, he thought as a chill of renewed dread pulsed down his spine. He crouched down as he hurried through the trees, bending away from the relentless fluttering above his head, the flapping wings, the shrill whistles that echoed through the woods.

The low, shingled beach house at the end of the path was completely dark. As Matt drew near, he saw that the windows had no glass.

Bats swooped over the low, angled roof. A bat hovered by one window, just inches from Matt's face, then fluttered away with a shrill cry.

Leaning against the oar, holding it firmly with both hands, Matt peered into the window. It was pitch-black inside, blacker than the night. He couldn't see a thing.

Having no choice, he transferred the oar to one hand, lifted a leg over the windowsill, and lowered himself into the house.

It smelled so musty in there, even with all the windows open.

Musty and . . . dead.

He gasped from the foul smell, then forced himself to breathe normally.

Waiting for his eyes to adjust to the darkness, he stood still, the fluttering of bat wings from outside following him into the house.

The room came into focus. A long, narrow room. A bedroom without a bed.

And then he saw April.

Against one wall. Slumped in an oversize armchair. Her head down on the large padded arm of the chair.

She's dead, he thought, hurrying to her, bending over the chair.

He's killed her.

But, no. He heard her soft breath, wheezing slightly, her lips parted.

Still alive.

Still alive—but what has Gabri done to her?

Outside, the fluttering suddenly grew louder, nearer. The room darkened as if bats were covering the window, shutting out all light.

What was that against the opposite wall, away from the window?

Was it a bed?

Matt turned away from April, squinting against the darkness, leaning against the oar, trying to think over the relentless flapping, the maddening fluttering, the flickering of the dim light—and realized that he was staring at a coffin.

Its lid closed tightly, the smooth-wooded coffin was set against the wall.

"Oh!"

Matt realized his entire body was trembling. He grasped the oar tighter, steadying himself against it.

The fluttering seemed to fade, then grow louder. He pictured the bats sweeping the sky over the house, preparing to attack through the paneless windows.

"April, we've got to get out of here," he said in a quavering voice that barely escaped his throat.

He hurried back across the room to April and grabbed her by both shoulders. "April? April?"

She shuddered but didn't open her eyes.

"April?" He shook her a little harder.

Again she shuddered, but her head slumped back onto the arm of the chair.

He picked up her head, tried to pry open her eyes, shook her by the shoulders again.

"April—wake up! Wake up!" His cries were choked by his fear. "April—please! We have to get *out* of here!"

April stirred.

Her eyes opened slowly. She stared at him groggily. "Huh? Matt?" She tried to focus, but quickly gave up and closed her eyes again.

"April—"

Matt felt a presence behind him. A heavy presence.

He turned—and cried out as Gabri advanced.

Fangs sliding down his chin, his mouth wide in open glee, his eyes glowing red with fury, Gabri lunged forward to attack.

Chapter 27

MATT DIES

*"N*ooooooooo!"

Matt didn't even realize that the hideous shriek that roared through the long room came from his own throat.

With an animal grunt, Gabri lunged at Matt, fangs plunging toward Matt's neck.

Matt wheeled around in terror.

He didn't have time to think. He didn't have time to make a plan.

Reflexively, he turned, pulled his arm back, and thrust the oar handle forward toward his attacking foe.

Gabri ran right into it.

With a sickening, wet crack, the oar handle punctured his chest.

Gabri's eyes bulged, their flame extinguished.

He opened his mouth to cry out, and a gray moth fluttered out.

The moth floated up to the ceiling, then out the open window.

Gabri's eyes closed. His head tilted back.

And as Matt stared in horror, Gabri's body collapsed to the floor, folding like an accordion. His eyes stared lifelessly up at Matt, and Gabri's face began to crumble, the skin drying and peeling, flaking to powder until the entire skull was revealed.

And then the skull too disintegrated. Fell apart and crumbled.

Matt continued to gape in disbelief until Gabri's dark clothes lay crumpled on the floor, empty except for a low pile of gray ashes. A gust of wind from the window fluttered the ashes, causing most of the pile to scatter.

"Oh!"

Matt finally found his voice.

"April—" he called, turning back to her on the chair.

"April—are you awake? Let's go! Hurry!"

"Where are you going?" a girl's voice—not April's—called.

Matt held up his hands as if to shield himself as Jessica stepped in front of him. Her hair floated over her shoulders. Her face was twisted in anger.

"Jessica—leave us alone!" he screamed in a terror-filled voice he didn't recognize.

She tossed back her head and laughed, a loud, scornful laugh.

"Jessica—please! Let us go!" Matt cried.

Without replying, she uttered a growl, grabbed Matt's face tightly with both hands—such cold, cold hands—and buried her fangs in Matt's throat.

I'm dead, Matt thought, helplessly sinking, feeling the pain of her deadly bite.

I'm dead now.

Chapter 28

FAILURE

*F*eeling the pain course down his neck and through his entire body, Matt closed his eyes, sinking, sinking under the weight of Jessica's fangs.

I'm dying now, he thought helplessly.

You win, Jessica. As you knew you would.

Then, to his surprise, the pain lifted.

He cried out, startled, opening his eyes, trying to focus through the blur of motion in front of him.

Jessica was no longer gripping his head in her frozen hands; her fangs were no longer in his throat.

A struggle across the room. Groans and cries. Shifting, wrestling, grappling bodies.

Finally it all came into focus.

"April!" he cried, falling back against the wall, trying to stand up, to regain his balance.

April had revived and pulled Jessica from him.

Now the two of them were wrestling by the

window, scratching at each other, pulling hair, grabbing and hitting, crying out their desperation.

Feeling a little steadier, Matt took a step away from the wall. He stumbled back, the room tilting. The crackling flutter of bats grew louder, louder, until the sound seemed to be coming from his own head.

"No!" he cried, holding his hands over his ears.

The fluttering faded.

He couldn't just stand there defeated. He had to help April.

Jessica was overpowering her frail foe, shoving April hard against the frame of the open window, pushing her chin with one hand, holding her head down with the other. Jessica opened her mouth in a victorious grin, her slender, pointed fangs sliding down her chin.

April cried out as Jessica lowered her head to bite.

What can I do? Matt wondered, his eyes darting frantically around the dark room.

What can I do?

I have to act—now!

Spotting the oar, still resting on top of Gabri's wrinkled heap of clothes, he grabbed it up, turned the handle toward Jessica—and charged.

She ducked under it easily, reaching a hand up and pulling the oar out of Matt's grasp with inhuman strength.

Startled, Matt fell back as Jessica heaved the oar out the open window. Then she turned back to

April, pressing her back against the window frame, her fangs lowering to April's pale throat.

Gasping for air, Matt stared in horror. His mind whirred faster than the room.

He had to save April. But how?

Fire, he thought.

Fire kills vampires.

And with that thought, he remembered the plastic butane lighter in his pocket. Todd's lighter.

Thank you, Todd, Matt thought. Thank you. Thank you.

His hand trembling, he jammed it into his jeans pocket and pulled out the lighter.

Thank you, Todd.

Thank you for rescuing us.

"Jessica!" Matt shouted. "Jessica!"

Inches from April's throat, Jessica turned her eyes to Matt.

His chest heaving, his hand trembling, Matt lurched forward and thrust the lighter in Jessica's startled face.

She cried out in horror as he flicked the lighter. "Oh!"

No flame.

Matt flicked it again.

No flame.

The lighter didn't work.

Chapter 29

LOSERS

Staring at the lighter in Matt's trembling hand, Jessica snickered, her eyes glowing triumphantly. "You're both losers," she sneered.

Tossing her hair behind one shoulder, she turned back to April.

Losers, Matt repeated to himself, squeezing the lighter.

And now we're going to lose our lives.

In frustration, he flicked the lighter one more time.

This time it caught. A bright yellow flame shot up.

Jessica screamed as the flame caught her hair.

Slapping frantically at her head as the flames spread, Jessica leapt back, away from April, who scrambled, dazed, from the window.

"Aaaiiiiiii!" Jessica's scream filled the air as the

flames ringed her head. Her wild cry faded only when her face began to melt, rivulets of skin dripping down like a burning wax candle.

The air in the room filled with smoke and a sour, sulfuric smell.

Matt and April stared in horrified disbelief as the flames raged over Jessica's head, as she slowly melted, her skin sagging, dripping, wet chunks dropping off under the heat of the flames.

Jessica's outraged expression disappeared as her face caved in. Her skull was aflame, melting as her face had, and the fire spread to her shoulders, crackling loudly.

Headless, she slumped to the floor in a fiery puddle. The fire consumed her body in less than a minute.

And then the floor was on fire.

And the fire had spread to the walls.

And the coffin was burning, the rising red and yellow flames performing a sprightly dance over the smooth wooden lid.

Matt stared at the flames as if hypnotized. In the flickering, orange glare he could see that April was frozen there too, her eyes wide, catching the darting, leaping light, her mouth locked in a tight O of terror and astonishment.

The walls, the ceiling, the furniture, the coffin— all burned under the leaping red flames, so bright, so exciting, crackling so loudly; the fluttering sound, the sound of the hundreds of bat wings overhead, had finally disappeared.

"April?" Matt called as the flames encircled them.

Staring into the red and yellow glare, she didn't respond.

"April. We have to get out of here!"

He leapt over a line of low flames on the floor and grabbed her hand. His touch seemed to snap her out of her spell.

"Huh? Matt? We're okay?"

"Yes, we're okay!" he cried, pulling her through the open doorway.

And now they were in the cool, fresh air.

And now the house, consumed in flames, collapsed behind them.

And now April was rushing into Matt's arms, throwing her arms around him tightly, pressing her hot cheek against his.

"Matt," she sighed, holding him close, "I'll never make fun of your horror movies again!"

Chapter 30

THE HAPPY ENDING

A few nights later Matt walked with his arm around April's shoulder on the curving path toward town.

"I feel much better," Matt said softly, kicking at a clump of sand. "How about you?"

"Much better," April said, reaching up to her shoulder to squeeze his hand affectionately. "What a dreadful summer," she added.

"The worst," he said, trying to force back the wave of painful memories that kept invading his mind, returning relentlessly like the tides.

"I don't think we'll ever be the same," April said in a soft, regretful whisper.

"Yeah," he quickly agreed. "I didn't think I'd ever say it, but I can't wait to get back to Shadyside."

"Me too," April replied, tilting near, brushing his cheek with her soft, golden hair.

They walked on for a while in comfortable silence. Then, as the beach cottages gave way to the large, grassy field before town, a large gray rabbit hopped boldly across the path.

"He thinks he owns the place," Matt joked—and then stopped, letting go of April's shoulder.

As the rabbit crossed, Matt spotted something in the dirt.

"Whoa," he said, bending down to retrieve it.

"What is it?" April asked curiously.

"Look," Matt said. He held up her silver cross. "Is this the cross you lost?"

"Oh, just leave it there," April said casually, turning away.

"Huh?" Matt wasn't sure he had heard right. "But, April—"

"Just *drop* it," she insisted sharply.

Confused by her request, Matt obediently dropped the cross and chain back to the grassy field.

As he stepped away from it, April turned back to him, reached up and grabbed his shoulders with surprising strength, and bared her fangs, slender and pale in the light of the half moon.

"No—" Matt protested, struggling without success to free himself from her powerful grasp.

She chuckled, staring deeply into his eyes.

"But, April—" he insisted, panic gripping his

throat. "It—you—*can't* be! Back on the island, you—you saved my life!"

"I know," April said softly, smiling at him behind her ivorylike fangs. "Why should Jessica have all the nectar? I was saving you for *me!*"

Holding him tightly, she forced back his head and bit deeply, thirstily into his tender, throbbing throat.

FEAR STREET®
SUPER CHILLER

Goodnight
Kiss 2

Prologue

A NICE TIME

A pale moon floated high over the beach at Sandy Hollow as Diana walked beside Eric. The wet sand felt cold under her feet. Diana took Eric's hand. "I love the beach at night," she murmured.

"Huh? What did you say?" Eric asked. He seemed distracted.

"Nothing. Come on." Pulling him toward the waves that broke gently on the sand, Diana began to walk faster.

The beach is so peaceful at night, she thought. So perfect for what I must do.

The stars gleamed, silvery against the clear black sky. It was at least an hour before dawn. Diana had plenty of time.

She studied Eric's face. His hair was black and

shaggy, his eyes dark and serious. Her gaze lingered on his throat, on the smooth flesh just below his jaw.

Any moment now, she thought. Any moment.

"It's late," Eric said. "I really should go home."

"Not afraid of the dark, are you?" Diana teased.

"Of course not."

"Then what's the hurry?"

"I had a crazy day. I'd like to get a little sleep before the sun comes up."

Diana stopped walking and peered down the dark beach. "Look!" she cried. "Someone left a beach umbrella. Let's sit down. Just for a minute?"

"But it's so late," Eric protested.

Diana hurried to the umbrella and dropped onto the sand beneath it. "Come on," she urged. "We've got our own private spot."

Eric joined her. She pulled him to her and kissed him. Just once. Quickly. His lips felt cool on hers. As cool as the night air.

"I really have to get home," Eric whispered.

"You're not going home, Eric."

For a moment, he said nothing, his face a frozen silhouette against the star-filled sky. "What are you talking about?" he finally asked.

"I brought you here to die."

2

He laughed. "Is this a joke?"

"No, Eric. It's no joke. A vampire murdered my cousin last summer. She wasn't just my cousin, Eric. She was also my best friend. I want all vampires to die."

Eric's fangs slid down. "You lose," he snarled.

"No. *You* lose," Diana snapped.

His eyes glowed with rage and hunger. He reached for her.

Diana rolled away. She yanked the beach umbrella from the sand. The special umbrella she had made for tonight.

Eric came after her, moonlight flashing in his eyes.

The umbrella top slid across the sand as Diana yanked the pole off.

"I can already taste your blood, the sweet nectar!" Eric proclaimed.

"Don't count on it," Diana replied.

Eric groaned as she jammed the pole's sharp wooden tip through his heart. His eyes bulged wide in shock. "No!" he gasped. "No. You *can't!*"

He collapsed onto the sand.

The glow in his eyes faded.

His body shriveled. Slowly at first, then faster, his legs shrinking beneath his jeans. His arms dissolving. His skin flaking, blowing away in the wind.

Until a skeleton lay sprawled on the sand in Eric's clothes.

Bones. White bones.

Then dust.

Diana stirred the dust around with her hand until it disappeared into the beach sand.

"Goodbye, Eric," she murmured. "I had a very nice time."

PART ONE

PARTY TIME

Chapter 1

VAMPIRE ISLAND

"There's the Pizza Cove," Billy Naughton announced, pointing to a small restaurant across the street. "Excellent sausage and mushroom pizza."

Jay Windley nodded.

"Best pizza in town," Nate Stanton agreed as he ran a hand through his sandy hair. "I ate it every night last summer. Really. I mean, *every* night."

Jay nodded again.

Billy glanced around for other Sandy Hollow landmarks to point out. He had decided to spend the first night showing his best friend around. After all, he had spent all of last summer here, and Jay had never been to Sandy Hollow before.

Jay's friend Nate seemed kind of boring. Nate

and his family had been at Sandy Hollow last summer. But Billy didn't remember much about them.

Maybe I was too busy with Joelle to notice anyone else, Billy thought.

"I don't like the Pizza Cove," announced Lynette, Nate's little sister. Billy had a feeling Lynette would be tagging along all summer. It was only the first night, and already Mrs. Stanton had made Nate take her with them.

"Who cares what you like?" Nate teased her. "You'd like Gummi Worms on your pizza!"

Billy felt the salty dampness of the ocean breeze on his cheeks. The wind ruffled his long, black hair. He shook himself out of his daze. "It gets cold here at night," he commented.

"No kidding," Jay muttered, shivering. The ocean breeze plastered his light brown hair against his cheek.

"It's fun even when it's cold," Nate declared. "This is going to be an awesome summer. Except for work."

Billy groaned. "Don't remind me." He turned to Jay. "What are you going to do while we're at work, Jay? Hang out with your parents?"

Jay laughed. "No way. I'm going to hang out at the beach and get a killer tan. But I'll be thinking about you poor working guys all the time."

"Yeah, right." Nate gave him a shove. Jay stumbled into a woman passing by.

Billy laughed. Nate was a big guy. Big and strong. He was nearly twice Jay's size.

Jay's taste in friends really changed while I was away this past year, Billy thought. He never used to hang out with jocks.

"The only thing I want to do this summer is meet girls," Jay said.

"This is the place, man," Nate told him. "I had three girlfriends last summer!"

Jay grinned. "If there are so many girls, how come we haven't met any yet?"

"He said there were a lot of girls," Billy replied. "He didn't say they'd be interested in *you*, Jay."

Nate laughed loudly and slapped Billy a high-five.

"All my friends think Nate's a jerk," Lynette announced.

Nate's smile disappeared. "Why don't you go play in the ocean, Lynette?"

Lynette skipped happily along behind him. "My friends *all* think you're a total jerk," she repeated.

"Who cares what your friends think?" Nate grumbled. "I'm talking about real girls—not little kids in elementary school."

Lynette stuck her tongue out.

Billy rolled his eyes at Nate in sympathy.

"Wow, look!" Lynette exclaimed. "An ice-cream place."

Billy followed the direction of her gaze. She had discovered Swanny's, the ice-cream parlor and video arcade.

"Ice cream!" Lynette demanded, tugging her brother's sleeve. "Ice cream!"

Nate snorted. "Maybe later."

They drifted down Main Street, then crossed to the other side and headed back the way they had come.

Only a few shoppers at the Mini Market, Billy observed. The summer season had barely begun. In a few days the Mini Market and every other shop in Sandy Hollow would be crowded night and day with summer people.

"This has *got* to be a great summer," Billy declared. "I deserve it after the year I had."

"Yeah, it was so weird with you being in that hospital," Jay replied. "I couldn't even visit you."

"So what?" Nate put in. "Look on the bright side, Billy. You got to miss a whole year of school!"

"Well, I'm better now," Billy declared. "And ready to party—big time!"

Nate stuck his hand in the air and Billy high-fived him.

"How are your jobs starting out?" Jay asked.

Billy and Nate groaned in unison.

"Mine's not too bad," Billy replied. "At least I'm outside all day on the boat. My boss says sometimes rich guys charter it to go deep-sea fishing. Maybe I'll get some big tips."

"At least you *wanted* a job," Nate complained. "When my dad found out the golf course needed help, he said I'd do it—without even asking me! I wanted to party this summer, not kill weeds and replace divots."

"Daddy says it will be good for you," Lynette chimed in. "Because you're a lazy bum."

Nate glared at her.

"Well, I'm not going to let work keep me from having a good time," Billy declared. "I can work all day and party all night. Who needs to sleep?"

"I can party all night, too," Nate agreed. "Bring on the girls."

Jay laughed. "Get serious. In two days you'll both be totally wiped."

"Not me," Nate insisted. "No way!"

Billy was only half listening to his friends. The sound of surf in the distance had caught his attention. "Hey, let's check out the beach!" he suggested.

He led the way off Main Street to locate a boardwalk that ran to the beach. The old wooden steps leading down from the dunes groaned and sagged under their weight.

They had the beach to themselves. Billy knew it wouldn't last. By the end of the week, the beach would be jammed with sunbathers and swimmers and kids making sand castles. And at night there would be clambakes and bonfires and parties.

I can't wait, Billy thought. I can't wait to get started.

"You're right, man, this is awesome," Jay agreed.

Billy glanced around. The crests of the waves glowed white in the silvery moonlight. Billy could see a stone jetty in the distance, stretching out from the shore until it disappeared into the sea.

"What's that?" Jay cried.

Billy jumped. He heard Lynette gasp.

The sky suddenly filled with noise. Flapping. Fluttering. Above them. In front of them. Behind them.

"Look!" Nate shouted, pointing toward the jetty.

Billy saw them. Bats. Dozens of them, flying low over the stone jetty.

A chill slid down Billy's spine. He stared at the

12

bats. So many of them, he thought. How can there be so many?

"Awesome," Jay whispered.

Lynette squeezed past Billy and hid behind Nate.

The bats fluttered up, blocking the moonlight, darkening the beach. Then they flew out to sea and disappeared.

"Where did they go?" Lynette asked in a tiny voice.

"To the island," Billy answered. "There's an island close to shore. Nobody lives there anymore. The bats use the abandoned houses."

"Bat island," Jay said. "Sounds like a place in a horror movie."

"The local people call it Vampire Island," Nate corrected him. "It's covered with burned-out houses. That's why no one lives there."

Jay laughed. *Vampire* Island? Give me a break!"

"Some people say vampires lived there—in the abandoned houses," Billy explained. "Some high school kids went out there after a graduation party. They dared one another to find the vampires and destroy them. Two kids found a coffin and set it on fire."

Lynette shivered. She moved closer to Nate.

"The fire killed the vampire," Billy continued. "But when the kids tried to leave the island,

13

other vampires followed them. The kids tried to set them on fire, too. All the houses burned, and none of the kids ever came back from the island.

"Some people say they died in the fire with the vampires. But other people believe that the vampires got them. So now nobody ever goes there."

"How many kids were there?" Lynette asked.

"Six. I heard that three of them tried to row away. But the vampires changed into bats and flew to the boat and killed them."

Nate laughed. "What a dumb story. Does anyone really believe it?"

"A lot of people do," Billy replied softly.

They stood silently, staring at the rock jetty.

Finally Billy turned away from the rolling, dark ocean. "Let's go back to town," he suggested, shivering.

His friends immediately agreed. Billy knew they had been spooked by the bats—and by his story. Lynette grabbed Nate's sleeve and wouldn't let go.

"How am I going to meet any girls with my little sister always tagging along?" Nate grumbled.

"If you don't want me here, I'll go home," Lynette declared.

"No!" Nate cried. "No way."

"Why not?"

14

"Because Mom will *kill* me."

"Buy me an ice cream, or I'll tell Mom you tried to lose me!"

"But that's blackmail!" Nate protested.

Billy chuckled. "She's got you, Nate."

"I'd buy her the ice-cream cone if I were you," Jay told him.

Nate gave in. "Okay. Okay. Ice cream."

Billy had to laugh. Nate was a big, tough-looking guy. And his little sister knew exactly how to push him around.

They walked along the beach in silence. But as Billy stepped onto the stairs leading up to the boardwalk, Lynette let out a piercing scream.

"No!" she wailed. "Let him go! Let him go! Nooo!"

15

Chapter 2

DOGGIE GOES FLYING

*B*illy gasped as he saw why Lynette was screaming.

Down the beach, two enormous bats attacked a small black dog. Terrified, the dog spun in circles, snapping at them.

But the bats attacked viciously. Swooping from the sky, screeching and snapping their jaws.

One flapping bat landed on the dog's back. It sank its teeth into the little dog's flesh.

The dog let out a yelp of pain.

The other bat swooped onto the dog's neck, biting deeply.

Billy watched, stunned, as the bats gripped the dog in their jaws and began flapping their wings frantically.

The dog twisted helplessly, letting out cry after cry.

This is impossible, Billy thought. *Bats can't do this.*

Their wings beat the air furiously. They lifted the yelping dog off the ground.

The animal struggled, twisting one way, then the other. But the bats held on.

Slowly they lifted the dog.

A foot off the beach.

Two feet.

Still higher.

Flapping hard, they moved toward the ocean.

Billy felt rooted to the sand, unable to move. Unable to take his eyes off the horrifying sight.

He heard Lynette's sobs. Saw her run after the squirming, howling dog.

"Lynette—come back!" Billy cried. He sprinted after her. Over the sound of his own breathing, Billy heard Nate and Jay running close behind him. Their footsteps sounded hollow on the damp sand.

Billy quickly overtook Lynette. He was gaining on the bats. They seemed to be having trouble carrying such a heavy load. Flapping furiously, they moved slowly along the shore.

The dog kicked its legs and howled.

Billy ran harder. Nate and Jay beside him now.

"Stop them!" Lynette screamed.

From the corner of his eye, Billy saw Jay stumble. Jay toppled facefirst into the sand.

Billy didn't slow down. Nate still ran beside him. They were close to the bats.

The dog wailed in fright. Blood poured from where the bats had ripped its throat.

The bats beat the air with their wings.

Billy ran until he was directly underneath them. He reached up. Tried to grab the dog. Missed by a couple of inches.

Nate jumped too. And missed.

Got to jump higher, Billy thought.

He leaped again. Missed again.

The bats flapped furiously.

Flying faster now.

Pulling away from Billy.

Billy ran as fast as he could. Nate chugged along beside him.

Something cold and wet grabbed Billy's legs. Swept him off balance.

Billy glanced down. He had run into the ocean. A tall wave splashed over him, pushing him back, startling him with its cold.

Billy saw Nate splashing in knee-deep water, still chasing the bats. A moment later, Nate began bobbing with the waves as they rolled in to shore. Nate's feet, Billy realized, were no longer touching bottom.

"Nate!" Billy shouted. "Come back! There's nothing we can do!"

Nate swam to Billy's side. They watched as the bats and dog became a ghastly silhouette against the moon. Growing smaller and smaller. Until they disappeared.

They're taking the dog to the island, Billy thought. Taking it home to feed on it. Sickened, he stared out toward the island. Feelings of horror and disgust filled him.

Just wait, he thought bitterly. I know you're not really bats. I know what you are. And I'll destroy you. I promise, before summer is over, I'll destroy you all.

Chapter 3

DINNERTIME

*L*ynette no longer felt like having ice cream. She just wanted to go home.

Billy, Jay, and Nate led the way along the path that led to the summer condos their families had rented. They talked quietly among themselves. They didn't want to frighten Lynette more.

"Those were vampires," Billy murmured.

"Vampire bats?" Jay asked. "I never knew they were so strong."

"Not vampire bats," Billy corrected him. "Vampires who turn into bats."

Jay snorted.

"Yeah, right," Nate muttered. "And Frankenstein rents the beach house next to mine."

"You saw what they did," Billy whispered. "You really think ordinary bats could do that?"

Lynette began to bawl again. "Are they going to kill the dog?" she wailed. She had been listening after all.

"Nice job, Billy," Nate muttered. He tried to comfort his sister.

"Look, I'm sorry, but it's true," Billy replied. "You have to believe me. Those were not ordinary bats."

"I don't believe in vampires," Jay declared. "Because they're a pain in the neck!" He roared at his own joke.

"It's not funny," Lynette cried. "It's scary!"

"She's right," Billy said. "And if you don't listen to me, you could be in a lot of danger."

"From vampires?" Jay rolled his eyes.

"From vampires," Billy repeated. He stared hard at Jay, trying to convince his best friend that he was serious.

Jay frowned. "Um, Billy, it's kind of hard to believe that vampires really exist."

He thinks I'm messed up, Billy realized. He gazed at the troubled faces of his friends. Noticed the glances they exchanged.

They both think I'm crazy, he thought. But I can't blame them. I would have thought the same thing . . . before last summer.

The memory tortured Billy even now.

But he was here to put an end to the evil in Sandy Hollow. If his friends were going to help him, they had to know the truth about last summer.

The truth about Sandy Hollow.

"I had a girlfriend last summer," Billy explained. "Her name was Joelle. I met her the first week I was here, and we spent the whole summer together."

"What happened?" Jay asked. His eyes shone with interest.

Billy took a deep breath. "The vampires killed her. They flew from the vampire island as bats. Then they returned to their human form and killed Joelle. They drank her blood until she died."

His friends stared at him. Billy could see that they didn't believe him.

"I know it sounds insane," Billy admitted. "But that's what happened. I saw the bite marks on Joelle's neck."

"Maybe they were mosquito bites?" Jay asked.

"I know what a mosquito bite looks like," Billy snapped. "These were different. Bigger and deeper."

Nate rubbed his chin. "Was Joelle the girl they found on the beach?"

Billy nodded.

"They said she drowned," Nate argued. "Nobody mentioned vampires."

Billy could tell from the three faces staring at

him that, no matter what he said, none of them would believe him. Nate wore a smug grin that seemed to say, *You don't really think I'm going to fall for this, do you?* Jay revealed no emotion at all.

Billy felt his anger rising. He forced himself to stay calm. "Jay, I didn't tell you the whole story about why I missed a year of school," he continued. "The reason you couldn't visit me is because I wasn't in a regular hospital. It was a mental hospital."

Billy lowered his eyes to the ground. Now they'll think I'm *totally* nuts, he thought.

He pressed on. "I was pretty messed up by what happened to Joelle. Shock trauma, they called it. I guess I—"

"Then I don't get it," Jay interrupted. "Why did you come back here? If something like that happened to me, I'd never want to see this place again."

Billy took a deep breath. "I came back to find the vampires who killed Joelle—to hunt them down and destroy them."

"Are there really vampires?" Lynette asked in a small voice.

"Yes," Billy replied.

"No," Nate declared.

"What about the dog?" Billy demanded.

"That was weird," Jay admitted. "But all we

know about bats is what we learned in biology. Maybe the bats they've got here are different. Maybe they fly off with dogs all the time."

Nate chuckled.

"It's not funny!" Billy exploded. "You didn't see what happened to Joelle!"

He spun away from them and started to stalk away.

The others hurried to catch up with him. "Whoa. Calm down," Jay urged. "We came here to party—remember?"

"Yeah, man," Nate agreed. "We want to get some sun and meet some major babes."

"It's too early to go home," Jay protested. "Let's head back to Main Street. Check out the action."

None of them believe me, Billy realized. But I'll make them believe if it's the last thing I do.

April Blair hid in the shadows. Waiting. Watching. Two bats landed on the soft sand a few feet from where she stood. Remaining perfectly still, she studied them.

They began to spin.

Faster and faster.

Until they became two whirling columns.

Stretching. Growing longer, higher.

Slowing, taking shape.

Developing shoulders, arms, legs.

24

Heads. Faces.

In seconds, two girls stood where the bats had whirled.

Awesome hair, April thought, gazing at the redheaded girl. So long and full. And it actually shimmers in the moonlight.

She turned her eyes to the other girl. A mass of golden curls framed her smooth, pale face. The curls swayed gently when she moved her head.

"I need human nectar," the one with red hair moaned. "Dog nectar is too thin. It isn't satisfying. And the dog put up too much of a fight. Humans don't resist the way animals do."

"Well, human nectar is in season," the other declared. "The summer people are all arriving."

"Just in time. I'm so hungry!"

It's time to show myself, April thought. She stepped from the shadows and moved toward the two vampires.

"Hey!" yelled the red-haired girl. The vampires advanced.

April waited for them. Met their eyes.

"We won't have to be hungry much longer," the redheaded one declared. "The nectar came to us. Home delivery."

April stopped. She watched the vampires' fangs slide down. Needle-sharp points. Ready to penetrate her neck. The hunger made their breath come in rapid, excited hisses.

The redheaded girl reached for her.

"Don't be stupid," April snapped. "Don't you recognize one of your own?"

They hesitated.

"I was here last summer," April told them. "And I became one of you."

"Who remembers the summer people?" the redheaded girl asked disdainfully. "They're all just food to me."

"All just food," the blond one repeated.

April saw the hunger in their eyes, the unquenchable yearning for nectar.

"Wait. I think I remember you," the blond girl declared. "It was Gabri who turned you into an Immortal, wasn't it?"

April nodded. "That's right," she agreed. "Gabri did it."

"What's your name?" the blond vampire asked.

"April Blair."

"I'm Irene," the blond girl told her. "And this is Kylie."

Kylie grinned at April, showing her fangs.

April realized that Irene was studying her, sizing her up. But Kylie seemed interested in only one thing. Nectar. Her eyes glowed with hunger. A glistening drop of saliva trickled from the corner of her mouth.

"Why are we standing around here?" Kylie

asked hungrily. "I need the nectar. I need it *now*."

"Let's go," Irene agreed.

They climbed the dune that rose to street level.

"I'm so glad summer is finally here," Irene murmured.

"I hate the winter," Kylie grumbled. "There is hardly anybody around. I get so hungry."

They reached the street. April waited as Kylie checked her appearance, adjusted the black scrunchie in her hair, smoothed her short denim skirt.

Irene caught April's eye and smirked. "Kylie thinks she has to look good to attract the nectar."

April shook her head. "Why don't you just cloud their minds?" she asked Kylie. "Make them helpless and drink all the nectar you want."

"It's more fun this way," Kylie replied. "I'm ready. Let's go." She strode onto the sidewalk near the dune.

April gazed at the scene as they wandered toward Main Street. People strolled along the sidewalks. A man and woman with a toddler. Two girls in Hard Rock Cafe T-shirts. A gray-haired couple walking slowly, gazing into the shop windows.

"Nectar," Kylie whispered.

Irene gripped April's arm. "Look."

Following Irene's gaze, April spotted three

boys across the street. A young girl tagged along behind them.

That guy is pretty cute, April thought.

The boy was tall, with long, dark hair. He pointed to something. He seemed to be showing the others around town.

Look at me, April thought, staring hard at the boy. Turn this way and look at me.

The tall boy shifted his gaze in April's direction. He stopped short, pulling his friends to a halt. All three boys turned to stare.

Kylie tossed her red hair and chuckled. "They're so easy to control, aren't they?" she murmured.

"Dinnertime," April proclaimed hungrily. "Let's go get them."

Chapter 4

DESSERT

"**W**hoa. Watch out!" April cried as Kylie pushed past her.

But the redheaded girl ignored her. She stepped up to the tall, black-haired boy. "Hi," she said. "You guys here for the summer?"

Wow, April thought. I guess we know which one she wants.

"Yeah. I'm here for the next two months," the boy replied.

Kylie cocked her head and smiled, her red hair tumbling over her shoulder. "I'll be here until Labor Day," she told him.

April realized that Irene had started talking to the big, athletic-looking boy. That left the short, thin one for her.

"Hi, I'm April."

"Oh, uh, my name's Jay."

Seems nervous, April thought. "Where are you from?" she asked.

"Uh . . . Holcomb. All of us are from there."

"I'm from Shadyside."

"Never been there," he replied, abruptly displaying a big goofy grin. "Is it nice?"

"It will never make the list of the top five hundred most fabulous places to live!"

Jay laughed. "Neither will Holcomb."

Good, April thought, he's starting to loosen up a little. Jay introduced her to his friends, Nate and Billy. And to the little girl, Lynette.

Kylie's tinkling laugh caught April's attention. She turned to see the girl slip her arm through Billy's.

Kylie tried to pull him away from the others. But Billy seemed to resist. He looked very uncomfortable.

April smiled to herself. Never thought I'd see any boy resist the charms of someone like Kylie, she thought.

She turned to Irene and Nate. At least Irene is doing well, she thought.

Nate seemed much more interested than Billy. He was grinning nonstop at Irene.

These boys will do, April decided. We can keep them around for a while.

"How would you guys like to be in a play?" she asked. All three reacted with surprise.

"Tryouts are this week at the summer theater," April continued. "A lot of kids have already joined the theater group. They've made sets and everything."

"What play are you doing?" Jay asked.

"Night of the Vampire," April replied. She saw Irene and Kylie glance at each other. She smiled at the boys. "We're really short on guys," she added. "We're *always* short on guys."

"What's it about?" Nate asked.

"Might be about vampires," Jay teased him.

"Duh. I know, I know," Nate grumbled. "I mean, what is the story like?"

"It's about two vampires who fall in love with their victims," April explained. "It's a comedy."

Irene laughed.

"It sounds kind of cool," Nate said. "But Billy and I both have jobs."

"No problem," April assured him. "Rehearsals are always at night—all the performances, too. A lot of us . . . can't make it during the day."

"You said a lot of kids are in the play?" Billy asked.

April turned to him in surprise. Why did he

sound so suspicious? "Yeah," she answered. "A lot."

"Then I'm in," Billy declared. "I really want to meet people this summer."

April narrowed her eyes at Billy. What's his problem? she wondered.

"Come on, let's walk," Kylie urged, tugging on Billy's arm.

They strolled along Main Street. Irene stopped in front of the Beach Emporium window. "Nice bikinis, huh?" she said to Billy.

He shrugged.

Irene shook her head. "A little too wild for me."

"For *you*, yeah," Kylie sneered. "You're so . . . out of it."

"It's called good taste," Irene shot back. "But I wouldn't expect you to know about that."

Kylie and Irene have only one thing in common, April decided. The need for nectar. It will be a long summer hanging out with them.

"I hear there are a lot of wild parties here during the summer," Kylie said to Billy.

"There are usually parties and bonfires on the beach," Billy replied. "They get pretty wild sometimes."

"I love to party," Kylie murmured, staring into his eyes.

32

Billy walked on without replying.

Wow, April thought. Kylie can *not* seem to get him interested. Not many guys would pass up a chance with a girl as beautiful as Kylie. What is his deal?

She turned back to Jay. "Have you come here before?"

He gave her another big lopsided grin. "Uh, well . . . no. It's my first time."

"Don't be so nervous," April teased him. "I don't bite!"

Jay blushed a bright red. "I'm not nervous," he insisted. He gave her a shy smile.

He's actually kind of cute, April decided. I guess I'll stick with him. Kylie wants Billy, anyway.

April glanced at the redheaded vampire. She was still holding onto Billy's arm. And he still appeared bothered by it.

Billy is too suspicious, April decided. Kylie will have a hard time with him. I'm better off with Jay.

"I want to go home." Lynette's shrill voice cut into April's thoughts.

"Now?" Nate growled.

"Mom said you had to get me back before eleven."

Nate glanced at his watch and sighed. "Okay."

"We'd better go, too," Billy declared. "Nate and I have to work tomorrow."

"Can we get together again?" Nate asked Irene.

"I'm going to try out for the vampire play," Irene answered. "Maybe I'll see you there."

"Excellent!" Nate beamed.

"I think I'll try out too," Kylie declared. She gazed up at Billy. "It's my kind of play."

Billy didn't answer. Jay and Nate said goodbye. The three boys left, with Lynette tagging along beside her brother.

Kylie sighed. "I'm so thirsty. I like that Billy. I wanted to sink my fangs into him."

"He didn't seem to like you too much," April observed.

Kylie whipped around to face April, her eyes flashing with anger. "It's because I'm so hungry! I tried to cloud his mind, but I was too weak. But tonight I'm going to drink *someone's* nectar! Anyone's."

"Take it easy," Irene cautioned. "We have all summer. If you drink too much and kill one of them, the summer people will be all upset."

"Who cares if they get upset?" Kylie demanded. "Do you think I care about hurting their feelings?"

"If too many dead bodies turn up," April pointed out, "the police will close the beach. The summer people will leave. All the food will go away."

"I hate taking just sips," Kylie complained. "Sips are never enough."

"But if you drink too much blood and kill them, there will be no nectar at all. They might even get wise to us—and hunt us while we sleep!" Irene insisted. "We have to take sips."

Kylie let out a growl. She shifted her smoldering eyes to April. "You sure were coming on to Jay. You're hungry too, aren't you?"

April nodded. "Starving."

"Remember," Irene warned. "Just take sips. After three sips, they become one of us. They become an Immortal. But that's the way it has to be. Don't kill anyone."

"Unless *they* attack you," Kylie added. She gave a hungry moan. "Why did those boys have to go home so early?"

"They'll be back tomorrow," April promised.

"It will be so boring, just taking sips from them." Kylie sighed.

April nodded. "I wanted to drink Jay up. Drink until he was dry!"

"Hey! How about a bet?" Kylie suggested. "That will make things more interesting! First one to turn one of those three boys into an Immortal wins."

April giggled. "You're on."

"Okay," Irene agreed. "It will be fun."

"I've won already," April declared. "Jay is so ripe, so ready . . ."

"Billy won't resist me next time," Kylie insisted. "This will be an easy bet to win."

The tips of Kylie's fangs slid into view. Her eyes blazed. April had never seen such intense hunger before.

"Kylie!" Irene snapped. "Watch it! We're on Main Street!"

Kylie's fangs disappeared. "I'm so hungry," she whispered. "So terribly hungry."

"What will be the prize if we win?" April asked.

"Yes," Kylie said, "what will I win for making Billy one of us?"

Irene chuckled. "I've got it. The perfect prize. At the end of the summer, the winner can have the other two boys for dessert!"

Chapter 5

VAMPIRE TRYOUTS

*B*illy leaned against the stage and gazed out at the kids who had shown up for play tryouts. There were about thirty of them—everybody talking at once, laughing, telling jokes, teasing each other.

Which ones? he thought.

He studied their faces. Were any of them vampires? Did the cute girl in the front row sleep in a coffin all day because direct sunlight would kill her?

How about the two boys giving each other high-fives?

Where are they? he wondered. Where are the vampires who killed Joelle?

A short, round woman with her blond hair in a bun strode onto the stage. "All right, every-

37

body!" she shouted, trying to be heard over all the noise. "Let me have your attention."

The noise slowly died down. "I'm Ms. Aaronson," she announced. "I run the community theater here at Sandy Hollow. And I'm thrilled to see so many young people here."

Billy tuned her out as she talked about the play. He stared intently at the other kids in the auditorium seats. Each friendly smile could hide sharp fangs, he knew. Each strange face could belong to a monster.

Ms. Aaronson cleared her throat. Billy glanced up at her again. "Let's see," she said. "Ah, here we are. Jay Windley, you're first. Please read from the script."

Jay stepped forward, looking very tense. Billy couldn't help smiling when Jay gave Ms. Aaronson one of his lopsided grins.

Jay took a deep breath and began reading. He was usually pretty soft-spoken, but now his voice sounded deep and powerful as he said the lines.

He's pretty good, Billy thought, surprised. He's really getting into the part.

Jay completed his reading without blowing a single word.

"Hey, you were great," Billy told him.

"I guess it went okay," Jay replied, smoothing back his brown hair. "I just wish I could do that well with girls."

"You seem to be doing okay with April."

Another lopsided grin. "Is she here yet?"

"Haven't seen her," Billy reported.

Jay nodded. "I hope she comes to tryouts tonight."

"Relax," Billy said. "This whole thing was her idea."

"Hi, Billy."

Billy turned to find Kylie standing next to him. She gazed at him with a smile. "I guess I'm a few minutes late."

"They just started. This will be going on for hours," Billy told her.

"Which part are you trying out for?" Kylie asked. She moved closer to him. He could smell her perfume.

"Just a little part. A delivery boy. He has five lines."

"I'm trying out for the lady vampire," Kylie informed him proudly. "I think I'm going to get it. I'm a natural."

"Is April here?" Jay asked eagerly.

Kylie frowned. "I didn't see her yet tonight," she answered.

"Was she at her house?" Jay pressed.

"Looking for me?" a voice called.

Billy turned, startled. April and Irene stood right behind them. I didn't even hear them come up, he thought.

Jay grinned. "Yeah, I thought you changed your mind," he told April.

"Not a chance," she replied. "Let's sit down." She dragged Jay to a seat in the auditorium.

Irene hurried over to sit with Nate.

"Looks like it's you and me," Kylie told him. She tossed her long hair over her shoulder and grinned.

Billy glanced at her. "I guess," he said. He wasn't sure he wanted to be stuck with Kylie. She seemed way too intense. But it wasn't as bad as he expected—Kylie seemed really into the auditions. She barely spoke to Billy as they watched all the kids read.

"Time for the part of Natalie," Ms. Aaronson finally announced, consulting her clipboard. "Let's see, who's first? Ah, Kylie. You here, Kylie?"

"Yes," Kylie replied, stepping forward.

"Do you have a last name, dear?" Ms. Aaronson asked.

"Yes," Kylie answered. "But I never use it."

Ms. Aaronson frowned, apparently trying to decide whether she should insist on having Kylie's last name. She sighed. "Okay, Kylie with no last name, you're up."

Kylie glided to the center of the stage, smiling, looking pleased with herself. Wow, Billy thought, she really likes being the center of attention.

"It's so hard being a vampire," Kylie began. "No one appreciates what we have to go through." She moaned about how much she needed human blood.

"Pretty good," said a girl's voice next to Billy. "But she's overacting a little."

Billy couldn't help laughing. "Don't tell her that!" he said. He turned to see a pretty black-haired girl standing next to him.

She smiled at him. "I shouldn't be mean. I'm probably just nervous," she admitted. "I want the same part!"

"Mae-Linn Walsh! You're up!" called Ms. Aaronson.

"Wish me luck," whispered the black-haired girl. She ran lightly up the steps to the stage.

Wow, she's really cute, Billy thought.

When she began to read, the auditorium fell silent. Mae-Linn paced back and forth, playing the part of someone faced with a major decision. She wrinkled her nose, cocked her head, smiled, frowned. Everyone watched.

I know who's going to be the star of this play, Billy decided.

Mae-Linn finished her reading. She blushed when the kids began to applaud. Then she climbed down from the stage and walked over to Billy. "You were great," he told her.

"You really think I did okay?" she asked. "I hope I get the part. It would be fun."

He studied her sparkling brown eyes. She had such soft, old-fashioned looks.

Billy felt his heart begin to beat faster.

"You doing anything after the tryouts?" she asked.

"Not really," Billy replied.

"Want to get a Coke or something?"

"Hey, great. I'd love to."

"I came with two other girls," Mae-Linn told him. "I've got to let them know." She disappeared through the curtains at the back of the stage.

This summer is looking better already, Billy decided.

Shifting his gaze toward the seats, he spotted Jay and April leaving together.

"Ms. Aaronson is supposed to announce who got the parts in a few minutes," Kylie said, coming up behind him.

"Think you'll get the lead?" Billy asked.

"Why? Do you think someone else did better than me?" Her expression darkened. Her green eyes narrowed.

"Uh, no," Billy answered, a little surprised by her reaction. "I was only asking how you thought it went."

"I got the part," Kylie assured him. "No problem."

"Well, congratulations." He wondered whether that was the right thing to say. "You were really excellent," he added.

"Want to take a walk around town, see what's happening?" she asked brightly.

"I can't."

"Why not?" Kylie demanded.

Her eyes met his. They seemed to grab him, pull him into another place. A strange, dreamlike place. He felt as though he were falling.

He forced himself to look away.

Kylie seemed surprised. And annoyed. "Why don't you want to hang out with me?" she demanded.

"I, uh, . . . I already told Mae-Linn I'd take her for a Coke."

Disappointment spread across Kylie's face.

"I'm—I'm sorry," he stammered, surprised at how upset she seemed.

Kylie turned and stalked off the stage.

"May I have your attention," Ms. Aaronson called. "Here are the names of the people I've selected for the play. Now, I want you to understand that everyone did a wonderful job. But there are only so many parts to go around . . ."

Nate, Jay, and Billy all got parts. So did April,

Kylie, and Irene. Billy wasn't surprised when Mae-Linn got the lead role.

But he saw that Kylie looked astonished.

"Hey, we both got parts," Mae-Linn called happily as she ran up to Billy.

"There was never any doubt about you," Billy replied.

"You really think so?" Mae-Linn asked shyly.

"You kidding?" Billy replied. "You were amazing."

She flashed him a dazzling smile. "Ready for that Coke?" she asked.

"Let's go," Billy answered.

He pushed open the theater door and gestured for Mae-Linn to walk ahead of him. As Billy followed her, he heard a strange sound.

A hissing sound.

Behind him.

The hiss of a snake?

"Look out!" he cried.

Chapter 6

NATE'S LUCKY SUMMER

Billy spun around, his heart pounding.

The angry hiss had sounded so close.

But he saw no snake on the ground.

Who was that, standing in the theater doorway?

He squinted into the light that flooded out from the theater. Was it Kylie?

Yes, Kylie. Standing there, so still.

Why was she *staring* at him like that?

Mae-Linn gazed up at Billy.

She looks really cute in the moonlight, he thought.

They drifted along the beach, not really going anywhere. Off to their right, waves crashed against the stone jetty.

"Is that your friend?" Mae-Linn asked.

Billy spotted a couple ahead of them on the beach. He recognized Jay and April, walking barefoot, letting the waves roll over their feet.

The moon disappeared behind a cloud, and April and Jay faded into the darkness. When the cloud passed, Jay and April had vanished.

Wow, Billy thought. Fast worker!

Mae-Linn slipped her hand into his.

I'm not doing too bad myself, Billy decided. They walked in silence for a few minutes.

"I think it's pretty late," Mae-Linn declared. "Do you know what time it is?"

Billy tried to focus on his watch, but it was too dark to see. "I can't tell," he replied.

"I'd better get back to the condo, or my parents will be worried."

"Are you doing anything tomorrow?" he asked. "Do you want to do anything? With me, I mean?"

Mae-Linn giggled at his awkwardness. "Okay," she replied brightly.

"I'll walk you home," he told her.

"Oh, don't bother," she protested. "I live right over there. I'll see you tomorrow."

She spun a complete circle, her shiny dark hair swinging out behind her. Then she dashed away, disappearing into the darkness.

It is going to be a great summer, Billy decided. A really great summer.

You didn't come here to have a great summer, he scolded himself. Remember the real reason you're here.

Billy took a deep breath and thought about Joelle. He would never forget her pale face on the sand. Never forget the two red marks on her white throat.

I will *never* forget what the vampires did to her, he swore.

Never.

He gazed down the beach. He wouldn't forget why he was here.

But Mae-Linn was certainly an added attraction.

"This is going to be a fun summer," Irene murmured, between the kisses she was giving Nate.

Fun for me, she thought. Not so much fun for you.

They sat on the porch swing in front of Nate's parents' beach condo. Irene kissed him again. The swing rocked gently. Back and forth. Back and forth.

I don't even have to cloud his mind, Irene thought. He's mine. All mine.

"It will definitely be fun," Nate agreed eagerly. "This is going to be the best summer of my life."

"I think so too," Irene whispered in his ear. "This will be a very special summer for both of us."

He studied her in the moonlight, a gigantic smile on his face.

Such a happy guy, Irene observed. He thinks he lucked out and found the girl of his dreams.

She kissed him gently on the neck.

Then slid her fangs down.

She prepared to sink them into his throat.

The need surged through her.

Hungry, she thought. So very, very hungry.

And now for a sip.

But only a sip. Don't get greedy, she warned herself. A sip. That's all.

Her fangs touched the softness of Nate's neck.

I can taste the nectar, she thought.

Taste it. Taste it. . . .

Chapter 7

BURIED TREASURE

*I*rene's fangs brushed Nate's throat.

A shriek exploded in her ear.

Irene jerked away from him, quickly closing her lips over the fangs.

She heard a giggle from behind the swing. Irene twisted around—and found Nate's little sister, Lynette.

Did the brat see my fangs? Irene thought. Did I hide them quickly enough?

"Lynette, what's your problem?" Nate demanded angrily.

"I gotcha!" Lynette cried happily.

Rage bubbled up inside Irene. She wanted to grab the little girl and drink her dry in one gulp.

But she had to stay calm.

49

She couldn't reveal herself. Couldn't upset Nate.

And couldn't lose the bet with Kylie and April.

But I was so close, she thought. So close to the nectar. She stared hungrily at Nate. If she stayed for one more minute she would lose control. She would kill Nate and his sister.

With a groan, Irene stood up. She muttered a quick goodnight, and hurried off into the darkness.

At least I don't think the little sister saw my fangs, Irene thought.

Behind her, she could hear Nate angrily scolding Lynette: "Thanks for chasing Irene away. You're dead meat!"

Thump! Thump! Thump!

Billy wandered through the dungeons of a big castle. The place was filthy. Empty and damp. Moisture glistened on the gray stone walls.

Thump-thump-thump-thump!

The noise came from above him. Someone was up there!

No one will stop me, Billy thought. No one will keep me from my revenge. Slipping the wooden stake from his bag, he started up the stone steps that led to the next level.

He reached the first landing—and stopped. An

iron gate blocked his way. He tugged on it. Securely locked.

He spotted a door hidden in the shadows. Stained, splintery wood with rusty iron hinges. He pulled on the door. It creaked as it swung open.

The room was dark and damp. Somewhere in the distance, water dripped.

Billy smiled grimly. This was exactly the kind of place they liked to sleep.

He stepped through the doorway. Spotted them instantly. Four coffins lined up against the wall.

Billy lowered his hands to the lid of the closest one. Be ready, he thought. Be ready for anything.

He slowly raised the coffin lid.

The vampire lay inside. A handsome young man with black hair. A square face.

Billy raised the wooden stake.

No hammer. Can I do it without a hammer?

Boom! Boom! Boom!

The noise again. Someone else in the castle.

Thud-thud-thud-thud!

The vampire's eyes opened. He snarled.

And lunged for Billy.

Billy jerked awake.

Bang-bang-bang-bang.

He stared around the small bedroom, breathing hard.

51

Someone knocking on the door. Billy shook his head, chasing away the last bits of the frightening dream. Yes. Someone was at the front door to the condo. Grabbing his robe, he stumbled to the door.

Two police officers stood on the doorstep.

"What's your name?" asked one.

"Billy."

"Your whole name."

"Billy Naughton."

"Were you out with Mae-Linn Walsh tonight?"

"Yeah," Billy replied, rubbing the last of the sleep from his eyes. "Why? What's wrong?"

"What time did you last see her?"

"Uh . . . about eleven-thirty, I guess."

"Are your parents here?"

"N-no," Billy stammered. "They only come up on weekends."

The two officers stared at him. One was a big tall guy. A walking pile of muscles. The other was a stern-looking woman. Both wore serious expressions.

"Did something happen to Mae-Linn?" Billy asked.

"She's missing," the policeman declared.

"Where did you last see her?" his partner asked.

"Uh, on the beach."

"Where on the beach?" she demanded.

"Near the edge of town. Coming from the community theater."

"Can you show us the spot?" the policeman asked.

Billy nodded.

"Get dressed and come with us."

Billy peered out from the backseat of the patrol car, watching the deserted town float by. Voices crackled over the two-way radio, but he couldn't make out what they were saying.

Mae-Linn, he thought. What happened to her? He pictured her shiny black hair, her bright smile.

Where is she?

"Slow down," he told the officers as they reached the edge of town. "It's only a little farther."

He stared at the smooth, silvery beach. "Right about here," he said. "Stop."

Billy climbed out of the patrol car. He slid down a small dune, cold sand spilling into his shoes. The police officers were right behind him, the beams from their powerful flashlights making wide yellow circles on the sand.

Billy glanced along the shoreline in both directions. "I think we walked over here."

The ocean breeze brushed back Billy's black hair. He could smell the sea. Salt air, decaying seaweed.

53

Mae-Linn, he thought, where did you go?

The two police officers spread out behind him, casting their lights in every direction.

Billy scanned the beach. Shadows hid within shadows.

Dangerous, he thought. The beach is dangerous at night.

A dark mound rose in front of him.

A pile of sand?

Billy started toward it. Glancing over his shoulder, he saw the beams of the police officers' flashlights. They moved down the beach, away from him.

"I found something!" he called to the police officers. He heard their footfalls as they hurried toward him.

Billy scooped away some of the sand with his hands, the cool, wet clumps spilling out between his fingers.

He touched something.

Something hard and smooth.

He brushed away the sand.

Something square.

Leather. A purse.

A purse?

"What did you find?" the policeman asked, shining his flashlight on Billy.

Billy gasped. "Mae-Linn?"

54

He shoveled the sand away, working frantically with both hands.

He stopped when his hand touched something cold. Cold and soft.

Billy leaned closer. Peered down.

"No—!"

He turned away. Felt his stomach lurch. And started to vomit.

Chapter 8

A SURPRISE ATTACK

Soft skin glowed white in the moonlight.

Billy recognized an arm. Mae-Linn's arm.

The officers helped to comfort Billy. Then they worked to uncover the rest of her body.

Her arms stretched out to the sides as if she were trying to make a snow angel in the sand. Strands of her shimmery dark hair covered one side of her face.

"Mae-Linn! Mae-Linn!" Billy choked out.

The officers pulled him back, away from Mae-Linn's body. "Don't touch anything," the policewoman warned.

Trembling, Billy stared at Mae-Linn. Her eyes were open, staring up at the night sky. So empty. So vacant.

Her mouth was wide open, and filled with sand. Her nostrils were filled with sand, too.

I have to know, Billy thought. I have to find out how she died.

He gazed at the police officers. They stood above Mae-Linn, speaking quietly. They weren't watching Billy.

In one quick movement, he threw himself onto the sand next to Mae-Linn. He heard the officers cry out as he reached for her shiny black hair. Pushed it away from her face. Away from her neck.

Billy studied her white throat.

In the moonlight he saw them. Two small puncture marks.

And a tiny drop of dried blood.

"No!" Billy cried, backing away from the body. "I don't believe it! Just like Joelle!"

The policeman pulled Billy back as his partner rushed to examine Mae-Linn's body. Billy barely noticed the weight of the man's hand on his arm. The two puncture marks lingered in his mind.

Vampires! The vampires did this, he thought. Mae-Linn would be alive right now if it weren't for *them!*

First Joelle, and now Mae-Linn. They have to be stopped!

57

I swear I'll destroy them, Billy pledged to himself once again.

I'll find them.

And I'll kill them.

Every last one of them.

Still feeling dazed, Billy sat in the cold sand. Other police officers arrived. They staked off the beach around Mae-Linn's body and strung yellow police lines around her. Finally one of them called Billy over to a cruiser.

Billy remained silent on the drive to police headquarters. The dark town whirred by as if in a dream.

The police station stood at the intersection of Main Street and Ocean Avenue. An old stone building. Bars covered the upstairs windows.

That's where the jail is, Billy thought.

He shuddered.

I'm the last one to see Mae-Linn alive, he realized. Does that make me a suspect?

Inside, a detective named Mullins grilled him, asking the same questions over and over. Where had he met Mae-Linn? When had he last seen her? Finally, about an hour before dawn, the detective let him go.

Billy walked along Main Street, passing the closed shops. No one out at that hour. Except him.

He walked faster, eager to get away from the police station, eager to get home. He wondered whether he had convinced the police of his innocence.

No way, he concluded. Detective Mullins considers me the prime suspect.

Billy thought about the barred windows on the second floor of the police station. And about Mae-Linn. And Joelle.

He shivered.

I'm going to find the vampires, he vowed. These aren't empty words. I'm going to destroy them.

He knew how to do it. He had spent a lot of time reading about vampires this past year. A lot of time preparing to kill them. He planned his revenge as he walked.

Sunlight destroys vampires. Fire does, too.

Or a wooden stake through the heart.

All I have to do is find them, Billy thought. That's the hard part.

But he knew what to look for. Vampires couldn't go out during the daylight. They couldn't eat regular food—only blood. They couldn't be seen in photographs or in mirrors.

I have all summer, Billy thought. All summer to find out which kids are vampires . . .

* * *

April stared up at the evening sky. She was annoyed.

Where are they? she wondered. Why are they always so late? I want to go into town and find the boys.

She pushed her straight blond hair out of her eyes and sighed. Kylie and Irene never seemed to hurry—no matter how hungry they were.

April pulled off her sandals. The cool sand worked its way between her toes, slid over the tops of her feet.

A whirring noise filled the air.

April watched as two bats twirled and became spinning cylinders, drawing up the beach sand and whipping it into miniature tornados.

Whirling side by side.

Dune grass thrashed the air. The wind whistled.

April shielded her eyes from the flying sand.

The whirling stopped suddenly. Sand fell back to the ground. The swaying grass became still.

Kylie and Irene stood on the beach, facing each other.

"It's about time," April snapped.

They ignored her and kept staring at each other.

"Mae-Linn went out on only one date with Billy," Irene scolded. "I can't believe you're so desperate to win our bet that you would kill her for that. You know what can happen if humans start to die."

"I *didn't* kill her," Kylie protested. "I didn't even go to the beach last night."

"Liar!" Irene replied. "You killed that girl. You're a liar, Kylie."

Kylie's eyes blazed. "Take that back," she growled.

Oh wow, April thought. These two will fight all night if I don't do something.

"The police will close the beach if we're not careful!" Irene screamed. "The food will go away! And you risked that just so you could go out with Billy and win the bet. Are you stupid or what?"

"I told you," Kylie snarled, "I didn't go near the beach."

April could feel Kylie's fury. It seemed to radiate from her, hot and intense. She took a step back.

Kylie hissed. Her fangs slid down.

Irene let out an ear-piercing screech. Her fangs lowered over her lips. Her face twisted in rage.

A chill of fear made April shudder. "Stop it!" she shrieked. "Both of you! Stop it!"

"Keep out of this!" Kylie growled.

To April's surprise, they turned on her—and attacked, snarling and hissing.

April tried to back away. But they held her tightly in place. Two pairs of fangs closed in on April's throat.

"What—what are you going to do?" she cried.

Chapter 9

ANOTHER SURPRISE ATTACK

"**I** have no nectar!" April cried. "You *know* I'm one of you!"

To her surprise, Irene and Kylie both tossed back their heads in laughter.

"You should've seen the look on your face, April!" Kylie declared.

"April Fools!" Irene declared. "Get it? It's April Fools' Day in June!"

They both laughed again, enjoying their joke.

April snarled and raised her long fingernails. "I'll s-s-slash you both to pieces!" she hissed furiously.

"Hey—it was just a joke," Kylie replied. "Put your claws back in. You don't have to totally lose it!"

"We're *all* losing it," Irene moaned. "Because

63

we're so hungry." She sighed. "Last night I was so desperate, I had to kill another dog."

Kylie and April shook their heads grimly.

Then Kylie turned to April. "Speaking of helpless creatures," she said, "how did it go with Jay last night?"

April couldn't hide her smile. "You two don't stand a chance," she replied coyly. "I'll win the bet before you even get started."

The next evening, Billy grabbed the phone as soon as he got home from work. He hadn't been able to reach Jay all day.

Jay's mom answered the phone.

"He's in his room," she told Billy. "He's been a little under the weather all day. I don't know what's wrong with him. Just a sec. I'll get him."

Billy heard the clink of the phone being put down. A few moments later, Jay came on the line.

"Hi. You hear about Mae-Linn?" Jay asked.

"Yeah, I heard." I didn't just *hear*, Billy thought. I saw her, too. "She was okay when we said goodnight on the beach. That's the last time I saw her. The police questioned me for hours. Like I'm some kind of killer. It was unreal."

"It's so weird," Jay said. "I mean, she was alive last night. And now . . ."

Jay's words trailed off. They both fell silent.

Billy wondered whether he should tell Jay about the bite marks on Mae-Linn's neck. Would his friend believe him?

"Uh—your mom says you're sick or something," Billy said.

"Yeah, I've been tired all day," Jay replied. *"Really* tired. Like I haven't slept for a week and a half."

"You sick?"

"I don't know. I'm just wrecked. And weak. Like I can't even move."

Billy drew in a breath. "Hope it isn't the flu. Are you going to make it to play rehearsal?"

"I'll try to get there. I want to see April again."

"You two got a thing going?"

"Maybe," Jay replied. "Sort of, I guess. I hope."

"Then I'll see you at the theater," Billy said. He hung up and stared out the window. *I don't like this,* he thought. *No way do I like this. It sounds too familiar.*

Joelle had always been tired last summer. Really tired. It got worse and worse as the summer went on. She walked around like a zombie. Pale. Dazed. Lost.

Until the vampire got greedy and drank too much.

And killed her.

Billy sighed. Maybe Joelle had been lucky. If

she hadn't died, she would have become one of them. Death had to be better than that.

Abruptly he slammed his fist down on the table. "I won't let them have Jay," he growled through clenched teeth. "I won't let them kill another friend."

He paced up and down the room. If he was right, if a vampire was sipping Jay's blood, the vampire had to be someone close to Jay, close enough to bite his neck.

April.

Billy tried to picture April. Her long blond hair. Her pale skin. I'll watch April, he thought. I'll look for the signs. And if she's a vampire, I'll do what I came here to do.

I'll destroy her.

Billy grabbed his script and banged out the door. He decided to stop by Nate's place on the way to the theater. If Nate was still there, they could walk to play rehearsal together.

Really dark tonight, Billy thought. Clouds filled the night sky, blocking out the moon and stars. Shadows seemed to seep out of the spaces between cottages.

Spooky, he thought. A good night for vampires to hunt.

He was glad when he reached Nate's place.

The condo was a new two-story brick building that looked as if it had been put in Sandy Hollow by mistake. Everything else in town was wood or stone. Nate's condo building didn't look as if it belonged on a beach at all!

The condo had a little park out front, with trees, a couple of swings, and a love seat. It was so dark Billy could hardly tell where he was going.

A loud snapping sound came from the trees.

Billy stopped. Listened. Silence now.

But he had heard something. Like a person hiding in the trees. Or a vampire.

Billy started for the condo, then hesitated. Someone . . . some*thing* was here. Watching him. He was sure of it. He could *feel* it.

Vampires.

Could they know why I'm here? Do they realize someone is hunting them? Will they try to kill me before I kill them?

He heard the snapping sound again. Billy whirled to face it. Nothing in the trees. Only darkness.

It's nothing, he told himself. Your imagination, that's all.

Black shadows lurked along the side of the condo. As he passed the spot where the darkness seemed deepest, he heard a scrape. Like a foot moving. Only a few feet away.

"It's nothing," Billy whispered.

Nothing.

He kept moving, eager to get to Nate's front door.

Another noise.

Scratching.

Like claws.

Tiny claws. Like a bat's claws.

An animal, Billy decided. An ordinary animal. A dog or a cat. A raccoon. Just an animal . . .

He cried out when it jumped him from behind.

Hands slid over his shoulders.

Closed on his neck.

Billy whirled to defend himself.

He saw the black shape.

Terrified, he cried out again.

GOOSEBUMPS GIVE YOURSELF GOOSEBUMPS

"Because it isn't funny," Billy told her, trying for Lynette's door.

"I'm going in anyway," Lynette insisted. "I bet you can't catch me."

Billy chasing her. A few seconds later Lynette disappeared into the...

"No, many your little sister nearby," Billy warned.

Chapter 10

REHEARSAL FOR DEATH

Billy threw his hands up to defend himself. He fell back a step.

And heard laughter in the darkness.

"Got you!" Lynette squealed happily.

Billy let out a long breath. "Wow," he murmured. "I guess you did." Would his heart ever stop racing?

"Bet you thought I was one of those vampires!"

Lynette's face was barely visible in the shadows, a dim outline. But Billy knew she was grinning at him.

"You shouldn't scare people like that," Billy told her, still feeling shaky.

"Why not?"

"Because it isn't funny," Billy told her, heading for Nate's door.

"I think it's funny," Lynette insisted. "I think it's a riot!"

Billy rang the bell. A few seconds later Nate opened the door.

"Hey, man. Your little sister is evil," Billy declared.

Billy and Nate were quiet as they made their way toward the theater. It's the first rehearsal, Billy thought. The first rehearsal, and already the star is dead.

And what about Jay?

Billy recalled how pale Joelle had looked last year. How she had been weak and tired all the time.

Would the same thing happen to Jay?

The theater stood on a small grassy rise at the south edge of Sandy Hollow. A rectangular wooden building, white with green shutters and trim.

Billy could feel the fear hanging over everybody as soon as he and Nate stepped inside. All the kids had gathered on the stage. They talked in low tones about Mae-Linn.

Are any of them vampires? Billy wondered. He looked around for April, but didn't see her.

"There's Irene," Nate told him. "I'll catch you later."

Irene stood with some other girls near the steps leading down from the stage. She smiled as Nate rushed over to her.

Billy turned away from them, scanning the crowd for Jay. He drifted toward the other side of the theater.

"Someone in Sandy Hollow killed her," a brown-haired girl declared as Billy moved past her. "Maybe even someone we know."

"Hey, you hear if they're going to cancel the play?" a freckle-faced boy asked Billy.

Billy shook his head. He studied the boy. Such pale skin. Vampires didn't have tans—not even at Sandy Hollow. Other kids went to the beach every day, but not the vampires. Could this boy be a vampire?

The freckle-faced kid moved away from Billy, glancing nervously over his shoulder.

Got to remember him, Billy thought.

The theater door opened. Billy turned to see Jay walk slowly into the auditorium.

Billy's heart sank. Oh, no, he thought. Jay looks really bad.

Jay moved like a sleepwalker. Staring at the floor, he shuffled toward the stage.

Billy started across the crowded room to his best friend. But April appeared before he could get there. She took Jay's hand and pulled him down into one of the seats, talking to him, giggling at something he said.

Billy stared hard at April. Is she a vampire? Billy wondered. Is she turning my best friend into a monster?

I have to check Jay's neck for bite marks, Billy decided. Then I'll know for sure.

Someone grabbed his arm. "Hi, Billy."

Kylie stood next to him. She wore denim cutoffs and a blue halter top. Her long hair was pulled into a ponytail that hung to the center of her back. Billy stared at her. She's really beautiful, he thought. A little weird, but definitely beautiful.

"I guess you heard what happened," Kylie said quietly.

Billy nodded.

"Isn't it awful? I'm surprised so many kids came to rehearsal tonight. I thought they might be afraid to leave their houses."

"You came," Billy pointed out.

Kylie grinned. "Well, nothing scares me."

Ms. Aaronson stepped to the center of the stage and raised her hand for silence. "Let me have your attention, please."

Everyone stopped talking.

Ms. Aaronson announced that the play would go on—and that the performance would be dedicated to Mae-Linn. "Kylie will be taking over the part of Natalie," she added.

Kylie smiled brightly. "Now I get to do a scene with *you*," she told Billy.

Billy didn't answer. He glanced around the theater, searching for Jay and April. They were nowhere to be seen. That's weird, Billy thought. Why would they leave at the beginning of rehearsal?

"Let's go. Act One," Ms. Aaronson called. "Places!"

Kylie took Billy's hand. "That's us," she told him.

He followed her to the stage, still thinking about Jay.

"All right," Ms. Aaronson said. "Begin from the beginning."

Billy moved slowly across the stage, eyeing the buildings painted on the backdrop. "Twenty-seven Bracker Street," he said. "Why can't I find it? Mr. Corkley will have my hide if I don't find it."

Billy carried a box of groceries. He was supposed to be a delivery boy trying to deliver an order. A *lost* delivery boy.

Kylie sprang out of the shadows. Acting startled, Billy nearly dropped the box of groceries.

"Looking for something?" Kylie asked with an evil smile.

"Uh . . . uh . . ." Billy stammered.

"Speak up! Are you lost?"

"I—I'm looking for 27 Bracker Street. Do you know where it is?" Billy asked.

"Right over here. I'll show you," Kylie said.

Billy followed her to stage right. His heart pounded in his chest. Why am I so nervous? he wondered. It's just a play.

But the danger seemed real. I'm good at pretending to be afraid of vampires, Billy thought. Because I *am* afraid.

Suddenly Kylie turned. Billy jumped—and dropped the groceries.

He flung up his hands. Kylie grabbed him with surprising strength.

Sharp white fangs appeared in her mouth. Her eyes glinted in the stage lights.

She pulled Billy to her and lowered her fangs to his neck.

"No!" Billy yelled. "Stop!"

He struggled to get out of Kylie's grasp.

"Not so hard!" he cried. "Hey—not so hard!"

But she buried her fangs in his throat.

Chapter 11

BIG SURPRISE FOR APRIL

"**H**ey! Let go!" Billy cried. "Not so hard!"

Kylie backed away. She pulled out her plastic fangs.

Billy touched the spot where Kylie bit him. No blood. The skin wasn't broken.

"I'm sorry," Kylie said. "I guess I was really getting into my part."

Billy rubbed his sore neck. Get a grip, he told himself. How will you deal with *real* vampires if you can't stay calm in a dumb play?

"Sorry I freaked," Billy told Kylie. "You really startled me. You're a good actress."

Kylie's eyes lit up. "Thanks, Billy."

"Okay. Good job," called Ms. Aaronson. "Next scene!"

Billy watched as Jay shuffled onstage. He remembered how smooth Jay had been in auditions. Today he seemed like a different person. He struggled through his lines without any energy.

"Jay is totally wiped," Billy whispered to Kylie.

"I'll say," Kylie replied. "Maybe he and April have been staying up late," she added with a smirk.

That's what I'm afraid of, Billy thought.

After rehearsal, Nate and Irene wandered over to Billy and Kylie. "Want to hang out?" Nate asked.

Before Billy could respond, Jay and April joined them. "Um, yeah!" Billy said quickly. "Why don't we *all* go down to Swanny's arcade?"

"You look as if you haven't slept in weeks," Kylie told Jay as they moved toward the theater exit.

"Just the opposite," Jay explained. "I slept all day, and then when I got up, I still felt tired."

Just like Joelle, Billy thought.

He studied Jay's neck. No bite marks. Unless they were hidden by the collar of his polo shirt.

Am I wrong about April? Billy wondered. Could Jay simply be sick?

April seemed nice enough. She and Jay held hands as they walked. So did Irene and Nate, Billy noticed.

"Hey!" called a loud voice. A tall boy wearing a maroon baseball cap stood in front of them, blocking the door to the theater. Surprised, Billy stopped.

The boy lifted his finger. Pointed.

At April, Billy realized.

He saw the color drain from April's cheeks. Her eyes went wide in alarm.

April took a step back. For a moment Billy thought she might scream.

The tall boy stared hard at April. "Hey—I remember you!" he said.

Chapter 12

BATS

What's going on? Billy wondered. Why is April so freaked out?

"Don't you remember me?" the boy asked her.

"I . . . uh . . ." April stammered.

"Rick Tyler," the boy announced. "From Shadyside."

"Oh, yeah," April replied. Taking his arm, she quickly pulled him away from Billy and the others.

"This is an old friend," she called back to them, hurrying Rick out the door. "I need to talk to him alone. Catch you guys later."

She and Rick vanished out the door.

"What was *that* about?" Irene asked.

"Beats me," Kylie replied.

"Should we wait for her?" Jay asked.

"I don't see her anywhere," Nate reported, stepping outside. "Looks like April found somebody new, Jay. Tough break, man."

Jay nodded sleepily, as if he couldn't find the strength to answer.

"Let's go," Nate urged.

They started into town. Halfway to the arcade, Jay stopped. "I can't go," he announced. "I've got to get some sleep. I can't even move."

"No way!" Billy protested. "Come on, Jay. Stay with us."

Until I figure out some way to see your neck, he thought.

"Can't," Jay mumbled. He trudged slowly away toward the beach—and his condo.

Billy rushed after Jay, the loose sand feeling spongy under his sandals. He caught up with Jay on the other side of the dunes.

"Wait up," he called.

Jay stopped. "What?"

"Let me see your neck." Billy reached for Jay's collar.

"Hey—" Jay protested, knocking Billy's hand away.

"I need to see your neck," Billy insisted.

Jay frowned. "Are you crazy? What is your *problem?*"

"I think you've been bitten by a vampire."

Jay stared at him for a long moment. Then he

gave a short laugh. "Billy, go away. I'm too beat to listen to this."

Billy reached for Jay's collar again.

"No way!" Jay shouted, pushing Billy away.

Billy stumbled back, nearly losing his balance. I didn't think Jay had enough strength left to do that, he thought.

"I don't want to hear this vampire stuff!" Jay cried. "I'm too tired."

What should I do? Billy wondered. Should I tackle him? Rip off his shirt?

"Billy, I don't know how to say this," Jay started. "But you were in a mental hospital. And now you're acting crazy. I mean, I'm worried about you. Are you sure you're okay?"

"You think I'm crazy," Billy muttered.

"You're talking about *vampires!*" Jay exclaimed.

"Jay, you have to listen to me—" he began.

But a voice interrupted him. "Hey, Billy! You coming?" Kylie stood on the crest of the dune with Nate and Irene, watching them.

Billy hesitated.

"Go on, man," Jay told him. "Stop thinking about your old girlfriend. There's no such thing as a vampire."

Billy glared at his best friend. But he couldn't force Jay to show him his neck. Not with the others watching. They would *all* think he'd gone nuts.

He walked back toward Kylie.

Jay will be okay for tonight, he told himself. He's too wiped to do anything but go straight home. And April is with that Rick guy.

By the time they reached the center of town, Nate and Irene had disappeared.

"Hey, where did they go?" Billy asked Kylie.

"Don't know," Kylie answered. "Maybe they wanted to be alone."

"I guess," Billy replied.

Their eyes met. Billy started to look away, but her gaze held him. Her eyes seemed to glow softly, pulling him in. Gently. Slowly.

Billy felt a weird tug in his chest.

He felt as if he were floating.

Gliding in a mist.

Alone with Kylie. Beautiful Kylie.

Drifting past the Mini Market.

The Pizza Cove.

The Harbor Palace movie theater.

Billy shook the weird dreaminess off. Kylie stared at him, frowning, her green eyes smoldering.

They stood in front of the Old Atlantic Chowder House, people pushing past them to get in and out. How did we get here? Billy wondered. Kylie's eyes still burned into his.

"Uh . . . want some chowder?" he asked awkwardly.

Kylie shrugged. "Sure. Why not?"

The place had fishing nets on the walls and red-checked plastic tablecloths. Waiters hurried past with steaming bowls of chowder, the tangy aroma drifting through the room.

"The menu is over there," Billy told Kylie, pointing to a large blackboard on a stand. The day's offerings were scribbled in chalk.

Kylie studied the menu, then shrugged. "I guess I'm not really hungry." She laughed. "I never eat. I never seem to have the time."

"We don't have to eat if you don't want to," Billy told her.

They left the restaurant.

"Come on," Kylie urged, grabbing his hand. "Let's check out the beach."

Billy wasn't sure he wanted to return to the beach so soon. He thought of Mae-Linn. He pictured her body again, half covered with sand. It was hard to shake such an ugly memory.

But Kylie *was* really hot.

He decided to follow her. As they crossed Main Street, he searched for April and Rick Tyler, or Irene and Nate. No sign of them.

Kylie chose a spot where they had to climb down to the beach through the dune grass. It clung to Billy's ankles as if the blades were covered with sticky glue.

The moon shone brightly in the star-filled sky, bathing the beach in silvery light. Billy stopped to scrape some beach tar from his sandals.

Kylie seemed distracted, distant. Billy thought she had a strange expression on her face. Needy? Longing?

"Let's sit down," she suggested.

"I want to keep walking," Billy told her.

Kylie's eyes flashed angrily. Then she smiled. Slipped her hand into Billy's.

What's her deal? Billy wondered.

They walked along the beach holding hands. Kylie gazed at him. "You're sort of . . . well, hard to get to know," she told him. "You never talk about yourself."

"I don't like to talk about myself," he replied.

"Well, we don't have to talk," Kylie murmured, moving closer to him. She tilted her face to his. Billy stared into her eyes. Felt himself falling . . . falling into Kylie's eyes.

Drifting.

Everything looks blurry, he thought. Can't see anything.

Only Kylie. He heard her whispering his name, pulling him down to the sand.

A loud flapping sound shook Billy from his

daze. Something fluttered past his nose, so close he could feel the breeze from its wings.

Startled, Billy looked up. Something black flashed past his head. A dark shadow in the moonlight.

Something slammed against his shoulder.

He ducked out of the way as tiny claws grazed his cheek.

Bats?

Yes, two of them.

They swooped down again, one clawing at his shoulder, the other going for his face. He ducked out of the way.

Desperately searching the beach, he tried to find some cover. A dock to hide beneath. An abandoned beach umbrella.

Something. Anything. But there was nowhere to hide.

He glanced up, searching for the bats. They flew over him.

Circling.

Hissing.

Then they swooped to attack.

Chapter 13

VAMPIRE ISLAND

Billy hit the sand. He scrambled to his knees and tried to roll away.

The bats uttered shrill shrieks as they attacked.

As Billy tried to roll away, he saw Kylie leap to her feet. She swung her hands wildly, thrashing the air.

She hit one bat. The sound of her hand hitting its plump body made a loud *thock*.

The bats stopped their ugly screeching.

The other one hovered over Kylie. She swung again, narrowly missing it.

She let out a loud victory cry as the bats rose up, then swooped away.

Billy sat up in the sand. "Wow," he murmured. "Wow. You were great!"

"I'm not afraid of bats," Kylie boasted.

"I'm not either—unless they attack me," Billy said. He felt embarrassed that Kylie had to fight while he rolled helplessly in the sand.

"There are so many bats on this beach," he said. "They all live on that island out there."

"Know what I'd like to do?" Kylie asked excitedly. "Row out to the island and explore! Want to?"

Billy stared at her in surprise. "You mean right now? Wouldn't it be better to go in the daytime?"

"No," Kylie replied, tugging on his arm. "Come on. Let's do it now. It will be cool."

"Well . . ." Billy hesitated. He didn't really want to go. But he didn't want to look any more like a total wimp.

"We need a boat," Kylie said.

"The guy I work for has some rowboats," Billy told her. "He said I can borrow them whenever I want. I guess we could get one and go out there now."

"Where are the rowboats?"

"Down by the wharf. Come on. I'll show you." They started jogging down the beach.

"Hey, there's Irene and Nate!" Kylie exclaimed.

Billy spotted them walking close together. I guess they *did* want to be alone, he thought.

"I've got to tell her where we're going," Kylie said. "She'll be so jealous!"

"I'll get a boat while you talk to her," Billy offered. "I'll pick you up at that long dock—the one everybody dives from."

"See you there," Kylie agreed. "I can't wait."

Billy let the rowboat glide slowly up to the long dock. No sign of Kylie.

Where is she? he wondered. Maybe she changed her mind.

He tied the boat to a cleat and jumped onto the dock, scanning the beach. Still no Kylie. He didn't see Nate or Irene, either.

Billy climbed back into the little boat. Waited.

"Hey!" Kylie's sandals thumped on the wooden planks as she hurried down the dock. "Ready?"

"What took you so long?" he demanded.

Kylie shrugged. "Sorry," she said absently. "You ready to explore the island?"

Billy felt the boat rocking beneath him, making small waves against the dock. "Let's go," he told her. Slipping the oars into the oarlocks, he propelled the boat away from the dock and aimed it at the island.

The vampire island.

Nighttime, he thought. They will be awake.

But they won't be home, Billy told himself. Night is when they have to feed, and there's no food on the island. They go to Sandy Hollow for food. For *human* food.

"The island isn't very far," Kylie commented. "It shouldn't take long."

Billy rowed, the oarlocks creaking and groaning.

Kylie sat in the stern, grinning excitedly at him, her eyes flashing. "I love to do things like this," she told him. "Weird, crazy things. Just because I feel like it."

Billy saw bats flying over the water. Bats swooped low over the boat. They rose to become black shadows in the star-filled sky. They circled and swooped in again, passing only a few feet over Billy's head.

"It's almost like they're warning us off," Billy declared.

"Yeah. Right." Kylie rolled her eyes. "Don't worry," she said. "The bats won't hurt you. Bats are good. Didn't you learn that in school?"

Billy glanced over his shoulder and caught sight of the island. A long, low shape against the dark sky. Waiting.

Waiting for me, Billy thought.

The island stood black against the blue-black water.

Not a single light anywhere.

Am I totally crazy? Billy wondered as he gazed at the vampire island.

Am I going to regret this?

PART TWO

BILLY'S QUEST

Chapter 14

A SURPRISE WELCOME

"**T**here!" Kylie exclaimed, pointing to an old dock, bobbing in the water. "We can tie the boat to that dock."

As Billy guided the boat toward it, he studied the island. Darkness hid everything beyond the end of the dock. Tall trees towered over the shoreline, blocking out the moon, making the night even darker.

"This place is too weird," Billy muttered.

Bats flapped overhead. The sky was full of them. They fluttered from tree to tree. From the dock into the darkness. Billy heard a low growl carried on the wind. Were there dogs on the island, too? If so, they had to be wild. Another howl made him shiver.

"Isn't this exciting?" Kylie asked breathlessly.

Only if you have a death wish, Billy thought.

He eased the rowboat up to the dock. Kylie tied it to a ladder.

"Come on," she urged. "This is so cool. Let's see what's here." She started up the ladder.

"Watch out," Billy cautioned. "Half the rungs are missing."

Kylie made it easily to the top. "Come on up," she urged him. "It held me okay."

The rung Billy grabbed was covered with some sort of slimy, dark goo. He reached down to rinse his hand in the water.

Something instantly splashed to the surface. Startled, he yanked his hand out of the murky water.

"It was just a fish!" Kylie exclaimed, laughing.

Billy took a deep breath, then climbed the ladder.

"Let's go!" Kylie urged.

They moved slowly onto the island, stepping cautiously in the darkness.

A shrill cry made Billy jump.

"What was that?" he gasped.

"Probably a bird or something," Kylie replied. "I bet there are all kinds of things living here." She glanced over her shoulder at Billy. "They're probably all harmless," she added.

Nothing here is harmless, Billy thought. Some

of the creatures on this island are very dangerous.

They killed Joelle.

Vines and bushes clogged the path leading inland from the dock. The plants felt slimy and cold as he pushed through.

Billy searched for the burned-out houses. But he didn't see any houses at all. Maybe that was only a story.

Maybe everything he's heard about the island was a lie. Stories told again and again. Stories that grew wilder each time they were repeated, until there was no truth left in them.

No way, Billy thought. He knew one story about this island was true. A horror story. About vampires.

"I see something up ahead," Kylie whispered. She crashed through the bushes and disappeared from sight.

Billy followed her. Kylie led the way up to a tall, dark ruin. The remains of a burned house.

Most of it had collapsed, but jagged boards remained standing. Dark and charred.

"We should have brought flashlights," Billy commented.

"It's more fun this way," Kylie insisted. Her eyes met his. "Are you scared?" she teased.

Before Billy could answer, he heard a low moan.

From the trees around the house.

He turned back to the woods. But saw only shadows.

Ignore it, he told himself. It's just an animal.

Kylie had already started down an overgrown path. Billy went after her. The path led to another burned-out house. This one was still a shell, gutted by fire.

Billy examined the door. Only a small piece of it remained. A charred chunk of wood attached by a single hinge. Blackness oozed from the doorway.

Kylie stuck her head inside. "Look," she breathed.

Billy peered into the house—and gasped.

Bats.

Everywhere.

Hanging from the ceiling.

The doorways.

A few clung to the overhead light fixtures.

Two of them detached themselves from the ceiling—and launched themselves at Billy and Kylie. Billy raised his hand to protect his face. But the bats flapped past him and vanished.

He clung to the door frame, his heart racing.

This is the vampire island, he thought. Every one of these bats could be a vampire. Any one of them could attack us. Kill us.

His gaze fell on a charred piece of wood. It looked like it had once been a table leg.

Billy reached down and grabbed it. The wood felt heavy in his hand.

"Let's get out of here," Kylie suggested. She pushed past him and continued down the path. Billy followed.

A long, loud howl made Billy stop. He searched the trees frantically.

Kylie had disappeared.

Another howl. Closer this time.

"Kylie!" Billy yelled. Where was she? Why didn't she answer? "Kylie, get back here!"

Silence.

Billy held his breath as he peered into the trees. No sign of Kylie.

No animal. Nothing there.

Then—branches snapped. Dry leaves crackled.

Footsteps.

An animal charging through the trees.

Billy spun to face the sound.

Too late. A snarling black creature sprang at him. Knocked him to the ground.

Its yellow eyes glowed as it sank razor-sharp fangs into Billy's neck.

Chapter 15

NOT A REGULAR WOLF

Billy rolled to the side as the creature fell on him. Its teeth grazed his neck, catching in his hair. He felt its hot, sour breath on his face.

Billy gagged. He couldn't breathe.

Yellow eyes stared down at him. He shoved the creature away with both hands.

What *is* it? he wondered. Is it a wolf?

The creature attacked again.

Billy held the charred table leg in front of his face. The creature's fangs sank into the wood.

With a yelp it fell back, shaking the stick from its mouth.

Billy scrambled to his feet. Yes—it's a wolf! he realized.

He dove for the wooden table leg. Grabbed it

off the ground. And spun around, holding it in front of him like a sword.

The wolf leapt again.

And Billy drove the wooden table leg deep into its chest.

The yellow eyes narrowed in pain. But the creature didn't cry out, didn't utter a sound.

Billy stared at the deep hole in the wolf's chest. No blood. It didn't bleed.

Not a regular wolf, Billy saw to his horror. *Not a regular wolf.*

Now the yellow eyes glowed with fury. The wolf twisted away, opening its jaws wide, yanking the end of the stick from Billy's hand.

Was it about to attack again?

No.

Its eyes rolled up and it crumpled onto its back on the ground. All four legs thrashed the air for a moment. Then the creature let out a long sigh— and lay still.

Billy stood over it, struggling to catch his breath. He had just killed a vampire, he realized. A vampire he had disturbed. One that decided to attack him in wolf form.

He lightly prodded the black fur with his foot. Clumps of fur fell off the body.

His heart still pounding, Billy turned away. The woods stretched silently all around.

The whole island must be filled with monsters like this, Billy realized.

"Kylie." He murmured her name out loud.

Where is Kylie? he wondered.

I've got to show her this creature. She's got to see a real vampire. She'll believe me. Then everyone will believe me about the vampires here at Sandy Hollow.

"Kylie!" He shouted her name.

"Kylie!" He cupped his hands around his mouth and called to her.

Following the path that had brought them to the burned-out house, Billy trotted into the woods. "Kylie—where are you? Kylie?"

He found her sitting on a log on a low, sandy hill overlooking the water. She turned as he ran up to her, and jumped to her feet. "Billy—what's wrong?"

"I—I couldn't find you," he cried breathlessly.

"Sorry," she said. "I thought you were right behind me. But when I turned around, you were gone." She smiled. "I knew you'd find me. I—"

She stopped, catching the alarmed expression on Billy's face. "What's wrong? You're all scratched. What happened?"

The whole story burst out of him in a flood of words. "A vampire, Kylie. In wolf form. It attacked me. Outside that burned-out house. But I drove a stake through its chest. I killed it."

He grabbed her hand and started to pull her to the house. "Come on. You have to see it. I want to prove to you there are vampires here. I want you to see with your own eyes."

"But, Billy—" She pulled back.

"Hurry, Kylie. I'm going to prove it to you."

She narrowed her eyes at him. "Did you hit your head or something? You're talking crazy. Everyone knows there are no real vampires."

"Come on. Hurry." He tugged her harder.

She rolled her eyes and groaned. But she followed him.

He led the way through the trees. The chittering of bats overhead grew louder as they neared the house. A distant howl floated eerily over the whisper of the wind.

Through the trees, Billy spotted the dark outline of the burned-out house. "Here it is!" he told her. "Right in front. You'll see, Kylie. You'll see I'm telling the truth."

He led the way out of the trees. Then he pulled her across the wet grass. "There—!" He pointed.

And then they both gasped in shock.

Chapter 16

ROMANCE

"There's nothing there!" Kylie exclaimed.

Billy bent down and examined the spot. No sign of his struggle. No sign of the vampire wolf. The grass wasn't even bent.

"It—it must have been over here," he stammered. He ran across the grass, first one way, then the other. He trotted up to the house, then back, trying to retrace his steps.

Nothing here. Not a sign.

Kylie rolled her eyes again. "Lame, Billy. Really lame," she groaned.

"You have to believe me—!" Billy cried shrilly.

"It's not a very funny joke," Kylie said. She took his arm and pressed her cheek against his shoulder. Then she spoke in a tiny voice. "Are you trying to scare me so you can be my big, brave protector?"

"No. Really—" Billy insisted.

Clinging to his arm, she rubbed her nose against his cheek. "Come back to the log," she whispered. "It's such a pretty spot."

She doesn't believe me, Billy realized. She thinks it was some kind of joke. If I keep insisting, she'll just think I'm some kind of a jerk. Or that I'm crazy.

He let her pull him back to the low hill overlooking the water. "We—we have to get back," he stammered, gazing out toward the water.

"It's early. Let's see what else there is to explore," Kylie suggested.

"No way," Billy answered. "We're going back to the boat. There's nothing here."

Nothing but vampires, he thought.

"Just sit with me for one minute," Kylie begged. "Then we'll leave, I promise. It's so beautiful here."

Billy stared at her. He wanted to leave. Wanted to run to the boat as fast as he could. But Kylie looked so beautiful sitting there, moonlight washing over her red hair.

She patted the log beside her.

Billy sat down. The bark felt damp and crumbly beneath him. The cold air pressed in around them.

When did it get so foggy? Billy wondered. He could barely see anything beyond the clearing. It seemed as if he and Kylie were alone in an island of fog.

Billy suddenly felt drowsy. A little dizzy.

Kylie moved closer to him on the log. "See? Isn't this nice?" she asked softly.

Billy tried to focus his eyes on Kylie. The pale moonlight played over her face. She was truly beautiful, he realized. Her face belonged on a fashion model—or a movie star. And the way her long red hair glowed . . .

Kylie leaned over and kissed him.

She pulled back. Gazed into his eyes, smiled, and kissed him again.

A long, slow kiss.

This is wild, Billy thought. She is really *hot!*

The kiss continued. Billy felt as if he were drifting . . . falling . . .

Bats fluttered overhead. Billy paid no attention to them.

He was drifting . . . drifting . . .

He felt Kylie's mouth move from his lips to his neck.

Chapter 17

"NOT JAY!"

Billy stood up. "I—I feel so strange," he said. "Kind of dizzy. We'd better go."

"Billy, sit down," Kylie insisted. "Billy—please."

He shook his head, trying to force away the strange dizziness.

Kylie jumped up. She stepped closer. And kissed him again.

The world seemed to be spinning. The dark trees whirled.

Billy wanted to give in to it, to let the spinning world take him, whisk him away. He wanted to stand in that moonlit clearing and kiss Kylie forever.

No.

He shook his head.

The spinning stopped.

"I've really got to get home," Billy insisted, pulling Kylie toward the boat.

Holding her hand, he pulled her through the trees. He could tell Kylie was annoyed by the way she slapped the branches out of her way, not saying anything. They passed the burned-out houses. Hurrying onto the dock, Billy climbed down the ladder, then helped Kylie into the boat.

Billy rowed toward the mainland in silence. Whenever he glanced at Kylie, anger flashed in her eyes.

She is spoiled, Billy decided. She pouts whenever she doesn't get her own way.

Bats fluttered overhead, swooping low over the tiny rowboat. A dark cloud inched its way across the face of the moon. The night grew darker and darker as Billy rowed toward the shore.

He guided the boat to the long dock and tied it up. Kylie hadn't said a word since they left the island. She seemed to be studying him.

Billy climbed onto the dock, then reached down to pull Kylie up. Her hand felt cold, as if the island's dampness had seeped into her skin. The last yellow sliver of the moon disappeared behind the black cloud as they stepped from the dock onto the beach.

Billy moved carefully, trying to see where he was going.

So dark.

"I don't know why we had to leave so early," Kylie complained, pressing her forehead against his shoulder.

"I do," Billy muttered. "That island was dangerous."

Kylie laughed. "Dangerous?"

Billy didn't want to be teased. He stomped on ahead.

"Billy—?" he heard Kylie call. Then he heard a small shriek. "Billy!" Kylie cried shrilly.

Billy spun around and ran back to Kylie. "What is it?"

"Billy, look . . ." Kylie whispered, holding her hands to her face, staring down in horror at the sand.

"Oh no!" Billy groaned.

A boy. Sprawled on his back in the sand. Staring up lifelessly at the sky. His neck twisted, twisted at such a wrong angle.

"Noooo!" Billy wailed, dropping down beside the boy. "Not Jay! Please—not Jay!"

Chapter 18

PIZZA FOR A VAMPIRE

*B*illy leaned over his friend—and gasped again.

"It—it *isn't* Jay!"

"I recognize him," Kylie said weakly, her hands still pressed tightly against her cheeks. "Don't you remember? He's the guy April went off with earlier tonight."

"Yes—Rick," Billy remembered.

He leaned over the body. Brushed swarming sand flies off the boy's face.

His eyes stopped at the throat.

At the two puncture wounds in the neck. A tiny drop of blood clung to each hole.

Rick's face was as white as flour.

He's been drained, Billy realized. Completely drained.

"This is so . . . awful," Kylie moaned.

"And what about April? Where is she? Do you think something has happened to her?"

Billy couldn't take his eyes off the twin red puncture marks.

No, he thought. Nothing has happened to April. Nothing has happened to that vampire.

Not yet.

The next night Billy met his friends at the Pizza Cove. Everyone was there—Nate, Jay, Irene, Kylie, and April—sitting at two tables pulled together.

"After we found Rick's body, Billy called the police from a pay phone on Main Street," Kylie explained. "I was really freaked out. I couldn't even talk. But he was great."

Yeah, great, Billy thought glumly. And I was questioned for more than an hour. It's a good thing Kylie was there to back up my story. That's the second murder I've been involved in. The second one . . .

Billy studied his friends' faces as Kylie told them about Rick Tyler. Jay seemed even more tired than last night. He sat beside April, staring at the others with bloodshot eyes.

He can hardly hold his head up, Billy thought. This is really bad news.

Billy studied Jay's neck. He didn't see any bite marks. But he was sure they were there.

Billy shifted his gaze to April. How many sips has she taken? he wondered. Three sips, and Jay becomes a vampire. How close is he?

April shredded her paper napkin, tearing off little pieces and putting them in a pile. Her hands shook.

She seems really upset, Billy thought.

But he knew she was acting.

"I can't believe I was the last person to see Rick alive," April said tearfully.

Jay offered her a slice of pizza.

"I can't eat," she declared, shaking her head. "I'm too upset."

Of course she can't eat, Billy thought. Vampires can't eat food.

He studied April's face. Her smooth white cheeks. Not a trace of a tan. She had never been out in the sun, he knew. If she saw sunlight, she would die.

Nate sighed. "You know, all I want is to have a great summer," he said. "But nobody is having fun. There are police all over the beach and the town. Everyone is so upset about the two murders. I even heard someone else say *vampires* are the killers!"

"I'm really sick of hearing about vampires," Irene declared.

"It's so stupid," Kylie agreed. "Everyone

knows there is no such thing. I can't believe people are so superstitious."

"They're real," Billy told her. He kept his eyes on April. "Don't let anybody tell you they're not."

April glanced at him, her expression blank, as if she wasn't interested in what he was saying. What a great actress, Billy thought. She should be the star of the play.

"You don't really believe that, do you?" Irene asked.

"Yes, he does," Jay chimed in. "Billy has been talking about vampires ever since we got here!"

Nate and Irene laughed.

Billy felt a hot ball of anger growing in his chest. He forced himself to stay calm. Ignore them, he told himself. Don't get into an argument about it.

Irene took Nate's arm and pulled him out of his chair. "You promised to take me dancing," she told him.

"I'm a total klutz," Nate protested.

"No problem," Irene informed him. "I'll show you everything you need to know."

Nate shrugged. "Anyone else want to come?"

They all shook their heads.

After Nate and Irene left, Billy turned his attention back to April. He studied her as she joked and flirted with Jay. She was pretty cute, with straight blond hair and beautiful emerald eyes.

She's a vampire, he reminded himself.

Not a cute girl. Not a nice girl.

A vampire.

"Have some pizza," Billy said. He shoved a slice of pizza in April's face.

She reacted with disgust.

He knew she would.

"No thanks," she said, waving it away. "I can't eat. Really."

"No. Try it," Billy insisted. He shoved it under her nose again. "It's really excellent." He wanted to make her squirm.

"No. Really," April said sharply, pulling her head back.

"Just a taste," Billy insisted.

"Give her a break, man," Jay cut in. "What's your problem, anyway?"

Billy slowly lowered the pizza slice to the plate. He kept his eyes on April.

She knows that I know, he realized.

She knows that I know the truth about her. She's probably thinking about how she can shut me up.

Billy felt a chill of fear.

I'm in danger now, he told himself. Real danger.

But not if I act first.

PART THREE

BILLY
AND KYLIE

Chapter 19

VAMPIRES EVERYWHERE

*T*he next evening, Kylie and Irene strolled on the beach.

Irene is looking really happy and excited, Kylie thought, studying her friend. I guess she's made real progress with Nate. She probably thinks she's going to win our bet.

Irene bent to pick up a horseshoe crab shell. She peered inside it, then tossed it back to the sand. "How is it going with Billy?" she asked.

Kylie sighed. "Billy has been a problem," she admitted. "He keeps seeing vampires everywhere."

Irene's eyes lit up. "That *is* a problem!"

Both girls laughed.

"I'm meeting Nate later at Swanny's," Irene

revealed. "I think tonight could be . . . delicious." An evil grin spread over her face.

"I came so close last night," Kylie told her. "So close I could taste the nectar. But . . ." Her voice trailed off.

"But what?" Irene demanded, brushing back her hair, letting the ocean wind flutter it.

Kylie shook her head. She frowned. "I don't want to talk about it. I'm so hungry, Irene. So hungry."

Irene started to reply. But Kylie dove to the sand.

Kylie struck quickly—and grabbed a plump sea gull off the ground. She tightened her hand around its feathery throat.

The bird flapped its wings. It let out a sharp squawk.

Its cry was cut off by Kylie's fingernails as they dug deep into its flesh and ripped out the bird's throat.

As dark blood flowed over the white feathers, Kylie buried her face in the open wound. Slurping loudly. Drinking frantically. Pressing the warm bird over her face as she drank.

"Hey—how about sharing?" Irene demanded, reaching out her hand.

Kylie hungrily drank some more. Then she dropped the gull into Irene's hand. Irene raised the bird's torn body to her face and drank.

"Save some for April," Kylie said, wiping blood off her cheeks with both hands.

"She can get her own," Irene replied, her face buried in the dead sea gull.

"Jay, hi. It's me," Billy said, balancing the phone between his shoulder and ear. He bent over and tied his sneakers as he talked.

"How's it going?" Jay asked dully.

"I've got to talk to you," Billy replied. Jay still sounds tired, he thought with alarm. I hope I'm not too late.

"Can't really talk now," Jay said, so low Billy could barely hear him. "Got to meet April. I've got to—"

"That's what I want to talk to you about," Billy interrupted. He finished tying the sneaker and sat up, grabbing the phone.

"April?" Jay asked, confused.

"Yes. Listen to me, Jay. I know it's hard to believe. But you're in danger. Real danger."

On the other end of the line, Jay let out a weak laugh.

"I'm totally serious," Billy insisted. "Don't laugh, Jay. Just listen to me."

"I'm not feeling well," Jay said, clearing his throat. "I've got to go, man. Really."

"Just listen to me!" Billy insisted. "Don't you

wonder why you're so tired? Don't you wonder why you feel so weak? It's because of April."

A long silence on Jay's end. Then, "Huh?"

"April is a vampire, Jay," Billy declared heatedly. "I know it's hard to believe. But she's a vampire. She's drinking your blood, a sip at a time. If you don't watch out—"

"Cut it out!" Jay snapped. "I told you, I'm late. I've got to go. These dumb vampire jokes—"

"It's not a joke," Billy insisted desperately. "I told you what happened last summer. It's happening again, Jay. You've got to listen. I'm trying to save your life. April will—"

"Billy, take a deep breath, man," Jay interrupted. "Listen to me. I'm feeling tired because I have the flu or something. All this vampire talk—well . . . Are your parents there?"

"Well . . . yeah," Billy replied.

"Have you talked with them about this vampire stuff?"

"No," Billy told him.

"Maybe you should," Jay urged. "Maybe you should tell them that you're troubled by thoughts about vampires. They can help you, Billy. You really should give your parents a chance to help you."

He thinks I'm crazy, Billy realized.

Here he is, in danger for his life—and he's worrying about me.

"I've got to go," Jay said. "April is here. At the condo. Maybe I'll see you later, Billy."

"No—!" Billy cried. "Don't go! Don't go with her, Jay! Please—!"

Billy heard a click. The phone went dead.

A raindrop hit Billy's cheek. The icy bead of water trickled down his neck, making his skin tingle.

The fog seemed to be thickening. It blanketed the town, turning the street lamps into misty blurs of yellow light.

Billy turned down Main Street. He searched for Jay and April in the Pizza Cove. Not there.

Billy pushed open the door of Swanny's ice-cream parlor and arcade. The damp night disappeared immediately. Loud music blared around him. Kids were laughing and talking over the music. Bent over video games.

Nate and Irene sat on a low bench near the jukebox, clinging together. Irene had her arms around Nate's shoulders. She was kissing him.

Billy walked quickly over to them. "Hey, do you guys know where Jay and April are?" he asked.

Irene turned. She had lipstick smeared over her mouth. Nate shot Billy an annoyed look. He signaled with both hands, as if to say, 'Get lost.'

"Have you seen him?" Billy demanded.

"Not since yesterday," Nate replied impatiently.

"I really need to find him," Billy said. "He's in danger."

That caught Irene's attention. She pulled away from Nate and raised her eyes to Billy. "Danger?"

"April is a vampire," Billy blurted out. "I tried to warn Jay. But he won't believe me. She's a vampire and she's—"

"Give it a rest, man," Nate said impatiently. He scowled at Billy.

"No. Really—" Billy started.

Nate narrowed his eyes menacingly. "I mean it. Give this vampire stuff a rest. You're starting to sound weird, Billy. You're starting to sound really messed up."

Nate turned back to Irene. She smiled at him and slid her hands behind his neck, pulling his face to hers.

No help there. Billy glanced around the arcade. He searched the crowd for Jay and April.

A familiar squeal of laughter caught his attention. Lynette. She was playing an old Ninja Turtles game at the back of the arcade, near the fire exit.

A lanky, older boy, dressed entirely in black, leaned over the game as Lynette played.

No! It's impossible, Billy thought, recognizing the boy immediately.

A face I'll never forget. Never.

The face of pure evil.

"Nate!" Billy cried. He grabbed Nate by the shoulder and tried to pry him away from Irene.

"Hey! Give me a break!" Nate protested angrily.

"Nate—your sister!" Billy cried. "There's a guy over there with your sister—that guy in black—"

"Oh, that's just Jon," Nate told him. "I know him from last summer. He said he'd watch Lynette if I got him an early tee time tomorrow at the golf club."

"Nate, you can't leave Lynette with that guy!" Billy shrieked. He tugged Nate's arm again. "He's a vampire, Nate. I know he is! He's a vampire! He'll—"

"Whoa! Let go!" Nate jerked his arm away. He jumped to his feet, and loomed angrily over Billy, bumping him with his powerful chest. "Back off, Billy. I mean it."

"Listen to me—" Billy wailed.

"You're messed up, man," Nate told him. "You're seeing vampires everywhere you look. Get home, Billy. Get yourself home, okay? You're really messed up."

"Maybe we should help him home," Irene suggested. "Or maybe we should get him to a doctor or something."

"Nooo!" Billy cried. "I'm telling the truth! I'm not crazy!"

He spun away from them—in time to see the tall boy pull Lynette out the fire door in back.

Chapter 20

CHEST PAINS

"No—stop!" Billy screamed.

A few kids turned from their games to stare at him.

Billy pushed his way through the crowded aisle to the fire door.

Jon is a vampire, he told himself. Jon is the vampire who murdered Joelle.

Now where is he taking Lynette?

He pushed the heavy fire door open with his shoulder, stepped outside, and let the heavy door slam behind him. The rain had stopped, but the air remained cool and wet.

He stood in a small alley behind the arcade. Where are they? he thought frantically. Where did Jon take her?

He let his eyes search up and down the alley. No vampire.

Would he really hurt a little kid? Billy thought.

"Help me!"

Lynette's cry. From nearby.

Which way? Billy wondered. He spun around. Tried to tell where the cry came from.

"Help me!" He heard it again.

He's taking her to the beach, Billy realized. The deserted beach.

Billy sprinted from the alley. The beach was a short distance away. But it seemed to take forever, even running full speed. Finally, he clambered down the wooden steps that led to the sand.

His sneakers dug into the rain-wet sand as he started to run.

"Lynette? Lynette?"

No reply.

He stopped short.

A dying fire still smoldered near the shore. Drenched by the rain. The last sparks of somebody's interrupted beach party.

And in the dim orange light of the low fire, Billy saw Lynette, sprawled on her back on the sand. Arms straight out. Head tilted at an angle. Not moving.

"Hey—!" Jon stepped forward to meet Billy. "Stay away from here!" he shouted, his voice deep and menacing over the steady rush of ocean waves behind him.

"I—I know you," Billy stammered.

The closer Jon came, the taller he appeared. His eyes flashed as he narrowed them on Billy. A dark orange flash, the same color as the dying fire.

You're dead, Billy thought. *You're dead, Jon. I killed you last summer. After you killed Joelle.*

But no.

Billy had obviously failed.

"I know you," Billy repeated. "You killed my girlfriend. You killed Joelle."

The vampire sneered. "Was that her name?"

"You—you—" Billy couldn't choke out any words.

The vampire snorted. "Bad break, kid. But that's the way it goes sometimes," he said with a smirk.

"You killed her—and you didn't even know her name," Billy managed to say.

"Sometimes I like fast food," the vampire said, snickering at his own joke. "I don't always have time for introductions."

Billy turned his gaze to the fire, thinking hard, the rage burning in his chest. "How can you joke about it?" he cried. "How can you joke about taking human lives?"

The vampire shrugged. "You're interrupting

my dinner." He motioned to Lynette, sprawled motionless on the sand. "Maybe I'll save the little girl for a late-night snack. You can be the main course." He let his fangs slide down over his lower lip.

His orange eyes flashed brightly. He began to rise up over Billy, floating off the ground.

"No—!" Billy uttered a sharp cry and dove past him.

Stumbling, sliding on the wet sand, Billy hurtled to the dying embers. A weathered piece of driftwood had just caught fire. It burned dully, purple-red flames licking up from the charred log.

Billy grabbed the burning log off the sand— and whirled around.

As Jon dove for him, Billy swung the flaming log at the vampire's chest.

"Die!" Billy screamed. "Die! Die! Die!"

But to Billy's shock, the vampire grabbed the burning log with both hands.

He tugged it easily from Billy's grasp. Held it by one end.

Billy's arms flew up to protect himself.

Too late.

With a howl of triumph, the vampire thrust the log forward—and shoved it through Billy's chest.

Chapter 21

DEAD ON THE SAND

*B*illy gasped and staggered back.

His legs collapsed, and he dropped to his knees on the sand.

He waited for the pain, for the crushing pain to sweep over his body. He waited for the darkness . . .

He glanced down at his chest, expecting to see the gaping wound. To his surprise, he saw no wound staining his shirt.

Instead he saw that the driftwood had crumbled. The log, soft and decayed, had fallen to pieces when it struck his chest. Tiny, burning chunks glowed on the sand in front of him.

Billy sucked in a deep breath of fresh ocean air. I'm alive, he thought. I'm alive—and I'm not giving this vampire another chance.

With a cry of rage, he rushed at Jon.

The vampire opened his fanged mouth in an angry hiss.

Billy leapt at him. Dug his fingers into the vampire's bony shoulders. Pushed him. Pushed him back.

Back.

The vampire hissed again and lowered his fangs to Billy's throat.

Driven by a rage he had never felt before, Billy pushed him. Back. Back.

And with a burst of strength, he heaved the startled vampire onto the purple, burning embers of the fire.

Jon landed hard on his back. The fire sizzled beneath him.

The vampire's eyes flared red. He shot his hands up to the sky as if reaching for something to pull himself up.

His mouth opened in a silent cry as the flames leapt around him.

And then, as Billy gaped in amazement, black smoke rose up from the sand. Billows of black smoke surrounded the thrashing vampire.

Billy took a step back, his heart pounding, his legs weak.

The smoke billowed into a thick curtain. It darkened the sky and the beach.

Behind the black curtain, Billy heard a fluttering sound. The fluttering became louder. Billy recognized the flap of wings.

Bat wings.

A red-eyed bat flapped up from behind the smoke. It rose over Billy, its tiny, round eyes glaring angrily. Dripping yellow saliva, the mouth opened in a shrill, menacing hiss.

And then the bat flapped away, swooping rapidly out over the sand, out to the ocean.

Billy stood watching it, swallowing hard, choking back his fear, his face drenched with sweat despite the coolness of the night.

Breathing hard, his chest heaving, he turned to Lynette. She hadn't moved, he saw to his horror. She lay lifelessly, sprawled on her back in the cold, wet sand.

"Hey!" A familiar voice made Billy jump.

He turned to see Nate and Irene running toward him across the sand. Nate, so big and powerful, came charging over the sand like an angry bull.

"What are you doing here? Where's Lynette?" he called to Billy.

Nate stopped a few feet from Billy. His mouth opened in a startled cry when he saw his sister on the sand.

"No—!" Nate cried, turning accusingly to Billy. "Oh no! What did you *do* to her?"

"Nothing!" Billy screamed. "I didn't—"

Nate dropped down beside Lynette on the sand. "No!" he cried. "No! Oh no! She's dead!"

Chapter 22

IS BILLY CRAZY?

Nate jumped to his feet, his features twisted in a rage. With a frightening roar, he grabbed Billy by the shoulders.

"No—stop!" Irene pleaded.

"What did you do to her?" Nate shrieked, spitting in Billy's face in his fury. "Are you sick? Are you *sick?*"

A low groan from the sand made everyone freeze.

Billy turned and saw Lynette's eyelids flutter. She turned her head and groaned again.

"She's alive!" Nate cried happily. He let go of Billy and dropped down beside her again. "Lynette? Are you okay? Did Billy hurt you?"

She gazed up, dazed, still unable to speak.

"I didn't do anything!" Billy insisted shrilly.

"It was that vampire. I tried to save her from that vampire!"

Nate glared up at him. "I'm warning you, Billy. Get away from here," he said through clenched teeth.

"I warned you that Jon was a vampire," Billy told Nate. "He dragged Lynette here. But I fought him off. I didn't hurt her, Nate. I saved her life. You've got to believe me!"

Billy heard Irene utter a "tsk-tsk" behind him.

"You're crazy, Billy," Nate cried, still on his knees beside his sister. "All this vampire talk is crazy. And sick. You left the mental hospital too soon. You're still sick. Now, get away from here. Go get help. Get yourself some help. Or I'll pound you. I really will."

"You've got to believe me!" Billy pleaded. "You've—"

Lynette opened her eyes wide. She sat up groggily, staring around. "Where am I?"

"Lynette will tell you the whole thing," Billy insisted desperately. "Lynette will tell you about Jon, about how he dragged her out here to the beach."

Nate leaned over his sister. "Is it true?"

"Tell him," Billy pleaded. "Tell him, Lynette. Tell him about the vampire."

Lynette blinked several times. She shook her

head hard as if trying to see clearly. "I . . . can't remember," she said finally in a tiny voice.

"Tell him what happened. Please!" Billy insisted.

"I was in Swanny's," Lynette said, thinking hard. "I was playing a Ninja Turtles game. And . . . that's all I remember."

"You don't remember Jon?" Billy demanded weakly. "Tell him about Jon, Lynette. About the tall boy dressed in black. He pulled you out here to the beach—remember?"

Lynette shook her head. "I remember seeing him in Swanny's. But I don't remember anything else." Tears welled in her eyes. "I don't remember coming out here."

Nate turned accusingly to Billy.

"She doesn't remember because Jon clouded her mind," Billy told him. "He clouded her mind. That's why she was lying unconscious on the beach. The vampire—"

"I'm going to cloud *your* mind!" Nate cried, jumping to his feet.

"It was the vampire!" Billy screamed. "You've got to believe—"

He didn't finish his frantic cry—because Nate's fist came crashing into his jaw.

Chapter 23

A PAIN IN THE NECK

*B*illy walked alone through town the next evening.

Fog floated low and thick over the street, hiding Sandy Hollow behind a misty white curtain. It pressed in on Billy, closing him inside his own private cloud.

He rubbed his sore jaw. His thoughts were bitter.

No one believes me, he told himself. Everyone thinks I'm crazy. I'm totally alone.

Something cool and damp grabbed his foot.

It oozed around the straps of his thongs.

Billy glanced down in surprise. Wet sand. He had reached the beach without realizing it.

Pulling off his thongs, he went barefoot, enjoying the feel of the sand as it squished up between his toes. The waves crashed against the stone jetty somewhere off to his left.

Flapping.

From behind him.

Billy spun around. This time he would be ready for the bats. But he saw only one. It swooped past him and continued on its way, a black speck in the fog.

Lost in his own thoughts, Billy drifted along the beach.

Now he heard another sound.

Behind him.

Someone following him!

He spun around.

No one there.

I'm letting myself get spooked, he concluded. There's no one here but me.

Billy took another step. Stopped.

A shape stood in front of him.

Shimmering in the fog.

"Who's there?" he asked.

"Just me," Kylie replied, stepping into focus.

"I—I didn't see you come up. What are you doing out here?" he asked.

"I didn't feel like being home alone. Mind if I walk with you?"

"No. Of course not."

They strolled along the beach, surrounded on all sides by a misty white wall of fog.

137

Kylie grabbed his arm. "Listen. Hear that?"

"A foghorn."

"I love that sound, don't you?"

"It's sort of mysterious," Billy replied.

Kylie stepped in front of him. She reached out and slipped her arms around his neck. "I love the fog," she whispered. "No one can see us."

Billy gazed into her eyes, thinking how beautiful Kylie was. Beautiful Kylie. Her perfect face framed by all that red hair. Her eyes seeming to shimmer even in the fog.

She kissed him. Long and slow.

I have no time for this, Billy thought. I have to find April. I have to save Jay.

Chapter 24

KISSES FOR JAY

"Ouch!" Billy pulled away. "What was that?" He rubbed his neck.

"Probably a mosquito," Kylie said. "They always come out when it's so wet."

"Sorry I jumped like that," Billy told her.

"I hate mosquitoes," she said. "Such miserable little bloodsuckers."

Billy rubbed the spot. "I have to get home," he told Kylie.

"You're always running off," she complained.

"I'm sorry. But I really have to call Jay. I'm kind of worried about him."

She leaned against him. "Maybe we can get together tomorrow night?"

"Sure," Billy replied. "Or the night after.

Where are you headed? I'll walk part of the way with you."

"Thanks, but I think I'm going to walk on the beach for a while."

Billy started toward his house. Glancing behind him, he saw that Kylie had already disappeared in the fog. A moment later a loud sound startled him.

A hissing screech.

Full of rage.

A cat?

A bat flapped over his head. Billy glanced up, but the creature was invisible in the fog.

Billy tried to phone Jay as soon as he got home. No answer.

He climbed into bed, thinking about Kylie—about her hot, hot kisses.

Am I crazy? he wondered. Most guys would jump at the chance to go out with such a beautiful girl.

But I can't get too close, he decided. I can't forget why I came back to Sandy Hollow.

That vampire came too close to hurting Lynette.

And April is too close to Jay. That's more important than all Kylie's kisses.

I can't let Jay become a vampire.

* * *

Jay sat on the beach, listening to the waves tumble and roar as they slid over the jetty and rolled onto the sand. The sound was distant, like a dream.

A girl slipped her arms around his neck.

Was she really there?

Or was she imaginary, nothing but wisps of fog?

She kissed his face. Then his lips.

"April," he whispered. "April."

The fog seemed to be lifting. Only patches now. Moonlight twinkled on the surface of the waves. Everything shimmered. Everything.

Jay tried to focus on the girl. The waves reflected the moonlight, making dancing lights in her hair. She seemed fuzzy, unreal.

Why was everything such a blur?

She kissed him. Again and again.

A gentle breeze stirred the night air, clearing away the last wisps of fog. But that one spot, right where he sat with the girl, seemed covered in mist.

Her kisses continued, as if they would go on forever. Yes, he thought. Forever. Forever.

He whispered her name again. "April."

Her lips left his, sliding down to his neck.

Jay felt twin stabs of pain in his throat.

But they seemed far, far away.

141

Part of a dream.

Not real.

"April," he murmured. "April, what are you doing to me?"

Chapter 25

BUG BITES

Billy drifted along Main Street, scanning the faces of the people coming in and out of brightly lighted shops, hoping to spot Jay.

He had been phoning Jay's condo endlessly. But no one answered. He had to assume the worst—that Jay was with April.

He knew Jay was under April's spell.

April had clouded Jay's mind.

Her hold on him would be hard to break.

I have to keep trying, Billy thought grimly. I can't give up. I can never give up.

A blond girl and a muscular boy with sandy hair stepped out of an antique store.

"Nate!" he called, hurrying toward them. "Irene!"

Two strangers turned to him with puzzled expressions on their faces.

Billy mumbled an apology, and the couple hurried away.

Where is everyone? Billy wondered. Why can't I find my friends?

He checked the beach. At least it wasn't foggy tonight. The moonlight made it easy to see everyone there. But he spotted only a few couples. No one he recognized.

He had thought a lot about how to destroy April. He knew he had to get her into the sun. Or drive a stake through her heart while she slept. But how could he do it alone?

If Jay would help him, he knew he stood a chance. Then there would be a way.

Billy decided to check Jay's condo. He made his way to the row of condos, found Jay's place, and rang the bell several times.

Nobody home.

He stood on Jay's doorstep, trying to figure out where everyone could have gone. He pushed the doorbell button again even though he knew he was wasting his time. He heard its muffled ringing from inside the empty condo.

Billy almost jumped when the door opened.

Jay gazed at him through half-shut eyes. He appeared weak and pale, as if he might fall down at any moment.

"Man, you look really awful!" Billy exclaimed.

"I *feel* awful."

Billy stepped inside. No one else there. "Where are your parents?" he asked.

"They're having dinner with some people they met on the beach. I couldn't go. I think I'd hurl if I tried to eat anything."

They sat down on the couch.

"Were you out partying last night?" Billy asked.

"Last night?" Jay frowned. "I don't think I was out too late. I can't remember. I went walking on the beach with April, and everything else is sort of . . . foggy."

Billy studied his friend. So pale. So fragile-looking.

Nothing on Jay's neck, but Billy knew the mark of the vampire was there, below the collar, out of sight.

"You can't remember because a vampire clouded your mind," Billy declared.

Jay shook his head. "Not that vampire junk again," he groaned.

"I'll show you!" Billy cried. "I'll make you believe me!"

He yanked Jay's collar down so hard the top button of his polo shirt popped off and sailed across the room.

"Hey!" Jay protested. "What are you doing?"

"There!" Billy announced. "I knew it!"

Two marks in the soft flesh of Jay's neck.

Red. Swollen.

Puncture holes.

"Look at your neck!" Billy cried. "Look at the bite marks!" He dragged Jay to a mirror.

"What about my neck?"

"Look at it! Don't you see it?"

"See *what,* man? I don't know what you're talking about."

"The bite marks."

Jay sighed. "You want me to believe that those bug bites are vampire bites?"

"Those are puncture marks."

"Those are bug bites!" Jay cried impatiently. "All this vampire talk is crazy, Billy. It's bad enough being sick during summer vacation. I don't need you cracking up again. I can't deal with this!"

"I'm trying to save you before it's too late. Before you become one of them."

"I'm not too worried, Billy. I've had lots of bug bites, and I haven't turned into a bug yet."

"April has messed up your mind so you don't see things clearly. They can do that, Jay. So when you look in the mirror you see bug bites. That's what she *wants* you to see."

Jay glared at him. "April? You think April is a vampire? You're crazy! You leave April out of this. She's the first girl who ever liked me. If you ruin it for me—"

"Listen to me," Billy interrupted. "I know why you've felt so bad lately. When April drinks your blood, she leaves behind some of her poison. It makes you sick. And eventually it will turn you into one of *them*—a vampire!"

Jay let out a hoarse cry. "Right. And if I go out during a full moon, I'll become a werewolf."

"I'm serious, Jay! You're in a lot of danger. If April drinks your blood one more time . . . that might be all it takes!"

"Leave me alone, man," Jay snapped. "Take a hike. Really. You're totally disturbed."

"I'm trying to help you!" Billy yelled. Anger surged through him. How can I make Jay listen? How can I make him see what's happening to him?

"Get out of here, Billy!" Jay repeated.

Billy leapt to his feet. "I tried," Billy said with a sigh. "I tried."

He whirled around and stormed out the door. I have to prove it, Billy decided. I have to find some way to prove I'm right.

How do you *prove* to someone that his girl-friend is a vampire?

"Hi, Billy," whispered a husky voice.

Billy raised his eyes to Kylie. She grinned at him.

"Where did you come from?" he asked in surprise.

"I was right here all the time," she answered. "There's a barbecue on the beach. Want to go?"

"Sure," he answered.

"Good," Kylie replied. She slipped her arm through his and licked her lips. "I'm starving."

Chapter 26

BILLY'S BIG NIGHT

*A*pril pushed the sand around with her bare toes. The sun had set half an hour ago, but the sand still felt warm against her foot. She heard voices. Glanced up. A boy and girl strolled along the beach, chatting.

Kylie and Irene had pulled her aside at the barbecue last night. The three of them had agreed to meet tonight on the beach as soon as it turned dark. To compare notes on how their bet was going.

Kylie and Irene were half an hour late. April wondered if they had forgotten. After all, they had been sort of distracted at the barbecue last night.

April grinned, thinking about it. She had enjoyed watching Kylie and Billy. Kylie did everything she could to get his attention. But Billy seemed distracted, upset about something. Kylie had been really angry, and it showed.

I'm surprised she didn't grab him and bite his neck right there, April thought.

Bats flapped overhead. April gazed up, thinking it might be Kylie and Irene. But they were just bats, flying from the island for a night of feasting on the mainland bugs.

It was a clear night. The moon was no longer full, but it still shone brightly. April could see the beach clearly.

She spotted two figures approaching across a large dune. Kylie and Irene.

"You're late," she informed them when they reached her.

"So what?" Kylie asked. "You're immortal. What's a little time to you?"

"We're going to be late for play practice if we don't hurry," April said.

"Kylie doesn't care," Irene stated. "I told her we were late, but she had to try on three different pairs of shorts and half a dozen tops."

Kylie yawned.

"It's too bad we can't see our reflections in the mirror," Irene went on. "Poor Kylie really misses admiring herself."

"At least I've got something to admire," Kylie shot back.

"Will you give me a break," April begged. "I don't want to waste the whole night while the two of you snap at each other. I'm hungry."

"She's right," Irene agreed. "We're supposed to be comparing notes."

"Okay," Kylie replied. "How are you two doing?"

April grinned. "I'm going to get Jay alone after play practice tonight."

Irene shook her head disgustedly. "I haven't gotten Nate alone long enough to get a sip. His bratty little sister is always tagging along! I'm so happy his parents took her home. They said she was having nightmares about vampires!"

April shook her head.

"You're both going to lose," Kylie declared. "Billy doesn't suspect a thing. I've been taking it slow." She smiled, showing the tips of her needle-sharp fangs. "But tonight is his big night."

PART FOUR

VAMPIRE TRAP

Chapter 27

APRIL IS CAUGHT

"**D**on't even talk to me," Jay told Billy as soon as he entered the theater for play practice. "I don't want to hear any more talk about vampires—unless you're talking about the play."

"Jay"—Billy began. But his friend strode away across the stage. Billy watched him, knowing he couldn't give up, no matter how angry Jay got. I have to keep trying, Billy thought.

Rehearsal was late getting started. Some of the kids hadn't shown up yet—including Kylie, Irene, and April. Ms. Aaronson paced back and forth along the front of the stage, glancing at her watch.

Billy shifted his attention back to Jay. He looks even worse, Billy saw. Jay's eyes were glazed and watery. He was so pale he was totally white, as if he'd never been in the sun in his entire life.

Like a vampire.

How many more sips before Jay became one of them?

After rehearsal, Ms. Aaronson asked Nate and Irene to stay for a few moments so they could work on their scenes.

Billy spotted Jay and April leaving together through the main exit. He started to go after them, but someone blocked his path.

"It's nice out," Kylie told him. "Want to take a walk?"

"Yeah," Billy replied. "Let's catch up with April and Jay."

They stepped out of the theater, and Billy looked around for Jay and April. He spotted a boy and girl making out by the corner of the building. Kids were strolling toward town on the narrow road. Others headed directly for the beach.

No sign of Jay.

Had April lured him behind the theater? Into the woods?

Was she drinking his blood at that very moment?

"Come on," Kylie urged. "Let's go into town."

Billy scanned the sidewalks as he followed her,

searching for Jay and April. He saw kids holding hands. Eating hot dogs. Checking out the window of the Beach Emporium.

"Do you want to rehearse our scene?" Kylie asked.

"I only say a few words," Billy muttered. "They're not hard to remember."

"But I've got a lot of dialogue to memorize," Kylie reminded him. "I could use the help."

"Okay," Billy agreed. "But I don't have my script. I left it at the theater."

"Run back and get it," Kylie said. "I'll meet you on the beach by the wooden steps."

Billy trotted back to the theater. He expected to find Nate and Irene still going over their scenes with Ms. Aaronson. But the theater was dark.

Bet Ms. Aaronson locked it up, Billy thought. He tried the door.

It opened easily. Billy stepped inside the lobby, letting the door slam behind him. The theater was black. He felt his way along the wall.

Billy tried to remember where the light switch was. He pictured the lobby in his mind. The ticket booth. A Coke machine. The doors leading to the seats. Where was the light switch?

A noise. Off to his left. A click.

"Who's there?" he called.

No one answered.

Billy's heart began to hammer in his chest.

Why is the theater open but all the lights off? he wondered.

He slammed against something big and hard. It clanked and rattled.

The Coke machine.

Billy let out his breath. He went back to searching for the light switch.

Another sound. A soft patter. It seemed to echo off the walls and surround him.

"Hello?" he called, surprised at how shaky his voice sounded.

Get a hold of yourself, he thought. It's probably just mice.

He moved along the wall, feeling for a light switch. Finally his fingers found the edge of a switch plate. Then the switch itself. He flipped it up.

The overhead lights came on.

Billy blinked rapidly, trying to adjust to the sudden brightness. He took in his surroundings. He stood in the lobby. Alone. If there had been mice, they had scurried for cover the moment the lights came on.

The rest rooms, Billy thought.

Was someone hiding in the rest rooms?

He pushed open the door of the men's room and stepped inside. Empty. He tried the women's room. No one there either.

Okay, he told himself, quit this messing around and get your script. Kylie is going to wonder what happened to you.

He stepped through the double doors into the auditorium. Rows of empty seats stretched out in front of him. All facing the empty stage.

His footsteps echoed in the deserted theater as he walked slowly toward the stage.

He had left his script in the wings, on a wooden stool.

He started up the steps to the stage. A large bundle of cloth lay on the floor toward the rear of the stage. Billy glanced at the material. Gray streaks on it. Familiar gray streaks.

It was a backdrop painting of a grimy basement where the vampires kept their coffins.

It had taken some of the kids hours to paint it. Who would have rolled it up like that and tossed it to side of the stage?

Billy hurried over to the backdrop. I should spread it out, he decided. It will get wrinkled if it is left all bunched up like that.

He grabbed the edge of the backdrop and pulled hard.

To his surprise, the cloth had not been rolled up. Merely placed on top of something.

On top of what? Billy wondered.

He peered down—and saw the body.

A woman's body.

Billy felt his stomach tighten into a hard knot. "No!" he gasped.

Ms. Aaronson. Sprawled on her back. Her face as gray as the backdrop that had covered her.

Billy climbed shakily to his feet. He leaned over her—and saw the two bite marks on her neck.

Not another one, Billy thought. Another vampire murder.

A movement caught Billy's eye.

Was the vampire still here?

His heart pounding, he spun around.

And saw a figure hiding in the shadows.

April.

Chapter 28

APRIL AND BILLY

She stood in the deep shadows, near the back of the stage. Her eyes wide. Her mouth open.

Fangs! Billy thought. Are her fangs still down?

April's hands flew up to cover her mouth. She made a gagging sound and turned away from the pale body on the stage.

Should I tell her? Billy thought. Should I tell her she doesn't have to pretend in front of me?

Should I tell her I know she is a vampire?

No. She knows that I know.

Billy strode across the stage to where April stood. He grasped her arm and spun her around.

April gave a little shriek when her gaze fell on the body. She took a stumbling step backward.

"What are you doing here?" Billy asked her. "I thought you were with Jay."

"I was," April said. Her breathing came in sharp gasps. "But he was too tired. He had to go home. I came back to the theater because I wanted to ask Ms. Aaronson something. But I . . ." Her voice trailed off.

She stood there, trembling, pretending to be bewildered and scared.

She killed Ms. Aaronson, Billy knew. Just as she killed the others.

"I just got here," April insisted. "Only a minute ago. I came in and found Ms. Aaronson. Then I heard a noise. And I hid—because I thought it was the killer. I was so terrified. But it turned out to be you."

"I'm going to call the police," Billy told her.

She nodded.

Billy ran to the phone in the lobby and dialed 911. The dispatcher promised to have an officer there in a few minutes. The police will be *thrilled* to see me again, Billy thought bitterly.

He slammed the phone down. Turned—and found April standing a few feet behind him. His stomach tightened.

It suddenly dawned on him.

She's a vampire. And I'm alone with her.

Billy tried to move back.

Banged into the wall.

April's eyes locked onto his. She took a step forward.

Another.

"Billy," she whispered. "Billy . . ."

Chapter 29

BILLY SETS A TRAP

*A*pril threw herself into his arms. "Would you hold me? I can't stop shaking. Just hold me?"

For a moment, Billy stood still. Is this a trick? he wondered. Does she plan to attack me, too? Then his arms automatically closed around her.

She really is trembling, he saw.

And cold . . . her skin is so cold.

Cold as death. The phrase repeated in Billy's mind. Cold as death.

Vampires are already dead.

April pulled back and gazed at Billy. He imagined her fangs sliding down. Her lips pulling back from her teeth.

Her fangs piercing his skin.

A siren shrieked outside the theater. Billy gave a sigh of relief. The police had arrived.

Was that disappointment on April's face?

"The police are talking about closing the beach and sending everybody home," Billy announced. He, Jay, and Nate were skipping stones over the water.

It had been three days since Ms. Aaronson's murder. No killer had been found. No connection between the deaths. No official word on how they had all died.

But the police know, Billy thought. They would never close the beach unless they knew about the vampires.

He had promised Jay that he wouldn't mention vampires anymore. Billy and Nate had made an uneasy truce. But Billy knew that Nate wouldn't put up with any vampire talk, either.

At least Jay hasn't gotten any weaker, Billy thought. He still looks terrible. But April must be leaving him alone.

For now.

Frustrated, Billy picked up a round, flat stone and skipped it off the top of a breaker as it rolled into shore.

Nate tried to imitate him. But Nate's stone went *plop* and vanished into the ocean. "How come yours skip and mine sink?" he asked.

"Skill," Billy replied.

Jay chuckled. But Billy knew it was forced laughter. Nothing seemed funny lately. Not after so many people had died.

"Will they really close the beach?" Jay asked.

"Wow," Nate said, shaking his head. "You mean we'd all have to go home?"

"That's right," Billy replied.

"But I have the condo to myself now that my parents took Lynette home," Nate complained. "If they send us home, I'd have to give it up. And I'll have to say goodbye to Irene."

It's better than seeing her murdered by vampires, Billy thought.

"Speaking of Irene," Nate said, glancing at his watch, "I'm supposed to meet her at the Beach Emporium. Catch you guys later."

Billy watched Nate trot down the beach. Then he turned to Jay.

"Did April tell you that Ms. Aaronson had bite marks on her neck?" he asked.

Jay kept walking. He didn't answer.

"I saw them," Billy insisted. "Did April say anything about it?"

"No," Jay answered. "Now drop it!"

Billy grabbed Jay's arm and pulled him to a stop. "Let me prove to you that April is a vampire—before she makes you one, too. I know a way to prove it."

"Oh, please," Jay moaned. "Give me a break."

"You know you're sick," Billy pressed on.

"I've got the flu or something."

"How about your neck?" Billy demanded. "Have those 'bug bites' gotten any better? Or are they worse?"

Jay groaned.

"If I can prove it, you have to believe me," Billy insisted. "And if I don't prove it, I'll shut up. I'll never say another word about vampires. And I'll leave April alone."

"Fine!" Jay yelled. "I give up! You won't drop this until I let you try, will you? Okay, go ahead. But don't blame me if you end up looking like a total jerk."

Great! Billy thought. Finally.

"What are you going to do?" Jay asked.

"First, you have to promise not to be alone with April until this is over," Billy told him.

"You're kidding, right?"

"Look, Jay, she's already bitten you once or twice. Three times and you're a vampire."

"I'm not going to quit seeing April."

"You don't have to. You just have to make sure someone else is there whenever you're with April."

"That's just what I need—a chaperone."

"Jay—"

"Okay, okay. I'll do it."

"Promise?"

"Yes, I promise. Tell me what you're planning to do."

"It's easy," Billy explained. "What kills vampires?"

"I'm not driving a stake through April's heart."

"We don't have to do that. What else kills them?"

"I don't know."

"Sunlight."

"Sunlight," Jay repeated.

Billy leaned forward to explain exactly what he had in mind. When he was almost finished, he heard a sound behind him.

He turned quickly. And saw April standing behind him. Her eyes burned into Billy's.

How long has she been standing there? Billy asked himself.

How much did she hear?

Chapter 30

GOODBYE TO A VAMPIRE

"Hey—what's up?" April said cheerfully. "I thought I might find you guys here."

Billy studied her face, trying to tell if she had overheard his plan.

She stepped close to Jay. "You guys just hanging out? Want to take a walk or something?"

Jay glanced at Billy. "I can't," he told April. "I'm still feeling really wrecked."

"I've got to get home, too," Billy told her.

"Okay," April replied. "Maybe I'll see you guys tomorrow sometime." She turned and started toward Main Street. "Oh," she cried, turning around. "I almost forgot. There's going to be a huge clambake on the beach tomorrow. Want to go?"

"Sounds excellent," Jay answered.

"See you then," April replied.

"It's okay." Billy sighed as soon as April had disappeared from view. "She didn't overhear our plan."

"She *better* not have," Jay growled. "If you mess things up between April and me, I'll never forgive you. Really."

"Hey man, where've you been?" Jay asked as Billy joined him the next night on the beach. "The clams are all gone."

Billy shrugged. "I got hung up. I'll pick up a burger somewhere."

"Hey, Billy," April called. She and Jay sat on the sand with some other kids.

It was well after midnight, and the beach party had spread out all over the beach. Billy was relieved that Jay seemed to be keeping his promise not to be alone with April.

He surveyed the scene. Kids talking and tipping back cans of soda. A pyramid constructed from the empties—six feet tall and growing. A group of guys and girls trying to play volleyball with a glow-in-the-dark ball. The steamy aroma of charcoal smoke and clams lingered in the air.

Tonight is the night, Billy thought.

Tonight is your *last* night, April.

He had to trick April into going somewhere

with Jay—but not just anywhere. It had to be a place without windows.

And then he had to keep April there until dawn. Until the sun came up.

Lightning flashed out over the ocean. Followed by a distant rumble of thunder. Dark, billowing clouds filled the night sky.

Rain, Billy thought. If it rains, my plan will work. If it rains, I can get April to go inside. And stay there until the sun comes up.

Billy saw that Kylie had joined them. She stood between Nate and Jay, listening to their conversation.

Rain, Billy thought. Please rain.

Kylie slipped beside Billy. "Let's go for a walk along the beach," she whispered in his ear.

"No. Sit down. I don't feel like walking right now," Billy told her.

I've got to stay close to Jay, he thought. So I can make sure April doesn't manage to get him alone. And I've got to be ready.

Kylie's eyes locked onto his, and Billy felt the urge to go with her. But he resisted. "I just want to hang out with everyone," he said.

Kylie lowered her eyes. Billy realized she was pouting.

Another rumble in the distance. More thunder.

Black clouds rolled low over the sky.

Please rain, Billy urged again.

But the thunder and lightning remained in the distance.

By three in the morning, the clambake had become a wild party.

"I think everyone is trying to forget about the murders," Kylie commented. Billy nodded.

"Billy, can we please go for a walk?" she asked again. "I don't know why you want to sit in one place all night."

Billy sighed. But his answer was lost in a sudden clap of thunder. He glanced up to see a flash of lightning rip through the sky directly overhead, followed by another rumble of thunder.

The downpour came an instant later.

Kids scurried for cover, shrieking and laughing. "Billy!" Kylie cried. "This way!" She sprinted toward Main Street with a group of kids.

Perfect!

Billy turned to Jay. "Let's do it," he said.

Jay nodded grimly. "April, come on," he shouted over the noise of the rain. "The theater is the closest place."

The two of them dashed for the theater. Billy followed. Rain pelted him, the wind-driven drops stinging his eyes. Billy glanced over his shoulder. Good. No one behind them.

He sped past Jay and yanked open the theater door.

April and Jay rushed inside as lightning sizzled overhead and a thunderclap shook the building.

They stood in the lobby, breathing hard. "What a wild storm!" April exclaimed. "I'm drenched."

"Me too!" Jay cried, stamping his feet. He looks totally wiped out, Billy saw. That run must have been too much for him.

"Let's go down to the basement," Billy suggested. "It's warmer down there."

The sign on the door to the basement read THEATER PERSONNEL ONLY, but it was never locked. Billy flipped on the light, and they started down a set of wooden steps.

Billy closed the door behind him. The basement had two exits. The one they had entered through. And the one that led directly outside.

No windows.

The perfect place, Billy thought.

It was crammed with props that had been used in plays over the years. Costumes covered in clear plastic hung on a rack along one wall. Hat boxes lined the shelf above it. One was marked ENGLISH TOP HAT. Another read GIRLS' BONNETS.

Billy sat down on a wooden box. April and Jay found a couple of stools. Now I stall for time, Billy thought. We've got to keep April here until sunrise.

They were all soaked. April fussed with her soggy hair. Billy saw that April was not wearing a watch. Everything was working out perfectly.

An icy look from Jay. Hang in there, Billy thought. I know you don't like tricking April. But you'll see that I'm right—the minute the sunlight hits her.

They talked for a while. But Jay seemed too tired to keep up much of a conversation.

"What time is it?" April finally asked.

"Three-fifteen," Billy lied, glancing at his watch. It was really much later—almost daybreak. Another few minutes, he thought. And the vampire will be history.

"I'd better go soon," she told Jay. "I'll really be in trouble if I don't get home before dawn."

You sure will, Billy thought. "You can't go out in this storm," he protested.

"We can't even tell if it's still raining," she complained. "There aren't any windows. Let's go upstairs."

"The storm couldn't be over this soon," Billy insisted. "Not the way it was coming down."

"I'll go upstairs and check," April declared.

"Let's send Jay instead," Billy suggested. "He'll fall asleep if he doesn't move."

April chuckled. "Yeah, go see if it's still raining," she told Jay. "And get me a Coke while you're there?"

Jay hesitated. Come on, Billy thought. Don't quit on me now.

Jay stood up slowly. He trudged up the stairs. He looked half dead.

He returned five minutes later with three cans of Coke. "It's still coming down," he announced, handing the drinks around. He nodded to Billy.

Billy knew what that meant. The rain had actually stopped. The sun had come up.

Time for April's test. A test Billy knew she would flunk.

"It's time," he announced.

He grabbed April. Coke sloshed out of her can and onto her T-shirt.

"What are you doing?" she demanded sharply. "Let go of me!" She dropped the can. Liquid squirted out, spattering his shoes.

Jay stood still, staring at April.

"Go on, Jay!" Billy shouted. "Open the door!"

"Billy!" April screamed. "Let me go!"

Jay strode to the door leading outside, turned the knob—and glanced back at April.

"Jay!" she cried. "Help me!"

Billy dragged her to the door. "Open it!" he instructed Jay.

April fought fiercely, kicking, scratching. Trying desperately to wriggle out of his grasp. "What are you *doing?* Let me go!"

Jay yanked open the door, revealing concrete steps leading up to ground level. Bright sunlight reflected off the steps.

April gasped. "You said it was still raining!" she cried. "What's going on here? What are you *doing?*"

She struggled fiercely to get away from Billy. He tightened his grip on her arms.

And shoved her through the open door.

Into the sun.

April screamed. Sunlight streamed over her.

And Billy watched her head burst into flame.

Chapter 31

APRIL IS DEAD

Billy gasped and shut his eyes. He could see the white light through his eyelids.

When he opened his eyes again, he cried out in shock.

April stood bathed in bright sunlight, staring back at him angrily.

"Huh?" Billy's mouth dropped open. April hadn't exploded, hadn't burst into flame.

Had he imagined it? Had he *wanted* it so much that he hallucinated it?

Her blond hair glowed in the bright morning sunlight. She glared at Billy, shielding her eyes with one hand. "Satisfied?" she demanded in a whisper. "Satisfied?"

Jay gave Billy a hard shove that sent him into the concrete wall. "You jerk," Jay snapped. "You stupid jerk. You almost had me believing you."

Billy opened his mouth to reply—but couldn't find the words.

April shook her head. She stepped past them both, back into the basement. "I'm not a vampire," she said flatly. "You guys satisfied?"

Jay scowled at Billy. "You really are messed up, man. You really need help." He shoved Billy again.

"Guys, give me a break," April murmured. "You're going to ruin everything."

She dropped wearily onto a tall stool. Billy and Jay sat down across from her. "You're going to ruin everything I've worked so hard on," April said with a sigh.

"I—I don't understand," Billy stammered. "I thought I did. But I don't understand anything."

"You're sick," Jay insisted, still scowling at him. "I feel like such a jerk for listening to you. I'm really sorry, April. I knew you weren't a vampire. There's no such thing as vampires. But Billy kept after me. He wouldn't give it a rest. He—"

"But there *are* vampires here!" April interrupted heatedly. "That's why I'm here. That's why I've pretended to *be* a vampire."

"April—" Billy started.

"My name isn't April," she revealed. "It's Diana. Diana Devlin. April Blair was my cousin."

"Your cousin?" Billy cried.

"My cousin and my best friend," Diana revealed sadly. Her voice caught on the words.

"What happened to April?" Billy asked softly.

"She came here last summer," Diana replied, staring at the floor. "The vampires got her. They turned her into one of them. April confided in me. She knew she could trust me. She . . ." Diana's voice broke.

She cleared her throat and started again, still keeping her eyes lowered. "When she came back to Shadyside after the summer, April was a vampire. She hated it. She hated what she had become—a creature, not a person. A creature who feeds on other people.

"She told me all about it. At first, I didn't believe it. But she made me believe. And then, I felt so helpless. There was nothing I could do for her. No way I could help her.

"Finally, April solved her problem for herself. The only way she could." A tear slid down Diana's cheek. "One morning she stepped out into the sunlight. She killed herself."

"Wow. Oh wow," Jay murmured sadly, shaking his head.

Silence for a while.

Billy broke the silence. "Why are you here?" he asked Diana. "Why did you take April's name? Why did you come to Sandy Hollow this summer?"

"I came back to kill the vampires who murdered my cousin," Diana replied through gritted teeth. She wiped another tear off her cheek. "I want to pay them back for what they did to April. I want to kill them all!

"They believe I'm April," she continued. "I look a lot like my cousin. They believe I'm April. And they believe I'm a vampire."

She sighed. "I've had a couple of close calls. That boy Rick—he almost ruined everything."

Billy remembered Rick. He had found Rick's body—his drained body—in the sand that same night.

"But Rick recognized you as April!" Billy said.

Diana shook her head. "No. He recognized me as *Diana*. He almost ruined everything. That's why I dragged him away as fast as I could. Before he could call me by my real name."

"And then—you *killed* him?" Billy gasped. "To keep your secret?"

Diana narrowed her eyes at him. "Of course not. I'm not a murderer. I didn't kill Rick. I think Kylie did."

Billy jumped to his feet. His heart thudded in

his chest. His whole body shook. "Kylie?" he cried shrilly.

Diana nodded solemnly. "Kylie and Irene are vampires," she revealed. Her eyes burned into Billy's. "You didn't guess that? You really didn't?"

Billy felt too shocked to reply. He shook his head, murmuring the two names. "Kylie? Irene?"

"I think Kylie killed that girl Mae-Linn. And she killed Rick."

"But—why?" Billy demanded.

"For the nectar. Kylie wasn't getting anywhere with you, Billy. And she was so thirsty."

"I can't believe this," Jay chimed in, shaking his head. "I can't believe we're sitting here talking about people we know being vampires. I must be dreaming this. I have to be dreaming!"

"I wish," Diana murmured sadly. "But Kylie and Irene really are vampires. And I have fooled them into believing I'm one of them. I've fooled them so that I could get close enough to kill them both."

"Whoa. Wait a minute." Billy stepped forward to confront her. "There's only one problem with your story, Diana or April, or whoever you are."

Diana jumped to her feet. "Well?"

Billy pulled down Jay's shirt collar. "See these puncture holes? These aren't *pretend* holes, Diana. You've been hanging out with Jay, going out with him practically every night. And look at him. Look at this wound on his neck."

Billy's features hardened into anger. "How do you explain *that*, Diana? How do you explain what you've done to Jay?"

"I didn't do that," Diana insisted heatedly. "I don't have fangs. I don't drink blood. I think Kylie or Irene did it to Jay."

"But I haven't been with them!" Jay protested.

"I think one of them has been following you and me, Jay," Diana explained. "Probably Kylie. I think Kylie has been doing this to you—late at night after I leave."

"But I would know!" Jay cried. "I would see Kylie. I would recognize her!"

Diana shook her head. "No, you wouldn't. She clouded your mind. She probably made you think that she was *me*. I—I think Kylie killed Ms. Aaronson too. Just for the nectar. The vampire's thirst is so powerful. I've seen Kylie and Irene do such *disgusting* things—just to satisfy their thirst."

Billy shook his head. "Kylie. Kylie." He murmured her name again. "I came back to Sandy Hollow to kill vampires, too. But I never suspected her. I was so stupid . . ."

He thought about his walks alone with Kylie on the beach. He thought about her kisses.

And he shuddered.

"Let's go get them," he said to Diana. "We'll do it tomorrow. Let's find them while they're asleep in their coffins and kill them both."

"It won't be easy." Diana sighed.

She had no idea how right she was.

Chapter 32

RETURN TO VAMPIRE ISLAND

Raindrops pattered softly on the dock as Billy untied the line, then jumped into the rowboat with Diana. The boat rocked gently from side to side.

He and Diana wore raincoats with plastic hoods. Billy adjusted his hood as he settled into the boat.

I'm finally doing it, he thought. I'm finally going to get my revenge on the vampires.

It was only noon, but the dark clouds hovering low in the sky made it nearly as dark as night. Billy slipped the oars into the oarlocks and began rowing.

Diana sat in the stern, facing him. Her jaw was set, her expression determined, her eyes hard.

Billy was sure that nothing would stop her from killing Irene and Kylie if she got the chance.

He wished Jay had come along. He knew they needed all the help they could get. But after staying up all night the day before, poor, weakened Jay had to get some sleep.

Billy studied the two nylon backpacks that lay on the floor between them. Each one contained the same items. Wooden stakes. And a hammer. The tools for destroying vampires.

He had bought the stakes at a local carpenter shop. Made of the hardest oak, they were long and slender, tapered to an incredibly sharp point.

"I would feel better with bright sunlight," Diana declared.

"It's supposed to rain like this all week," Billy replied, dipping the oars into the water and leaning back as he pulled on the handles. "And I'm off from work today. This is the only day we can do it."

Diana nodded. "But it's such a dark day . . ."

"Most vampires can't stand *any* daylight," Billy assured her. "The sun doesn't have to be shining. That's what the books I read all say."

The rain continued to fall in a steady drizzle. The raindrops pattered on Billy's rain slicker. The ocean seemed as calm as a lake. The boat rocked gently as it glided toward the island.

"Are you scared?" Billy asked.

"Yes," Diana replied. "But I can do it. I've already killed one vampire. I know can do it again."

"You mean here?" Billy cried. "This summer?"

"Yes. His name was Eric. I killed him with a wooden stake."

Billy stared at her in astonishment. She looked so fragile and sweet. And she had already killed more vampires than he had. She didn't say anything more about it, so he didn't ask.

Glancing over his shoulder, Billy saw the island looming above them. This was the first time he had seen it in the daylight. It seemed dark and menacing even now.

"It looks evil," Diana observed.

"It *is* evil," Billy replied.

Before long he could make out the tall trees that lined the shore.

An icy drop of perspiration slid down his forehead. He shivered.

Billy rowed toward the spot where he thought the old dock stood. He scanned the shore.

Where's the dock? he wondered. Why can't I see it?

The boat drifted closer to shore.

"It's gone," he muttered.

"What is?" Diana asked. "What's gone?"

"The dock. Look."

A few sawed-off pilings poked out of the water, marking the spot where the dock had stood. He couldn't find a place to tie up the boat.

"Vampires must have destroyed the dock," Billy decided. "They wanted to make it harder for anyone to sneak up on them while they sleep."

Diana's eyes narrowed in fear. "Do you think the vampires suspect something? Do you think they might suspect someone is coming here to get them?"

It wasn't a question Billy wanted to think about.

He rowed along the shoreline, looking for a spot to beach the boat. There seemed to be nothing but big rocks and sheer drop-offs.

"Can we swim ashore?" Diana asked.

"No anchor. The boat would drift away. We'd have no way to get back."

Billy pulled on the oars, heading for the ocean side of the island. The waves grew bigger, the rowboat riding high on the swells, then dropping into the troughs. Ocean water burst over the bow, splashing into Billy's face.

"This little boat wasn't made for going into the ocean," Diana said tensely. She held onto her seat with both hands.

He spotted a change in the shoreline. "Look!" he exclaimed. "An inlet."

He rowed toward it, the boat rising and dipping, rocking and twisting. It felt like a roller coaster ride. Only more frightening. No one ever drowned on a roller coaster.

The water calmed as the boat slid into the inlet. Trees rose above them, sending gnarled branches over the water.

The water here looked black. The boat glided through it silently. Billy remembered the spooky howls and cries he had heard the last time he was here. But this time an eerie quiet had settled over everything.

"Over there." Diana pointed to a spot where the forest floor sloped gently down to the water. The perfect spot to leave the boat.

Billy guided the rowboat to the spot, its bow sliding onto the soft earth. He leapt out of the boat and tied it to a tree.

Diana tossed him the two backpacks, then climbed onto shore.

Billy took a deep breath. The air felt damp and stale. "You ready?"

Diana nodded. Her eyes glowed with determination.

Billy hadn't realized how small the island was. It only took a few minutes before he spotted one of the burned-out beach houses. He and Diana started toward it. As they walked, more of the blackened houses came into view.

"How will we ever find their coffins?" Billy wondered out loud. He glanced at his watch. "It's already afternoon. We should probably split up. It'll be faster."

Diana shifted her backpack. "You really think that's a good idea?"

"You afraid to be alone?"

She hesitated, then nodded. "Yeah, I guess I am. A little. When I killed that vampire Eric on the beach, I was on my own territory. This is different. This is *their* world. It's a lot scarier than a beach."

"Can you still go through with it if we find them?" Billy demanded.

She fixed her gaze on him. "Yes," she declared. "For April."

"It really would be faster if we split up," Billy insisted. "Don't worry. The vampires are asleep. If you find them, all you have to do is call me, and I'll be right there."

Diana nodded. "You're right. I'm sorry. I'm being a wimp." She smiled bravely. "Come on. Let's find Kylie and Irene. I'll go this way. You go that way."

They separated and Billy watched as Diana

stepped into the blackened shell of a cottage. Then he picked out a charred house on his right, strode boldly to the doorway—and stepped inside.

So dark inside. He blinked, eager for his eyes to adjust to the dark.

And realized he was not alone.

Chapter 33

WHO IS IN THE COFFINS?

Billy gasped.

And stared at the face that peered back at him from the shadows.

No time to grab the backpack. No time to pull one of the wooden stakes from the pack.

Billy staggered back—then realized he was staring at a painting.

A large painting, tilted on the charred wall. A woman, open-mouthed, screaming. Her hair flying around her head.

Billy swallowed hard. I just let a painting terrify me, he realized. What am I going to do when I come face to face with a *vampire?*

He studied the painting for a moment. She looks the way I feel, he thought.

He turned away from it, his heart still pounding. Most of the interior walls had been reduced to ashes, so he could see the entire structure from where he stood. Nothing there. Nothing but ashes.

He turned and made his way quickly from the house.

The island was less creepy in the daylight.

But only a little.

Fear made his heart pound and his legs feel weak. But he forced himself to keep moving.

He made his way from house to house. Many had been completely gutted by fire. He searched them quickly, knowing he wouldn't find anything.

He carefully examined any houses that were still intact, peeking into cupboards, peering into closets. No signs of Kylie or Irene.

Where could they be?

He stopped in a small clearing and glanced at his watch. Three forty-five. Billy shook it. It had read three forty-five the last time he looked.

The second hand wasn't moving. The watch had stopped.

How long have I been here? he wondered. How soon does the sun go down?

The rain had stopped, but dark clouds still filled the sky, making it hard to guess the time. Billy figured it must be almost evening. If they didn't find Kylie and Irene soon, they would have to get off the island.

He wondered where Diana was. He had not seen her since they split up.

Billy turned slowly in the clearing, trying to decide on his next move. A distant animal cry, shrill and frightening, floated to him from the woods. The first animal he'd heard since coming ashore.

Does that mean it's almost night? he wondered. Do the animals come out only after dark?

He checked his watch again, just to make sure. Three forty-five.

Should I yell for Diana? he wondered. They still had to make their way back through the trees to the boat.

The boat! Billy thought. Where is it? Which direction is it in?

Suddenly feeling panicked, he let his eyes search the trees. He stood in a small, grass-covered clearing. On one side the grass lay flattened.

Some kind of path?

Yes. Someone had worn a trail there. Recently.

I don't know how long we have before the vampires rise, Billy thought. Should I follow the path, or try to find Diana?

Would the path lead him to the vampires?

Maybe . . .

He followed the path through the woods, knocking branches out of the way. Thick vines grew along the sides. They clung to his skin and clothing as he made his way through.

He stopped in front of a tall tangle of vines and bare tree branches. Thick as a wall.

A wall?

Had someone built this here?

Billy peered through the vines. Yes. He could see something on the other side. He reached into the wall, pushing branches aside.

"Oww!" He cried out as thorns sank into his palm. Billy snatched his hand back and stared at it in horror. Two small dark holes. Deep punctures. Like a vampire bite.

How am I going to get in there? he wondered.

The wall of vines curved around some kind of structure. Protecting it.

This has to be their house, Billy thought. I have to get through.

He pulled a wooden stake from his backpack. Thrust it through the thorns. Working it around, he made a hole large enough to see through.

Yes! A house.

A charred house behind the wall of vines.

It was burned, but not badly. The walls and roof appeared to be solid. Working furiously,

Billy enlarged the hole until it was big enough for him to crawl through, then put away the stake.

Thorns snagged his backpack and clothes, leaving long scratches on his skin. He ignored them. He didn't take his eyes off the burned-out house.

Billy glanced up at the sky. The rain had stopped. The clouds moved quickly, as if a strong wind were blowing them.

How soon till sunset? he wondered. How much time do I have?

He ran to the door of the house. He grabbed the knob. It turned easily. The door swung open about an inch, then stopped. Something on the inside was holding it closed.

Billy pushed. The door opened a little farther. He shoved it with all his strength. Whatever blocked the door scraped across the floor.

The door stood open about a foot. Billy squeezed through the opening.

Total darkness, except for the light from the open door.

Billy waited for his eyes to adjust. The first thing he was able to see was a dresser that had been shoved against the door.

Slowly the room came into focus. Billy stood in what had been the kitchen. It smelled stale, like an old campfire.

His eyes darted around the room. He couldn't see much. The room seemed to be completely bare.

Billy stepped through the doorway into the next room. It was even darker here, damp and musty. Deep shadows crept from the corners, pools of blackness that seemed to absorb the dim light spilling in from the kitchen.

He examined the walls. Someone had nailed boards over the windows.

From the inside.

Billy peered around the room, trying to see into the shadows.

"Whoa," he whispered. In the corner. What was that?

The shadows were so deep that Billy could barely make out the three shapes. He moved quickly across the room—and saw three long, rectangular boxes.

Coffins.

Billy's breath caught in his throat. A wave of terror swept over him, holding him in place, holding his eyes on the coffins.

Yes. Yes. I have found what I am looking for, he told himself. I have found the resting place of the vampires.

But when does the sun go down? Do I have enough time to destroy them before they awaken?

Billy stared at the coffins, his pulse racing.

I cannot stand here gaping. I have to look inside, he told himself.

He took a deep breath. Reached out with trembling hands. And lifted the lid on the coffin closest to him.

Chapter 34

HAMMER TIME

Billy tugged the coffin lid up. Forced himself to stare inside.

Girls' clothes.

Nothing but clothes.

He picked up a short skirt, a midriff top. He rummaged around, sifting through bathing suits and jeans.

Did the clothing belong to Kylie and Irene? Some of it did look familiar.

Had he found Kylie and Irene's coffins? Had he been lucky enough to find the right place?

Open the other coffins, Billy instructed himself. Hurry! You've got to see. You've got to know.

The remaining two coffins rested end-to-end, only a couple of inches apart.

Billy grabbed both lids at once, one in each hand.

With a hard tug, he yanked the lids up. Then he bent to peer inside.

Trembling, his breath coming in ragged gasps, Billy stared into the coffins.

Kylie and Irene.

Yes.

Sound asleep. Eyes shut. Faces calm, at peace. Sleeping in ancient dirt.

Hands folded across their chests.

Billy stared at them, swallowing hard. Stared as if he'd never seen them before.

They appeared so innocent.

Kylie stirred, shifted her position slightly. She smacked her lips, revealing the tips of her fangs. Dreaming of food? Billy wondered. Dreaming of human blood? *My* blood?

Don't stand there! a voice inside Billy screamed. *Time is running out! Do something! Before it's too late!*

But the sight of them seemed to hold him in place. He couldn't take his eyes off them. Kylie with her beautiful red hair. Irene's golden curls glowing even in the dim light.

Billy stared at them, stared without moving, without breathing—as if the two vampires were able to cloud his mind even in their sleep.

Snap out of it! he warned himself.

199

Billy blinked, shook his head.

Hurry!

Frantically, Billy slipped off the backpack and tossed it to the floor. He ripped at the cloth, unable to get it open.

I've got to calm down, he thought. Calm down.

The zipper tore. The bag fell open, spilling wooden stakes onto the floor. Billy snatched one up and grabbed the hammer.

Gasping for breath, he held the pointed tip of the oak stake over Kylie's heart. Extra-hard wood. Sharpened to a point as deadly as the tips of Kylie's fangs.

Billy's hands shook so hard he wasn't sure he could swing the hammer. Or hit the stake with it.

Can I do this? he wondered. Can I really do this?

He raised the hammer.

Chapter 35

BREAKFAST

*B*illy raised the hammer. It felt so heavy in his trembling hand. As if it weighed a hundred pounds.

He lowered it.

I can't do this, he thought. I can't pound a pointed stake into a person's chest.

He peered down at Kylie.

She's not a person, Billy told himself. She used to be a person. But now she's a deadly vampire. She could be a thousand years old!

And how many innocent people has she murdered in all her years?

He took a deep breath. Once again, he leaned over Kylie and placed the tip of the stake in the center of her chest.

He positioned the hammer over the stake. He raised the hammer. Held it shakily over the stake.

Counted silently to three.

And Kylie opened her eyes.

"Oh!" Billy uttered a shocked cry and staggered back. The hammer and stake fell from his hands and clattered loudly on the floor.

Kylie sat up, instantly alert. Her eyes narrowed on Billy.

An angry hiss escaped her throat. "Billy . . ." she whispered. "Billy . . ."

The whisper appeared to wake Irene. She sat up alertly, wide awake in an instant, and gazed at Billy.

Billy took another step back. He opened his mouth to speak. But realized he had nothing to say.

"Billy . . ." Kylie whispered, a smile spreading across her face. "Billy . . ."

"Billy . . ." Irene echoed in a harsh whisper. "Billy . . ."

The two vampires floated up from their coffins.

"Billy . . . Billy . . ."

He tried to run—but stumbled over the hammer and went tumbling into the wall.

"Billy . . . Billy . . ."

They floated over him, both chanting his name.

"Billy . . ." Kylie whispered in his ear.

She ran her tongue over her lips. "Billy . . . so glad you decided to drop in for breakfast."

Chapter 36

KYLIE'S TURN

*I*rene held one arm. Kylie gripped the other.

Billy struggled frantically to free himself.

"Billy . . . give up, Billy," Irene whispered. "You can't get away from us. We are stronger than you can possibly imagine."

Billy ignored her. He fought desperately, twisting, turning. But their fingers dug into his flesh, their powerful grip unbreakable.

He took a deep breath, pulled back his arms—and shoved Kylie with all his strength.

She stumbled, letting go.

He swung his whole body, slamming Irene with his shoulder.

Her grip loosened. Only a tiny bit. But enough.

Billy whirled to his left.

He was free!

"You're strong for a mortal," Irene growled. "But not strong enough." She lunged for him.

Billy turned, started to run—and tripped over the backpack.

He fell hard, landing on his elbows and knees.

Wooden stakes clattered across the floor in all directions.

The vampires floated over him, hissing and drooling.

Their eyes glowed with rage, with hunger.

Irene sprang at him.

Billy rolled to the left. His fingers wrapped around one of the stakes. He snatched it up.

Irene flew down on him, her fangs aimed at his throat.

And Billy shoved the stake up toward her chest.

He closed his eyes.

Irene's weight crashed down on him.

I missed, he realized. I missed her heart.

I'm dead.

Silence for a moment.

And then Irene let out a piercing howl. As Billy opened his eyes, she flew to her feet. Then she staggered backward, the wooden stake jutting from her chest.

No blood, Billy saw. Not a drop.

Irene screamed. She tossed back her head in a long howl of pain.

And as she howled, she began to age.

Her hair turned white.

Her face wrinkled and sagged.

As Billy stared in amazement, Irene's hair fell out, until nothing remained but a few white wisps, wriggling like snakes on her pink scalp.

Irene collapsed to the floor.

Her legs shriveled to stumps. Her face caved in. The skin flaked off, revealing gray bone.

Her screams continued from her open-jawed skull.

And then the skull crumbled into dust.

And the room was silent.

Billy stared at the puddle of dust on the floor.

Kylie's shriek of rage made him spin around.

She grabbed Billy under the shoulders and lifted him off his feet.

"My turn," she whispered. "My turn."

Chapter 37

KYLIE HAS EYES FOR BILLY

Kylie's nails dug into Billy's skin. He felt the hot tips of her fangs on his neck.

"Billy!" Diana's voice. From outside. "Billy, the sun is setting! We have to go!"

Still holding Billy, Kylie spun around in a circle, her long red hair flying behind her. "Who is that?" she demanded.

Diana burst into the room. "Billy!" she screamed.

Kylie whirled to face Diana. "April—what are you doing here?"

"Let him down!" Diana cried.

"But, April—" Kylie protested. "You're one of us. Why are you helping Billy?"

"I'm not April—and I'm not one of you," Diana told her.

Kylie's eyes flashed. "You will be," she snapped. "As soon as I finish with him." Her fangs slid down all the way as she lowered her face to Billy's throat.

Billy's hand shot out. With all his strength he held Kylie away. Her fangs hovered inches from his throat.

Kylie's face twisted with rage. She snapped her jaws like an animal, trying to sink her fangs into the soft flesh of Billy's neck.

With a terrified gasp, Billy raised his right hand—and jabbed two fingers into Kylie's eyes.

"Yeowwwwwwww!" She opened her mouth in a howl of pain.

Her hands flew up to her eyes. Billy plunged to the floor.

Howling, Kylie covered her eyes with both hands.

Billy turned and saw Diana at the window. "Now, die!" Diana shrieked at Kylie. "Die! Die!"

With a cry of rage, Diana ripped a board off the window.

A bright square of afternoon sunlight slanted into the room.

The orange light washed over Kylie.

She never uncovered her eyes.

As her skin began to shrivel and peel off, she

held her eyes tightly, bending in pain, howling, howling.

Until her head rolled off her body. Her body tumbled to the floor, across the square of orange light, melting, flaking, shriveling.

To dust.

Billy swallowed hard, staring in disbelief as Kylie's body fell apart. Only the eyeballs remained, staring up accusingly at him.

Staring. Staring. Until they too melted and became wet, green puddles on the floor.

"It's over," Billy said with a sigh, moving quickly across the room to Diana. "It's over." He hugged her, hugged her tightly.

They stood there, still shivering, still trembling, hugging until the sun disappeared behind the trees.

Chapter 38

THE PARTY IS OVER

"Come on," Diana urged, dragging Billy into the Pizza Cove.

It was nearly ten o'clock, and the place was still packed. Kids were talking and laughing and gobbling down pizza. Billy spotted an empty booth in the corner, and they slid into it.

Billy felt upset because Jay was still so weak. Jay's parents had taken him home so the family doctor could examine him.

"I don't know what's going to happen to him," Billy told Diana. "Kylie never finished turning him into a vampire. But he's so weak. And he never seems to get any better."

"Jay will get well," Diana assured him, as she studied the menu. "Now that he's away from here."

"I hope you're right," Billy told her.

"Cheer up," Diana said brightly. "We did it. We destroyed the vampires. We won!"

"We only destroyed two of them," Billy replied glumly.

"I can't believe you're acting like this," Diana scolded.

He managed a laugh. "You're right. I should be happy. What kind of pizza do you want?"

"Pepperoni with lots of green peppers."

They ordered it.

Billy watched the waiters scurry back and forth, taking orders and delivering steaming pizzas.

The tangy aroma of baking pizzas from the big ovens in back filled the restaurant.

Finally the waiter delivered their order. "Enjoy," he told them, as he set down the steaming pie and two plates.

"Give me your plate," Diana told him. "You get the honor of having the first slice."

Billy didn't want any pizza, but he handed her his plate.

"Uh-oh," Diana complained. "They didn't cut it all the way through." She fumbled with a slice of pizza, twisting it this way and that, but it refused to come loose.

"Let me," Billy offered. He picked up a knife from the table.

He pulled the pizza over to his side of the table. Inserted the blade into the pie, and pulled the knife toward him.

"Oww." The blade slid off the pan—and sliced into Billy's finger.

A bad cut. A deep one. Billy tried to hide it.

Too late. Diana had seen it.

She stared at him, her mouth open, eyes wide. "Billy—no blood," she cried. "Such a deep cut, and there was no blood."

"I'm sorry you saw that," Billy told her.

Diana leapt up with a startled cry.

But Billy grabbed her wrist. He pulled her back down into her seat.

"Let me explain," he pleaded, not letting go of Diana. "I lied about working on a charter boat. During the day, I'm asleep in my coffin. Direct sunlight will kill me. I can go out in daylight only if it's dark and cloudy—like when we went to the island and killed Kylie and Irene."

Diana stared at him in silent horror.

"I missed a whole year of school," Billy explained. "My friends all thought I was in the hospital. But I had to sleep in my coffin every day."

"A vampire," Diana whispered. "You're a vampire."

"It happened here in Sandy Hollow last summer," Billy explained. His voice cracked with emotion. "Last summer. That's when they turned me into a vampire."

"If you're a vampire," Diana demanded, "why did you help me kill two others?"

"To pay back the vampires. To pay them back for turning me into one of *them*. I hate them for making me crave the nectar. I killed Mae-Linn. For the nectar. I needed it so badly. I couldn't help myself. And I killed that guy Rick, too. I was so hungry!"

Diana shook her head. "It can't be," she whispered. "It can't be!"

"Now you know everything, Diana," Billy whispered. "Now I have no secrets. And I'm so hungry. So terribly hungry."

Diana cried out.

Too late.

Billy pulled her close. He sank his fangs deep into her throat.

Screams of terror filled the restaurant.

Billy barely heard them.

He was so hungry.

So terribly hungry.

THE
VAMPIRE CLUB

Starting at a new school can be a real pain in the neck.

I never wanted to leave Shadyside. I mean, who wants to move your senior year in high school?

I had to leave all my good buddies behind, including my pal Josh Miller, who owes me thirty dollars I know I'll never see again.

Josh promised to mail it to me next month. Do I believe that? I don't think so. He couldn't even keep a straight face when he said it.

And do you think it was easy to say goodbye to Kelly? Kelly and I had been going out since tenth grade. She is so great. I thought about her the whole long drive to Forest Grove. I kept picturing her smile and the dreamy look she'd get in her eyes when I kissed her.

Oh, man. I want to go back to Shadyside High. don't want to be the new kid in school at sixteer

Want to hear about a great first day? I went to a the wrong classes. I couldn't find the lunchroor or the bathroom. And of course I couldn't get th combination on my locker to work.

How did I feel? Three guesses. I felt like a jerk, total geek—like a five-year-old just starting kir dergarten.

Forest Grove High is an old brick buildin; three stories tall. It has ivy growing down on wall. Thick ivy that looks like a heavy curtain. even covers some of the classroom windows.

The high school stands on the edge of a fores Through the classroom windows, I gazed out a tangled trees and thick shrubs. It reminded me the Fear Street Woods back home.

The kids seemed nice enough. I met a few guy in gym I thought I might like hanging out witl And my Spanish teacher was kind of funny an nice.

Of course there was a problem with my sche ule. My schedule card said I had two lunc periods in a row. A little computer mistake. took half an hour to straighten that out in th office. By that time, I'd missed most of my Cre ative Writing class.

By the end of the first day, I was toast. I couldn wait to get out of there. I wanted to go home an rest my brain. Maybe work on the tree house I'n building for my little sister.

Working with wood always relaxes me. Actu

lly, I'm a pretty decent carpenter. Last summer, I
ad a job as an assistant at my uncle's construc-
on company. I actually got to build part of a
ouse. I was really into it.

So when the three o'clock bell rang, I was
ıinking about my workshop down in the base-
ıent of our new house. Thinking about the lum-
er I needed to start the tree-house platform.

But, whoa. To my surprise, no one left school.
'he other kids all picked up their stuff and
urried to other classrooms and places in the
uilding.

I stood in the middle of the hall, feeling really
onfused. Finally, I stopped a girl I recognized
om my Spanish class and asked her what was
oing on.

"You're the new guy," she said.

"I guess that's pretty obvious," I replied. "My
ame is Pete Barton."

"I'm Nan Garner," she said. She had long,
raight black hair and green eyes. Just like Kelly
ack home. She wore a dark blue sweater, pulled
own over black leggings.

She was really hot looking. I mean, my tongue
'as practically hanging out! On a scale of one to
n, she was definitely a hundred and fifty!

"Are you a senior, Pete?" she asked in her
elvety, soft voice.

I nodded. "Do you *believe* starting a new school
 senior year? It's really bad news."

She agreed. "It must be hard not to be graduat-
ıg with all your friends. Where are you from?"

3

"Shadyside," I told her. But she wasn't really listening. The hall was emptying out. She seemed eager to get someplace. "Where is everyone going?" I asked.

Her green eyes opened wide in surprise. "Didn't they tell you? Everyone has to be in a club. You know. For extracurricular credit. The clubs all meet at three."

"Everyone is in a club?" I'd never heard of that.

Nan nodded. "What are you into?" she asked. "I'll help you find a club to join."

"Well . . ." I had to think about it. "Is there a woodshop club? Or a carpentry club?" I asked. "I like working with my hands. I'm building a tree house for my sister behind our new house."

"I think there's a woodshop club," she replied. A teasing smile spread over her face. She put her hand on my shoulder. Her touch made my skin tingle.

"But wouldn't you like to try something a little more interesting?" she asked, lowering her voice to a whisper.

Whoa!

Sign me up for anything you've got! I thought. I mean, who could say no to those sparkling green eyes and that soft, purring voice? Not me, man.

She took my hand and started to lead me down the hall. "Follow me," she said. "I'm taking you to the club I'm in."

"What's it called?" I asked.

Her eyes flashed. "The Vampire Club."

* * *

4

Nan led the way out the back door of the school. I followed her into the forest, along a narrow dirt path that led through the tangled trees.

She had a bouncy walk, and I loved the way her black hair swung behind her with each step.

She is definitely *okay,* I thought. I wondered what she thought of me.

Pushing a clump of tall reeds aside, I could see a small, grassy clearing up ahead. And I heard voices, talking softly.

I felt a sudden chill. Maybe it was just the cool forest air. Maybe it was something more.

I stopped and tugged Nan's hand. "You don't really believe in vampires, do you?" I asked.

Before she could answer, a guy burst out of the clearing. He was big and blond and athletic looking, with a neck like a tree trunk. He wore a blue and gray Forest Grove sweatshirt over baggy khakis.

"Nan, you're late," he scolded. He glanced at me and frowned.

"I was just talking to Pete," Nan replied. "He's new. It's his first day." She introduced me to the guy. His name was Lee Baker.

He nodded but kept his blue eyes trained on Nan. He slipped a heavy arm around her shoulder. "You know I don't like you talking to other guys." He said it in a teasing way. But I could tell he wasn't joking.

Nan blushed and pulled out from under his arm. "Hey—give me a break, Lee. You don't *own* me, you know."

He turned to me. "You coming to the Vampire Club meeting, Pete?" It wasn't an invitation. It sounded more like a challenge.

I swallowed. "I guess. Nan said it was more interesting than—"

He didn't wait for me to finish. He turned her around, put his hands on her shoulders, and guided her into the clearing.

I felt a little awkward. I mean, I could tell that Lee was the jealous type. And that he didn't like me. But still I followed them into the small, round clearing.

Four tall, red candles had been set up in the grass on wooden candlesticks. The candles were placed at the corners of a large purple blanket. Eight or nine kids sat cross-legged on the blanket. The yellow candle flames flickered low in the steady forest breeze.

Most of the kids turned to watch us as we made our way to the blanket. A few of them stared at me. It made me feel kind of weird.

"Think fast!" a guy shouted. He heaved a tennis ball at Lee. It bounced off Lee's shoulder and hit the ground. Laughing, Lee dove for the guy and messed up his hair with both hands.

"Very mature," Nan muttered.

She stepped up beside a plump, brown-haired girl who stood on the grass. "This is Margaret," Nan told me. "Margaret is the president of the Vampire Club. Hey, everyone. This is Pete. He just started at Forest Grove today. He might want to join our club."

Everyone stared at me. I tried to give them all a casual wave. But I really felt like a geek standing there. Being the new kid in school was turning out to be a lot tougher than I'd imagined. I felt so awkward and uncomfortable the whole time.

"Does he know about the initiation?" Lee asked. He was kneeling on the grass at the side of the blanket.

"Lee, not now," Nan scolded. "Let Pete sit in on the meeting before we talk about that."

Some other kids murmured agreement with Nan.

Nan took a seat on the edge of the blanket and motioned for me to sit next to her.

I stared at her for a moment. The candlelight flickered in her green eyes. I dropped down beside her, wishing we were all alone out here. Wishing I could wrap my arms around her and . . .

"Come on. Don't be shy. Sit down!" Nan urged, impatiently patting the blanket beside her.

I could feel myself blushing. I dropped onto the blanket, and thought about what Lee had said.

What *was* the initiation? I wondered. What do you have to do to join the Vampire Club?

I glanced at Nan. She was smiling at me. What an awesome smile!

I'll do anything! I suddenly thought. *I don't care what the initiation is. I'll do it—if it will impress Nan.*

Margaret stood in front of everyone and called

the meeting to order. "Welcome to the Vampire Club," she said to me. "If you have any questions during the meeting, Pete, you can—"

"You—you're not all vampires, are you?" I blurted out. I meant it to be a joke. But it came out like a serious question.

Some kids laughed.

But Margaret didn't crack a smile. "No. We're not vampires," she told me. "We *hunt* vampires, Pete. We hunt the vampires at Forest Grove, and then . . . we take care of them."

I opened my mouth to say, "You're joking!" But I stopped myself when I looked around me and saw how serious everyone was.

The wind suddenly blew colder. I shivered beneath my sweater. Clouds darkened overhead. The candles flickered low.

"Do you believe in vampires, Pete?" a girl dressed all in black asked.

"Are *you* a vampire, Pete?" Lee chimed in. Everyone laughed. Everyone except Nan.

I turned to face everyone. "I don't think I believe in them," I said honestly. "I think vampires only exist in books and movies."

"That's because you just moved to Forest Grove," Margaret said. She motioned in the direction of the school. "As I'm sure you noticed, our high school was built on the edge of this forest. The forest stretches for miles and miles."

"And there are vampires in the forest," a guy said from the back of the blanket. "They were the first settlers in Forest Grove. They've lived in the forest for nearly three hundred years."

"How do you know?" I asked.

"Because we've *seen* them!" Lee declared. "We've hunted them down, Pete. And we've destroyed a bunch of them."

Nan jumped up angrily. "Stop it. You're saying too much!" she declared. "Why do you want to scare Pete to death on his first day? Give him a break, guys!"

"I'm not scared," I said. "I just think—"

"Let him decide for himself," Lee interrupted. "He doesn't have to join the club. He can join some baby club—if he's too big a wimp to go through the initiation."

"Whoa! I *said* I'm not afraid!" I insisted. "But I really don't believe if I got up from this blanket and took a walk, I'd find a bunch of vampires hanging out in the forest."

"They're not just in the forest. They're in our school!" Margaret declared.

My mouth dropped open. "Excuse me?"

"Forest Grove High is built on the edge of the forest where they live," Margaret explained. "So the vampires send their kids to the high school. Haven't you heard about the school's reputation, Pete?"

I shook my head. "No. What reputation?"

"Haven't you heard that other teams won't play us?" she continued, her voice rising excitedly. "They're too afraid of the vampires. Didn't you know that we're not invited to any of the state tournaments or competitions? Other schools are too frightened of us."

"Wow," I murmured. Could it be true? Should I believe them? Or was this all a big joke they always played on new kids?

I couldn't decide.

"Enough, guys," Nan insisted. "It's Pete's first day. He doesn't want to hear—"

"Let him hear the truth," a girl in black cried out. "He should know why we formed this club."

"We formed it to change the image of the school," Margaret told me. "We formed it to help give Forest Grove High a normal reputation."

"We formed it to hunt down vampires and destroy them!" Lee cried.

Several kids cheered.

"That's the initiation," Lee said, staring hard at me, challenging me again. "That's what you have to do to become a member of the Vampire Club. You have to kill a vampire."

"You're joking—right?" I demanded. "You guys are really good at keeping straight faces. But you're just playing a big joke on the new guy—right?"

"It's no joke," Margaret replied solemnly.

Lee stood up and moved in front of me. Gazing up at him, he looked like the Incredible Hulk!

He put his beefy hands on his waist and stared down at me. "Pete—do you want us to prove that vampires are real?"

I hesitated. "Well . . ."

His eyes locked on mine. "Do you want to see a

real vampire? Do you want to see one with your own eyes?"

"Yeah. Sure. I guess," I told him.

"Meet us tonight," Lee whispered.

I gasped as a burst of wind blew all four candles out.

After the club meeting, I hurried in to my locker to get my backpack. I couldn't wait to get home. What a long day!

My head was spinning. Some kids passed by laughing about something. I watched them, wondering if they were vampires.

This is crazy! I told myself. Why am I falling for this?

I felt a tap on my shoulder. I turned and found Nan gazing at me, her face tight with concern.

"Hi," I said, flashing her a smile. "You were right. That club was a lot more interesting than woodworking."

She didn't return my smile. "You really don't have to come tonight," she said. "Lee saw me talking to you before, and he's jealous. So he's trying to frighten you away."

"He's jealous?" I replied. "That's ridiculous!" *I'd like to give him a reason to be jealous!* I thought. *I'd like to steal Nan away from him— today!*

She nodded. "He's trying to frighten you," she repeated.

"Hey, no problem," I replied. "I'm not scared at all. I *want* to come."

11

Mainly, I want to spend time with you, Nan, I thought. *Mainly, I want to impress you.*

"But—" She started to say more. But Lee turned the corner and came lumbering toward us.

"I'm sorry—I've got to go," Nan whispered. She adjusted her backpack, spun around, and hurried to meet Lee.

I watched him slide his big arm around her shoulders. He leaned on her as they made their way out of the school.

She belongs with me, I thought. Not with that big hulk.

But what could I do? I was the new kid. The kid who couldn't even find his way to the gym. How could I ever win Nan over?

I met up with them at ten that night in the parking lot behind the school. It was a clear, cool night with a tiny sliver of a moon high in a blue-gray sky.

The building lights were all turned off. The darkness of the forest stretched in front of us. The whisper of the trees was the only sound.

I found five or six kids huddled at the edge of the parking lot. I jogged across the concrete to meet them. I waved my flashlight in greeting.

"Put that away," Lee snapped. He grabbed it from me. "Are you nuts?"

"I thought we needed to see—" I started.

"Do you want to tell the vampires you're coming?" Lee demanded. "Why not just call out, 'Hey, vampires—over here!' "

12

The others laughed.

I felt glad it was so dark. That way they couldn't see me blushing.

Nan was laughing at me too. I really hated that.

Lee tossed my flashlight on the ground. "Did you bring a camera with a flashbulb too?" he demanded nastily.

I ignored that. "Let's get going," I said, trying to sound tough. "Where are these vampires?"

Lee moved his face close to mine. He squinted hard at me. "Last chance to turn back," he said. "We won't blame you."

"The vampires look like normal people," Margaret chimed in. "But some of the things they do in the forest . . . well . . . it can get pretty gross."

I saw Nan watching me. I felt a little shaky about the whole thing. But *no way* was I going to act the least bit afraid. "Show me where they live," I said.

"They don't *live* in the forest anymore," Lee snapped, as if I'd just said the dumbest thing ever. "They live in houses, just like us. They come to the forest at night to feed, to drink the life from others."

"Let's go. I'm ready," I said, stepping up close to Nan.

"Sshhhh," Margaret warned. "Don't make a sound."

"Keep back with us," Lee instructed, pulling me away from Nan. "If the vampire sees you, don't expect us to protect you, Pete."

His words sent a shiver down my back.

Up till then, I'd been sure this was all a big joke. But now, as we stepped between the trees and began to make our way over the clumps of wet leaves and prickly, low weeds, I didn't know what to think.

Nan, walking beside Lee a few steps ahead of me, kept flashing me warning glances. I could tell that she didn't think it was a joke.

She seemed to be worried about me. Really worried.

My throat tightening, my heart pounding, I followed them, trying to be as silent as possible. We stepped over a fallen tree, then made our way through a patch of tall reeds, creaking as they bent in the soft breeze.

Silvery beams of moonlight shimmered down between the tree branches, making the forest floor sparkle. Walking so silently through the eerie, unreal light, I almost felt as if I had entered another world.

We stopped when we heard a loud scraping sound. A cough. Heavy, animal-like grunts.

Lee raised a finger to his lips. Then he pointed across a circle of tall grass.

And I saw a guy. Crouched in the grass.

I stared hard. He was pretty big. He wore a dark windbreaker with the hood pulled up.

As I watched him move across the grass, the wind blew the hood back—and I recognized him! A guy from my gym class.

"It's Jason," Lee whispered. His hot breath brushed my ear. "It's Jason Manus. From our

14

class. He lives in the big, white house directly across from school."

"Wh-what's he doing out here?" I stammered.

We all ducked low and watched him. Jason appeared to be wrestling with something. He disappeared in the tall grass for a moment.

The grass bent and snapped.

When Jason returned to view, he was gripping an animal in his hands. A dog. A big dog.

The dog squirmed and pulled. But couldn't free itself from Jason's grasp.

I leaned forward. Held my breath. Struggled not to make a sound.

But I couldn't help myself. I gasped as Jason pulled the struggling dog to him—lowered his head—and sank his teeth into the dog's furry throat.

"No—!" I gasped.

"He's drinking the dog's blood," Lee whispered, his eyes wide with excitement.

I sank to my knees on the wet ground. I suddenly felt sick.

This was real. All real.

I stared at Jason—the *vampire*—drinking noisily from the dog's throat.

I felt my stomach lurch. My throat tightened. I knew I was going to hurl. I couldn't hold it back.

Staggering to my feet, I clamped my hand over my mouth. And I ran.

I heard them laughing at me. I glanced back and saw Nan laughing along with the others.

I felt terrible. She must think I'm a total coward, I realized.

But I couldn't stop running. I didn't want them to see me heaving up my dinner on the ground.

Ducking under low limbs and branches, I ran until I reached the parking lot behind the school. Then I rested my hands on my knees and sucked in several deep breaths.

I didn't feel queasy anymore. But I was so embarrassed, I wanted to die. I pictured Nan again, heard her laughter. Heard them all laughing at me.

I pressed my hands over my ears, but it didn't shut out the laughter.

Then, suddenly, I knew what I had to do.

I had to go through with the initiation.

I had to kill the vampire.

It was the only way to stop the laughter. The only way to show Nan that I could be brave, that I was not a loser.

The others had all destroyed vampires. Nan, Lee, Margaret—all of them.

I could do it too. And then maybe I'd stand a chance with Nan.

I knew exactly what I had to do. It suddenly came so clear to me. I ran all the way home. Grabbed a firewood log from beside the garage. carried it down to my workshop in the basement.

We had lived in the new house for only a week. But I set up my tools first thing—before I even unpacked my clothes. That's how important they are to me.

I put the log on the lathe and cut it down. I cut a fine point on one end. Sharp. Sharp enough to penetrate a vampire's chest. Then I filed the point even sharper.

I waited till just before daybreak. I knew vampires had to return to their homes when the sun started to rise.

I thought about Nan as I waited.

I imagined her green eyes gazing into mine as I pulled her close. I imagined how her silky, black hair would feel as it brushed against my cheek.

I imagined holding her. Kissing her . . .

I can do this! I told myself as I stared at the night sky out my bedroom window. *I can do this—for Nan.*

A red morning sun was barely rising over the trees as I crept out. I hurried to Jason's house. The big, white house across from school.

No cars passed. I saw no one on the street. I slipped around to the back of the house.

Jason's room was the second one I peered into. From outside the window, I could see the vampire asleep on his back, covers up to his chin.

Silently, I slid open the window and dropped into the room. He stirred. His mouth opened and closed. The mouth he had used to drink the blood of that poor dog.

He didn't awaken.

My heart thudded. My hand shook as I raised the sharp-pointed stake high.

But I knew I had to do it. Had to. Had to.

17

I swung the stake down with all my strength Slammed it through his heart.

Killed the vampire. Killed him.

He didn't even move.

A second later, I was out of there. Running for home. My sneakers slapping the pavement. Feeling so good, so . . . joyful.

I had to call Nan. I had to tell her. I had to let her know I was a member of the club.

I knew it was early, but I didn't care. I got her number from Information and called her. She answered on the fourth ring.

"It's me. Pete," I said.

"You woke me up." Her voice sounded hoarse sleepy.

"I have to tell you something," I cried eagerly

"Me too," Nan said, suddenly sounding very awake. "Don't let Lee and the others fool you Pete. That was such a mean trick they played on you last night."

"Huh? Trick?" I murmured.

"Yes," Nan replied. "Jason isn't a vampire He's a friend of ours. There *aren't* any vampires None. Lee got Jason to pretend last night—to give you a big scare. But Jason is perfectly okay Actually, he's a great guy."

Nan took a breath. "Now—what did you want to tell me, Pete?" she asked.

About the Author

"Where do you get your ideas?"

That's the question that R.L. Stine is asked most often. "I don't know where my ideas come from," he says. "But I do know that I have a lot more scary stories in my mind that I can't wait to write."

So far, he has written nearly five dozen mysteries and thrillers for young people, all of them bestsellers.

Bob grew up in Columbus, Ohio. Today he lives in an apartment in New York City with his wife, Jane, and teenage son, Matt.

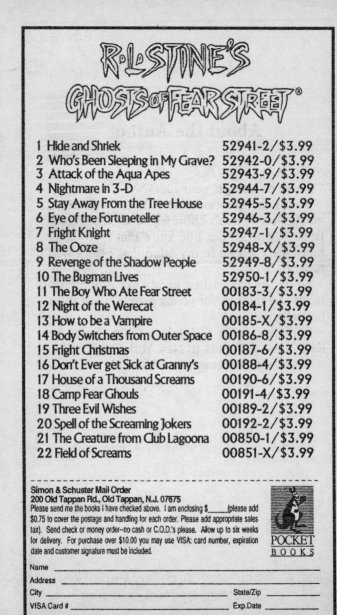

R·L·STINE'S
GHOSTS OF FEAR STREET ®

1	Hide and Shriek	52941-2/$3.99
2	Who's Been Sleeping in My Grave?	52942-0/$3.99
3	Attack of the Aqua Apes	52943-9/$3.99
4	Nightmare in 3-D	52944-7/$3.99
5	Stay Away From the Tree House	52945-5/$3.99
6	Eye of the Fortuneteller	52946-3/$3.99
7	Fright Knight	52947-1/$3.99
8	The Ooze	52948-X/$3.99
9	Revenge of the Shadow People	52949-8/$3.99
10	The Bugman Lives	52950-1/$3.99
11	The Boy Who Ate Fear Street	00183-3/$3.99
12	Night of the Werecat	00184-1/$3.99
13	How to be a Vampire	00185-X/$3.99
14	Body Switchers from Outer Space	00186-8/$3.99
15	Fright Christmas	00187-6/$3.99
16	Don't Ever get Sick at Granny's	00188-4/$3.99
17	House of a Thousand Screams	00190-6/$3.99
18	Camp Fear Ghouls	00191-4/$3.99
19	Three Evil Wishes	00189-2/$3.99
20	Spell of the Screaming Jokers	00192-2/$3.99
21	The Creature from Club Lagoona	00850-1/$3.99
22	Field of Screams	00851-X/$3.99

Simon & Schuster Mail Order
200 Old Tappan Rd., Old Tappan, N.J. 07675
Please send me the books I have checked above. I am enclosing $_____ (please add $0.75 to cover the postage and handling for each order. Please add appropriate sales tax). Send check or money order--no cash or C.O.D.'s please. Allow up to six weeks for delivery. For purchase over $10.00 you may use VISA: card number, expiration date and customer signature must be included.

POCKET
BOOKS

Name _____

Address _____

City _____ State/Zip _____

VISA Card # _____ Exp.Date _____

Signature _____ 1180-18

At the stroke of midnight...you are on Fear Street. Your footsteps echo as you walk past rows of houses. Houses with blank windows that seem to stare down at you. That seem to know your deepest, darkest secrets. Confide those secrets here...

R·L·STINE
FEAR STREET®
Midnight Diary

Find out more about yourself, your friendships, your loves and your fears.

Take your first step onto Fear Street—if you dare.

Coming in mid-July

Available from Archway Paperbacks
Published by Pocket Books

1367

FEAR STREET ®

R·L·STINE

GOODNIGHT KISS

◆Collector's Edition◆

Includes

Goodnight Kiss
Their first kiss could be her last....

Goodnight Kiss 2
It's the kiss of death.

Plus...

The Vampire Club
A NEW Vampire story by R.L. Stine

 Available from Archway Paperbacks
Published by Pocket Books

1360-01